Maps Full of Borders

Maps Full of Borders

Published by The Conrad Press in the United Kingdom 2020

Tel: +44(0)1227 472 874
www.theconradpress.com
info@theconradpress.com

ISBN 978-1-913567-45-3

Typesetting and Cover Design by:
Charlotte Mouncey, www.bookstyle.co.uk

The Conrad Press logo was designed by Maria Priestley.

Printed and bound in Great Britain by Clays Ltd, Elcograf S.p.A.

Maps Full of Borders

Todd Dedman

To Caz and Dick

CHAPTER 1

The painting

Molly stared hard at the page. This big, empty stretch of A3 whiteness somehow seemed to be an insurmountable object of disquiet and seething possibility. The vastness of the page momentarily weighed her down.

Molly knew what to do without fully knowing why. The emptiness of the page was all of a sudden mirrored by her mind with all of the previously well considered ideas now a vacuum of creativity and the numbness that comes with the fear of self-expectation.

She had talked herself through this, time and time and time again. This was really no big deal. There was no pre-ordained imagery that she was looking to transfer from her mind's eye to the page – she knew that to do so would only inevitably lead to frustration and compromise when the ability of her body did not match that of her brain. Ideas were all well and good until it was obvious that they could not be realised and then what was the point in that? What was the point in having a head full of potential?

Nobody was looking, nobody could hear, nobody would ever know unless she chose for them to know. And yet… still, Molly hovered the brush over the page and froze. The first stroke would, she assured herself, be the one least noticed by any future viewer, that lecherous bastard of criticism and chin stroking polite assassination.

Why, if not to be admired and discussed and dissected in a positive manner, would an artist commit the first meeting between paint and paper that meant some work was forthcoming?

The first cut may well be the deepest but the first mark on the page would determine all others – the initial leading to the eventual. How, Molly thought, do other artists begin? Is the beginning truly in the act or in the thought that precedes it? Does a beginning need to be noticed by others, thereby substituting the thought to a form of pre-beginning, the primordial soup before the big bang of activity?

The fears of commencement started to be replaced with questions of her continued commitment to painting.

Molly reasoned that she hated the process and, more often than not, despised the outcome, yet there remained a sense deeply entrenched somewhere within her that this was still something worthwhile, something to chase the time away, to bury the monotonous and melancholic thoughts and voices in her head and to actually do something.

Perhaps it was Miss Wolmsley, one of Molly's old English teachers, who had once told her that she was a human doing, not a human being. That sounded great, she thought, but it took her ages to work out what was actually meant by it.

At first Molly thought it was a negative phrase and that the person who had said it was in some way mocking her and was being less than entirely kind as perhaps it meant that she was too busy in her actions which were of little or no consequence and she was therefore losing time in 'being' – maybe being at one with herself? Whatever.

She didn't know, and her head just couldn't get a proper fix on the meaning, but she liked the sound and the rhythm and the cadence of the phrase. Molly more recently thought that actually, maybe, the phrase was a positive one and that being active and pursuing acts, i.e. doing, was so much better than merely existing, being. But was Molly active in her own being, or was she just trying too hard to project this idea of herself as arty, as pained, as isolationist? Did any of this matter to other, more normal people or was this just an aspect of Molly that made Molly the person she was?

Not only did the phrase play on her mind in an irresistible and painfully petulant manner, but she was also frustrated at her own inability to remember exactly who it was that planted this seed of an idea into her burgeoning intellectual curiosity. How could she not recall exactly who said something that she ruminated on over and over and over again? It was lapses like this that Molly knew would keep her awake at night. Time to refocus.

The scene had been set – paper put on the kitchen table, six colour paint pots placed in order of their position in the rainbow, and three brushes of different thicknesses were laid out in a meticulous manner in front of her. All were cheap, and all were readily available, but this was to be some sort of commentary on working-class access to tools, something about the means of production or some other things like that. A decent enough starting point.

Molly had read some of the books that Dan kept in his room in a shoddy, seemingly random pile by his bed and phrases like this leapt out at her. She liked them as she felt this meant there was a perpetual battle going on – a battle of doing and of being – that pleased her.

Molly would often watch the evening news and see tales of murder and money, of power grabs and lust and war and she would look out of her window and wonder where this all was taking place. Her life was quite dull, but she liked it that way.

She needed to see more of the world to truly understand the pages in books not necessarily intended for her that she rifled through, or maybe those ideas weren't relevant anymore. Perhaps men with stupidly big beards wrote this kind of stuff in the hope that others would pick up on it and do the work of revolution for them. Maybe being a human thinking is better than a human being but less important than a human doing.

The paintbrush had been put into the dark blue pot. Molly took more pleasure in setting the scene than committing the act; of this she was entirely certain.

Maybe other artists knew what they were going to create before they started. Was that where she was going wrong, with no pre-beginning? Was not having a clue what was going to be the finished product a bad idea? She had nobody to guide her and, anyway, all the great artists of any era didn't belong in that era as their work transcended it.

How does one go about creating work that transcends an era? Molly reasoned that it would be hard for her to know seeing as she didn't really understand what was going on in the art world in her own time to know what exactly it was she could do to move away from it or to push it in new directions or to oppose it.

Molly had heard the term 'post-modern' a few times on the radio but she decided that she was going to be seen to reject this concept, if anyone asked, and she would just have to try to find a convincing way to argue the case without actually getting into a fully-fledged discussion on its nuances as she didn't actually have much of an idea what it meant.

Perhaps that's the point with terms such as this, that they mean different things to all people and therefore language is fluid as meaning isn't fixed apart from by white, middle-class and middle-aged heterosexual men who can go screw themselves. Whatever. *Get on with it, Molly.*

What was the point of an idea that wasn't realised, of a pre-beginning which was encased in the inertia and muddle-headedness of its thinker? Would they come back again, either at some later date when inspiration was lacking, and such memories would be seen as welcome and worn projections, or would young ideas be consigned to the dustbin of aging mortality that so often seemed to envelope those over forty?

On the few occasions that Molly had watched television on Sunday evenings, she became aware of a religious programme that centred on old people singing in various churches and cathedrals around the country as they worried about the afterlife as the clock towards their taking up occupancy of their shitty, soon to be untendered, little burial mound was ticking for them.

They would gather in these places in their best clothes and sing empty words set to a forgettable melody to their chosen deity, a medieval sky wizard who had to be spoken to really nicely and, for some reason, with your eyes closed, if he was to make your hopes and wishes come true. Wish fulfilment via Higher Being intervention, of course, never happened because there was not and could not be such a thing as a god and those who kneeled down to pray were probably ill in the head in the same way that people who saw visions or ghosts were. God seemed to be at the root of a lot of wars. God and oil – often in tandem, but never too far from one another.

Molly could only make out one connection between these two that made sense. Plastic bags came from oil (she had heard this to be true, but didn't know exactly how this was the case, something about long polymers or something) and if she ever felt god talking to her she would end it all by placing such a bag over her head and self-asphyxiating.

She knew that god was an excuse for acts of criminal barbarity and that most of these people committing evil had clearly never actually read the Bible or any of the other religious books because she was sure that if they were in fact all full of instruction to kill everyone who didn't believe in a particular god-brand then the whole world would be dead by now.

Anyway, people seemed to always want to be defined by which side they are on as if this somehow helps them to narrow down all of the infinite possibilities of human existence – if we label ourselves then we help others to decide on whether we have something to offer. After all, friendship is simply about lining people up who give us something in return. Nobody has to work too hard on friendships as you either 'get' the other person or eventually you drift away. Molly 'got' people, but they tended to drift away from her, and that was okay. She never really felt much by way of an attachment to anyone else, apart from Dan, but that was only from time to time.

The brush had been hovering, motionless, over the paper for some time. This led to the inevitable eventuality of a splodge of paint landing on the page from on high. Molly saw this as some sort of sign that she just needed to stop thinking and get on with it and place the paint in a designated space on the page and then move the brush in whatever manner seemed most appropriate.

But the fear had her. Not the kind of fear she felt when she thought of killer clowns of scary nuns or indescribable monsters who may be following her closely when she was walking up the stairs in her house, but a fear that she knew was always with her. The fear of doing wrong, the fear of being wrong and the fear of caring about being wrong.

It was not so much in the judgement of others that Molly felt a mortifying grip of anxiety, but in the self-awareness that always came with action. She wanted to be better than she was, and she knew that she would probably live out her days with this persistent, unbearable and crushing disappointment in herself that others would share if they only had the time and effort to consider her more than they did. If only one other person could be bothered, that would be quite the thing.

She looked up and saw her fat hand holding the brush. At that moment, she hated her hand and the way it gripped the crappy shaft of the stupid brush. It was a useless appendage, a good for nothing piece of shit that needed to be told what to do like a bunch of remote-controlled sausages that lacked finesse. She wanted a free-flowing, autonomous hand that didn't have to wait for instruction from her all too often weak and befuddled brain.

It was the tablets that made her mind wander, and it was the tablets that made the sharpness of her thinking not what it previously was, but it was her fat, useless hateful spiteful hands that could not deliver the goods as she fleetingly saw them in her mind's eye.

She could feel, possibly sense, the required limb motion in her brain and went through the subtleties of the movement several times, but although she felt she knew how to move her body failed to respond with the required level of intricacy that the task demanded.

She hated her hands. And her feet, and her legs, and her arms, and her shoulders, and her face, and her hair, and her freckles, and the puncture mark on her left arm from some sort of jab she had had without even being asked her permission, and she hated her thoughts and her inability to turn her thoughts into anything solid that she could leave behind for people to marvel at after she had gone and to wonder why they had never understood her magnificent intellect while she lived. Damn all the people to hell.

Molly recalled a moment, years before when she was four, maybe five, maybe younger, when she was watching the television in the same mildly vacant and less than focused manner that she would still watch the television today. There were flailing presenters and flavour of the month manufactured pretty people talking about their insignificant 'art' pop music, but Molly's mind drifted to her hand. Strangely, not both; just her right hand.

She held it up towards the screen so that she could see it more clearly and she moved it around, swirling her fingers around their joints so as to more clearly see the bone structure under the skin that became more pronounced when each minilimb was moved. It was then that she realised this was *her* hand, nobody else's. This was the hand that would always be hers and would no doubt change as she changed.

Although the television screen pulsed with the rhythmic editing of the superfluous video that accompanied the saccharine music and therefore made the light on her hand irregular, she noticed a pleasing smoothness to her hand that she didn't think she saw on her dad's hand. With the hindsight that being a teenager brings, Molly thought that this was the moment when she became self-aware, like the waking moment of a sentient robot in some science fiction film or other. And Molly knew full well how such occurrences ended. She started to hum *Daisy Bell*, smug in the knowledge that most people didn't know its proper name.

Molly appreciated that memories have the tendency to change with the passing of time as she would often think about this childhood epiphany of the personal in the following years and realise that in that original moment she would likely have thought of her mother's hands first rather than her father's, yet here she was reconstructing the past to fit the current narrative of her life.

At age four, or five, or however old she was when this weird ritualistic act of assigning her hand to herself took place, Molly realised that she was going to grow old and that her hand would change accordingly. Molly reckoned that as her hand was the part of her body she saw most, she would be able to age herself by how old her hand looked. Even now, Molly couldn't quite work out why she had only considered her right hand, not her left or both, but there were times when she thought it was because she was, as were most people, right-handed so it made sense that her field of vision would be more dominated by her right hand than her left. She was right dominant, and more often than not, dominantly right.

When she was just a little older, Molly had heard someone explain that left-handed people were often seen as witches and although this was a long time ago perhaps there remained some seed of truth that everyone in the culture recognised. An old teacher of Molly's from primary school, maybe Mr Jenkins, or maybe Mr Watson who had had the car crash and limped and slurred his words afterwards, had once said that left-handed people found things like drawing lines on paper harder as numbers ascended from left to right on measuring tools which affected left-handers. The same teacher had also said how the Latin words for left and right were of interest. Molly could remember that the Latin for left was 'sinister'. It was probably Jenkins who said it.

Molly knew that her own mortality was linked to her hand, a symbol of years passed and opportunities that slip through your fingers. Molly knew at that young age that people used creams and lotions to hide signs of aging as the television told them in no uncertain terms that this is what they must do if they are to be seen as worthwhile people who others would care about. Molly vowed then never to moisturise her right hand, never to hide away from the fact that she would rely on it as she got older in helping her to realise that life was fleeting and that she should seize the day. Things were harder to seize with greasily moisturised fingers. Molly also knew at that moment that this was possibly the first memory that she would actively try to keep, and she was sure that she would remember this moment for the rest of her life if she tried hard enough. It was a gift to herself.

She looked around her and went through the things in the room worth remembering to sustain this memory as accurately as possible – the colour and texture of the carpet (red and worn in places), the pattern of the wallpaper (like a blue and green kaleidoscope), colour of her t-shirt and trousers (beige and pink respectively), the weather that was visible through the window in the room (grey with a promise of rain), the temperature in the room (quite mild), the presence of others in the room (she was alone) and the sounds she could hear (well, maybe that was a sacrifice to her memory she was not willing to make). She also realised at that moment that her vow to never moisturise her right hand meant, through reasons of physical practicality, that her left would be left to decay naturally, too.

But that was then. Molly looked at her still stationary hand with the paintbrush and willed it into action. Her hand was, depending on her mood, either too thin or too fat, as now, like a gelatinous mass thrown casually into the end of a pair of tights where its limpness took on a new definition of torpidity. Molly somehow knew that what she would paint would be fine, but this issue of the first stroke was a common one that often paralysed her into inaction for however long it took to get over this bullshit. What if the first stroke was somehow deemed to be wrong? How could there be such a thing as 'wrong' in a piece of work that Molly had commissioned in her own head which nobody else would ever, ever, ever (probably) see? She knew there was no rational and straightforward answer to this that other people would understand, but seeing as she hardly ever saw other people she felt this was not her main concern at this precise moment in time.

When Molly was at school, she would often spend hour upon hour upon hour in the art room working on anything that took her fancy. Molly missed having access to the required tools for lino printing in particular.

The art teacher was one of those who often let the kids explore their inner-selves and so the art room was open every minute of the school day. Molly regularly took herself there to escape the daily teen soap opera infused melodrama that was the lunch break. Spare time in this room was rewarded by the teacher with engagement, challenging conversation and oftentimes respectful peace and quiet as space was afforded to the development of artistic expression. It was in timetabled lessons that the teacher became a blunted automaton.

One day, Molly was spending the fifty-five minutes of lunchtime in the art room and another teacher who taught the A Level kids came in and asked the screwiest of screwed up questions that had gone around and around and around her head ever since. She was sure he meant well, but it just wasn't on for a teacher to drop a bombshell like he did and then walk away to get on with his own miserable/happy life (Molly could never work out whether teachers were failures or success stories – definitely one or the other, no inbetween).

He said 'I have never asked an art student this – when you are creating a piece of work, how do you know when you're finished?' Molly thought the obvious answer was to state that you stop just before you go insane, but schools seemed so tight on language like that that she felt it inevitable that she would wind up in front of her Form Tutor and her dad discussing her mental well-being. She would have much preferred to have been talking about her mental well-doing as she felt the circuits in her brain were firing away all of the time and she was certain that this was one of the reasons that she was different to everyone else as she was constantly on the move in her head, thinking over things from a million and two different angles to ensure that she had an answer for every occasion, regardless of whether she was saying what she thought or just saying something, anything, to get a rise from people. Molly, Molly, quite contrary. She hated her name.

Molly didn't know the answer to how artists knew when they were finished and, right now, she didn't even have a clue as to how she would know when she had properly started. Molly was reminded of a comment that Lizzie Doran made. She had been to see her granny who had asked her, quite out of the blue, how lesbians knew when they were finished having sex. Lizzie said she didn't know what to do or where to look and from the story Molly felt sorry for old Grandma Doran as this question clearly said more about her own sex life than anything else. It was difficult navigating other people's ignorance, let alone her own intellectual inadequacies and ineptitudes.

The unwanted blue paint splat on the page wasn't going to deter Molly from putting something over the top of it, or to the side of it. Maybe she could wait for that one solitary mark to dry before turning the page over and starting again, safe in the knowledge that the ghost mark from the dropped blob would be faint enough only for her to see, even though it would be invisible to the eye yet starkly present in Molly's haunted memory of the phantom smudge which nearly screwed everything up for her.

Nobody else felt or perceived or constructed ideas and life in the same way that Molly did, of that she was sure, and so nobody else deserved to see her artwork as there could possibly be no way in which they would be able to view it as her equal and she sure as hell wasn't having people who saw themselves as being superior to her looking over her work and wanking themselves into a frenzy of pre-prepared descriptors and overly rehearsed actions of the ritualised movements of ponderous musing and critical appreciation. Molly had learnt the word 'onanism' when she was about ten and although she had no idea really what wanking was at the time, she thought that 'wanking' was a silly word as it sounded like the person doing it was hurting themselves – the harsh sound of the K resonated too much and brought to mind images of people hitting themselves in the body part that was used for wanking. Self love as flagellation. Onanism, Molly decided, was a much better term as rather than sounding violent she thought there was a sense of sadness to it as it really hit home that those people were on their own – *own hand jism*. Also, nobody else seemed to know what the word onanism meant which more than added to the sense of secrecy that the term alluded to.

What, Molly reasoned, would be the worst-case scenario if the first stroke of the brush left something to be desired? It seemed like such a petty thing to worry about, but Molly knew that this was how her brain worked and she had, to some degree, started to become comfortable with this realisation and idea that she would always take an age to get something started because the first step was the one that scared her most. And yet… and yet there was just no way of making this process simpler and less fraught with contradictions and wild assumptions of the range of possibilities that one simple act, the placement of brush on paper, would afford. Molly knew that every single action that she performed would have a knock on effect and so each action, in and of itself, was significant and perhaps the most insignificant were simply looked over by the conscious aspect of the brain yet would have a long term, accumulative result which should not be overlooked as it would not be remembered but would help to shape every subsequent action and reaction.

If the first stroke were pleasing, would she become over confident and self-assured in a way that she had previously never experienced? Would the action lose importance due to its success, or was Molly the kind of person who merely dwelt on those actions that provéd less fruitful? There was no easy way to explain the significance of an insignificant act to someone who didn't think in the same way, but Molly knew that there was reason in her thinking. Reason enough, anyway.

By being transfixed on such thoughts was she a true artist? Didn't artists take risks? Had she suffered enough in her life to be considered a true artist or was she simply replicating, without knowing, the work of others whose souls had been put through the unrelenting grinder of existence? Actions may speak louder than words, but where do thoughts come in the hierarchy of human doing? Is thinking an act of human doing or human being? Molly thought that none of this mattered and if she could just plead with her hand to rest on the paper and do or be as it wanted then she would be over the shock and awe of starting whatever it was that she was starting.

Her thoughts were a stumbling block to her own plans of achieving something, even though she realised that she found no pleasure in achieving what she herself could do. Is this how everyone else felt? What about those people who were looked up to – doctors, actors, pop stars, lawyers, teachers (no, probably not teachers) – were they all filled with self doubt, self loathing and overt onanistic tendencies in the face of the pressures of being a human doing life. Do humans happen to life or does life happen to humans?

Please, Molly thought to herself in the harshest tone her mind could muster, *just put the brush on the paper and just bloody well start.* Molly always hated hearing her own voice talking directly to another part of herself and was happier wrapped up in the abstract and tangential thoughts that were her day-to-day life where the narrator for her thoughts was present but silent, a telepathy that existed between her inner and outer selves.

The moment of appreciation, all those years ago, that it was her hand that she was looking at gave Molly a spark of life; the realisation that one day the hand in front of her, her hand, would be dead and in a grave or, hopefully, burnt in a furnace along with the rest of her or maybe chopped off and sent in the post to a relative as a means of her kidnapper demanding a ransom be paid for the safe delivery of the rest of her body or buried in a shallow grave in the woods along with twenty six other mounds of earth where her killer had scattered the body parts, only for a lonely old dog walker to find them as the dog retrieved a leg from near the foot of a birch tree or an ash or whatever trees grow in woods. If her hand was alive then, by process of logic and statistical inference, so was she.

The hand would age as she aged and would develop wrinkles, darkened spots like she had seen on old Mrs Fry next door in the days before she was found dead in her chair, rough patches and orange bits from smoking on the doorbell poking finger and the one next to it (would she smoke when she got older? She hadn't made her mind up at this point and Molly thought that this was something that really needed to be planned ahead.

Was there a taste to cigarettes and, if so, was it better than the smell of the smoke that people blew out of their bodies?).

She would watch the years go by in her hand and she would see the decay that was inevitable in all life. Maybe the prime time for her hand was when she noticed how it would wane. Maybe a five-year-old's hand was peak hand. Perhaps all five-year-olds, or four-year-olds, were programmed to look at their hands at this point in their life and realise the futility of it all as people who had no real concept of time passing were supposed to develop a sense of linear erosion. Was it fair that people who measured time in sleeps and just wanted to know when Christmas was were given the task of rationalising their own sense of self-awareness through a body part? Perhaps it made most sense that children of this age would have some sort of pre-ordained instruction to observe their own mortality in their hand as they were not yet susceptible to the machinery of the advertising industry which told people, women in particular, that aging was a crime punishable by being alone and microwaving frozen meals for one and crying into your rosé for eternity as everyone with any sense would have walked away the moment the first wrinkle, grey hair or stretch mark appeared on their disgusting and undesirable body.

Of course, adverts were clever and didn't say such things in an explicit way, but Molly knew that they subtly suggested that only the young were worthy of being loved. Old people, or those who showed signs of being old, were abhorrent and everyone knew it. This was why, Molly thought, old people often died alone or surrounded by family members who tried hard to suppress a cry of 'KER-fucking-CHING!' when Great Aunt Maude surrendered her last wheezy, disgusting smelling breath to the ether. *Do old people even know they are old? No, Molly – stop it. Get on with it.*

This painting wouldn't paint itself. Molly pleaded to her hand. Her ineffective hand. A lump of flesh, bone, ligaments and blood and whatever else that was as static as a gargoyle on a cathedral wall. Molly had heard stories of female gargoyles who had their vaginas showing in some sort of display that most people nowadays were completely unaware of. In fact, she knew that one of the songs that Dan often listened to was about this. Well, maybe not about it exactly but the title was the name of these things (whatever they were called, she couldn't remember which annoyed her no end at this moment in time) and it was about showing off in some way. Molly did wonder whether these gargoyles were supposed to be symbols of female empowerment or men's general fears of the vagina. She realised, after all, that the stonemasons who would have made these things would most likely have all been men and so maybe, men being men, these carefully worked pieces of sculpture were demonising women. That would be most likely. Probably.

Men today used language in a way to keep women in their place, so Molly didn't think it would have been any different hundreds of years ago – much worse, if anything. Was life, therefore, a constant battle between men and women? Was the man who made the first gargoyle like this so scared of women that he spent what would have been an age painstakingly constructing and honing a block of stone into a carefully contoured shape as a critique of women and their body parts? Would that have made him feel better for his shitty little life that all he did every day was use his years of experience to carve a defamation to around half the population?

Was this how power worked? Rather than striving to build and develop relationships so that people could work together for the greater good – *THE GREATER GOOD* – one half of the population would try to maintain their power by just weakening the position of those who were perceived as a threat? Rather than trying to secure power (what was the point of power?) by your own means it was better, perhaps easier, to tell those beneath you that there was a sense of logic, however twisted, to the power structures of society. Men were in charge because, as the sculptor had so beautifully framed it, women could not be trusted not to shove their vaginas into the open air at the drop of a hat. A man's hat, most likely. The world made sense from that perspective. Sort of. But also not at all.

Women had always been vilified, Molly thought, since forever. There was the obvious virgin/whore dichotomy at play in the stories that Christianity developed from, Mary the virgin mother and Mary Magdalene the repentant sex worker (although Molly had paid enough attention in some Religious Studies lessons at school to know that this portrayal of Magdalene as a prostitute was inaccurate as she was confused by many to be the 'sinful woman' who washed Jesus's feet). Although a misinterpretation, the idea was still clear that in popular culture women were either entirely pure or imperceptibly impure with nothing in between and were not allowed to be the conflicted, multi-dimensional and complex characters that men were entitled to be.

Witches were another sign of men's fears of the potential power of women. Female murderers also were treated differently to their male counterparts. People like Myra Hindley or Rose West or that babysitter in America who shook the baby until it died were somehow portrayed as more evil, less humane and more hate filled than men who committed the same acts (or worse). This could be, Molly reasoned, for a number of reasons.

Firstly, in Molly's limited experience she felt that most people unwittingly seemed to only really value women as a vehicle by which the human race could continue. She was surprised by terms such as 'biological clock' which seemed really to suppress any women who had no interest in, or for biological reasons had no chance of, conceiving. This idea being used in every day talk made it pretty clear that women served one over-riding role in this culture. The patriarchy had subtly pushed women towards seeing themselves as receptacles of motherhood, enabled by an emphasis on women as being innately and naturally caring, and so therefore societal ideas of female violence were anathema to this idea of female passivity and nurturing. Women were vessels. Secondly, this was probably just a continuation of the concept that witches as evil women were to be feared more than evil males, which probably was a conflation of the first point, anyway.

Time to focus again.

So, this was it. Molly realised that, quite without her consent or in some ways her knowledge, her hand was engaging in movement towards the now not-so virgin paper. What would be the consequence of this? Had her hand made sense of the situation and decided to act, or was it just tired from being propped up in an unconventional position for so long while Molly's mind wandered this way and that? No matter, the hand was coming down.

Molly knew the significance of this act and saw it as the

beginning of the end of the painting rather than the start of the project. The work was in her head somewhere, yet it was not fully realised in a visual way but in an emotional manner there and so would come out on the paper in an almost stream of consciousness way even though Molly didn't know if this term could be used for anything other than writing or talking. And maybe thinking. The exciting part – though maybe that wasn't the correct term - for Molly was seeing what her brain had been concocting without consent from her consciousness. Nothing would now be done by accident but would be completed as designed in the quiet parts of her brain, those sections where the thoughts were so resilient and assured that they did not need to make themselves known.

This was where Molly felt her true essence existed, away from the buffering effects that life had dealt her. Her thoughts were framed by her experiences to date whereas her brain, her true brain, was simply an unemotional machine calculating all variables due to sense, not reliant on the frailties of human perception or personal values.

Those unfeeling and dispassionate parts of the brain weren't 'Molly' as she felt that only the parts of her thoughts that were able to interact, the decision making elements, were constructed as a part of whatever it meant to be Molly and how her own sense of self identified, and therefore hindered, itself. Her mind raced with all of the fears and ideas of the previous few minutes, a revision of the scenario that stopped herself from starting before her hand took control and got on with it. Her hand knew no shame and had no real sense of dignity or knowledge of other's criticisms of the rest of the body that they identified as Molly. The fast forward style of her thoughts didn't put her off as much she feared they might, and before Molly knew it there was a definite and somewhat determined brush mark on the page.

It was a non-descript line that tapered towards the end, more a sign of the paint running out that an artistic flourish. This, Molly knew, meant that the work would be functional, possibly compromising the outcome. But that was it, the work had begun, the paint was on the page. The page. Still big, but finally no longer empty.

She looked at the back of her hand holding the brush.

The world continued to turn.

CHAPTER 2

Family

Molly only knew sketches of her ancestry, a broken family tree whose leaves were all tattered and torn, strewn to the winds of genetic mishap. When people asked, which wasn't often, Molly would say what she knew – her dad met her mum when they were both quite young, married a few years later and had a kid who they named Molly before her mum upped and left. And no, she didn't know where her mother went or where she may be now. As far as Molly was aware, nobody knew of her absent mother's whereabouts and she wasn't even sure if anybody cared either.

That was it. No other questions, no emotions felt (eventually), no concessions to the memory of a woman who may well have suffered something quite considerable which provoked her into leaving her daughter who was only seven at the time. There was an emotional coldness in Molly when it came to matters of her mother, a detachment that served as a tool for the lobotomising of unwanted thoughts while also creating a hardened shell of apathy around her to ensure that nobody would be able to get to her like this again. It was a protective measure, a hardened skin to ward off the potential and unnecessary emotional influences of others.

The stark reality now was that Molly had been mother-free for longer than she had lived with one. She wasn't overly keen on dwelling on how this event had affected her personality as she was sure that other things would play a part in forming something which she felt still needed nurturing before it was complete, although Molly thought that perhaps there was no such thing as the finished article in this area. Humans were the opposite of lucid.

People, other people, those people who don't really count, felt that Molly had coped remarkably well given the circumstances. Those people know nothing but tend to say it loudly all the same.

Molly didn't want her mother to attain a sense of martyrdom. After all, it was the daughter who was the real victim here when looked at from the cold and calculated perspective of honest-to-goodness reality. This, though, was another viewpoint that Molly shied away from – this was an event in Molly's life that just happened, and it would be best for everybody if they all just shut up about it and got on with their squalid little happenings. Molly had no doubt that these things would all tumble out of whatever suppressed brain mechanism she was using to hide them once her own (definitely adopted) children came along but, until that time, best to keep them as buried as possible in the darkly entombed recesses of her being.

Molly understood the contradiction that the more she actively fought against and hid the memories of her mother, the more she was engaged in those recollections, but such moments were only brief and rarely ruined her day. The thing that did ruin her day was referring to Caroline as her mother, a habit she was not yet able to control to her satisfaction.

Molly had learnt strategies such as tone of voice and direct eye contact when confronted with questions about Caroline that ensured that when anyone raised this subject matter they would be left in no doubt that other topics of conversation would likely prove more fruitful and comfortable for all involved. Molly knew that her emotions abided by Newton's First Law, that they would remain at rest or in a constant state unless acted upon by an external force. In other words, she remained somewhat neutral about this matter until someone intervened and asked questions that they had no business asking.

The pretence of assuring others that she really was okay about all of this without their perceived kind interventions took a degree of energy from Molly as she found it difficult to sustain a pretence of not caring and having no answers herself. She was exhausted enough by the perpetual suppression of her own conscious thoughts about Caroline and, by extension, what that meant about herself, without having to unwillingly delve into the labyrinthian recollection and trauma that she had worked so hard to rid herself of. Maybe she missed a trick by not asking to see a counsellor, but Molly felt that there was nothing more self-indulgent, nothing more achingly a first world problem, than asking a stranger to listen to you bang on about stuff that was probably best left alone or best dealt with alone. No need to bring in other people to this mess.

Molly knew that she was at constant war with herself over this, which reassured her that burying and pushing back the fading images and sounds of the battle were the only sensible options she had.

She had watched a documentary about the Second World War and how many of the men who returned from military action never spoke of the hardships they had seen, the conflict they had been involved in and the deaths of their friends they would have surely witnessed. Molly got the feeling from the programme's male narrator that this was quite an honourable approach, that their stoicism was something to be applauded, and so she decided to follow suit. Now she was a little older, she felt that maybe the documentary was helping to perpetuate the idea that men do not, and in fact should not, talk of the things they have seen so as not to bother their womenfolk who would not have had the emotional armour to deal with such things. Patriarchy works in increasingly complex and subtle ways.

Molly often felt that perhaps it would be better for her if she did actually engage in discussion about this, but this would have likely affected Dan in ways that she was not comfortable with. Molly felt that in keeping her thoughts, ideas and emotions about all of this business locked up then she was doing a good deed for all as she would only be adding to other people's worries and their own response to these events and she did not want to be the centre of anyone's world. She did not want people's pity. She did not need people's sympathy. She felt no desire to allow others to understand her.

Molly thought that her dad, Dan, was an old-fashioned man in many ways. He kept his emotions in check whenever she was around, and she often visualised him in the trenches of his marriage, like the men in the documentary, picking out the shrapnel wound of a discouraging look, sheltering from the incoming bomb of an argument which was about to hit, or cowering in the dark with the PTSD from the toxic warfare that was Caroline. Perhaps those ideas were a little harsh on that woman who Molly could hardly remember, but it made it easier for her to nurture the notion that Dan was the resistance to the imperial war machine of womanhood that Caroline had been shaped into.

Molly knew that it was something of an understatement to say that Dan's life was a mess and that he was intensely unhappy. The number of beer cans in the recycling, along with the pizza boxes, and empty bottles of rum, crisps and menthol cigarette packets led Molly to believe that he sought solace in ways which were opposed to his previous life of marathons, gym membership, kickboxing and generally being a competitive arsehole. Now he was just a lonely, unhealthy, unbearably kind arsehole.

What you do is not who you are, Molly thought. *Unless you murder someone, in which case that one act will determine how others perceive you. And that is all they will ever want to talk about. Murderers must get bored of being murderers in the same way that Neil Armstrong must have got bored of people constantly wanting to talk to him about the moon. 'That was just one thing I did, and it was a long time ago' he would want to say. Labels are so limiting and being constrained to one act must be so dull, as if that is all a person is – a specific action. Is Neil Armstrong still alive?*

Dan never voluntarily spoke of Caroline, but then Molly rarely asked and probably had never enquired with any serious intent of getting a nostalgic conversation up and running. Had she asked, then her father would have told her all that he could remember – and he could remember it all. Dan knew that one day he would have to tell Molly everything, for his own sense of mental well-being if nothing else, and he would mull over the potential conversation that would rid him of his emotional baggage but perhaps weigh Molly down even more.

He struggled with coming to a decision on how best to approach it. He didn't want Molly to be the initiator of the conversation as there was a feeling that that wouldn't be fair. Equally, Dan didn't want to second guess when the moment may be right as he was very good at getting things wrong. In fact, that was one aspect of his personality that he was sure about – when someone needed him to say the right thing he would almost certainly, inexplicably and inadvertently say the exact opposite without meaning to.

* * * * * *

In 1970, Dan was born to Karen and Tom, the grandparents that Molly rarely met before they moved away to Spain in 2009. She remembered that they bickered in ways that people didn't understand, thinking that they were actually having a full-blown argument when in fact it was simply the way that they had become accustomed to communicating with one another over the years.

Despite Karen and Tom's perpetual raising of their voices over the most trivial of matters, Dan later had a younger brother and then a sister which means that his parents must have at least been cordial and appreciative to the other from time to time. Whenever Molly asked questions about Dan's parents she rarely got a reply which gave her more insight into what they were like as people. He just gave her the outlines of people – what they did, rather than who they were. This made Molly realise that he had no idea what his parents were really like as people, he had no obvious knowledge of their political views, their cultural tastes or what made them laugh. Perhaps the way in which Dan described his parents was the way most people saw others, as centrally being defined by what they do in life. Perhaps people aren't that interested in views and ideas.

Dan met Caroline at what his parents called 'a do'. While in Sixth Form at the local Grammar school, a group of friends chipped in to get a PA system that could be used for bands and DJs – enterprising young things who would all end up bored out of their minds in menial administrative jobs while casting a misty eyed nostalgic glance to the heady days of the late 1980s and early 1990s when they had hair.

They would put on parties as a loose collective in numerous places – rugby clubs, village halls and, once or twice, at their school. Some teachers were required to be present to act as chaperones/bouncers and Dan and his friends knew exactly which ones to target their requests towards. He had been taught in recent years by all three of the teachers he asked and knew one or two things about them that helped establish them as the likely candidates to accept such a task.

All three were well-known, by both the students and the parents, as considerable drinkers and Dan made it clear when he spoke to them that the event would be a strict alcohol-free affair and that the staff members would be able to confiscate any booze they found and get rid of it in whichever way they saw fit. It was abundantly clear by the end of the night from the glazed eyes and slightly staggering gait of these three that more than a few bottles had been 'dealt with'. Fair play to them, Dan thought. Surely all teachers of any worth had drink problems to anaesthetise the stress, noise and smell of their professional lives.

Stories were circulated that Dunlow, the persistently wonky Maths teacher, had cheerily got into his car at the end of the night which led to him getting arrested by Kent's finest, but there was no evidence of this other than the fact that he did not seem to have a car for a week or so after the gig. Rumours like this always went around the school about the personal lives of the teachers – their potential affairs, sexual orientation, drinking habits and whether or not any of them were kiddie fiddlers were the hot topics of the day. Nobody at that time used the word paedophile, or even paedo. Nobody had ever asked Dan, and he had not thought about it, but if someone did raise the question of when he first heard the word 'paedophile' he would have to take his time over it and guess that it would have been around the mid- to late-1990s.

While the tabloid press were whipping up a moral panic that all teenagers were taking Ecstasy and driving endlessly around the M25 in the hope of being fortuitous enough to become connected to the illegal rave scene before the Criminal Justice Act cut the fun, Dan and his friends were into the much more serious art of copying bands like The Cure, Joy Division, The Smiths and other miserabilists of the era.

Fun was the least of their concerns. All that was needed to engage in their music of choice was a rudimentary understanding of guitar tone – not necessarily of notes or chords. In this scene, the sound of the guitar was often more valued than the playing and often more important than the sound was the look. Skinny black jeans, paisley patterned shirts and collar length hair were the order of the day, a mish-mash of 60s psychedelia, 70s metal and 80s post-punk. This dress code was invariably wrapped up with a painted leather jacket. Jeff in the year above was particularly skilled at adorning the back of these coats with whatever band logo the wearer requested. This was the uniform of this subculture but those who were in bands realised after some time that they needed to slightly alter their look so that they would stand out from their audience (i.e. their mates).

Hour upon hour was wasted/spent fiddling with combo amp settings to find the sound which was just trebly enough to be piercing without being overly annoying and tinnitus inducing. All that was then needed was a rhythm section that could be consistent enough in their time-keeping yet invisible enough in their physicality not to distract from the lead guitarist and singer.

The frontman - it was always a man in this scene at this time - was the embodiment of what the band stood for. Often aloof, always commanding, with a projection of undeniably alluring sexuality which simply involved wearing a jumper that was at least three sizes too big and a charity shop bought trench coat with massive holes in the pockets, this man was the tortured poet of his generation who also had to hold down a job at Dixon's on Saturdays. Bass players and drummers were often to be found working in Our Price, singers in Dixon's or Timothy White's, whereas the guitarists would be at home due to his resistance towards selling out to The Man. Some bands also had keyboard players but these, Dan reckoned, were used when the guitarist wasn't really up to it.

Dan knew Caroline before he had the chance to speak to her – or rather, Dan was aware of Caroline before he plucked up the courage to drunkenly talk in her direction about an array of topics that he thought might impress her. Caroline was in the year below Dan at the girl's school which was about a twenty minute walk from his house.

He became aware of her through a friend of her cousin when they all used to hang out with each other in the streets before any of them looked old enough to be allowed to sit in a pub.

Before he was aware of his interest in her, some friends of Dan's had tried it on with her and, to his surprise, Dan found that this made him jealous and so therefore he assumed that he liked her. Not that any of them had got anywhere; she seemed to be something of a cold fish. Some of the more idiot boys in his year would have no doubt decided to call her frigid or a lesbian had they been on the receiving end of one of her polite but firm rebuttals but, thankfully, Dan's friends were made of better things and they just shrugged, put it down to some personality defect that they would work harder on more fully projecting to enhance the stench of failure that surrounded them, and got on with things.

These boys wanted to instil and encapsulate a sense of loneliness and separation from the world yet their untamed masculine lust, coupled with the Siren like whiff of patchouli oil and heavy set, Patricia Morrison style mascara, made such things difficult.

Dan had stories from school but few, if any, were about lessons and academic aspirations. There was one story that did the rounds at the boys' grammar that Angus Haye had been locked in the school with Lisa Proctor after a rehearsal for the school play and rather than do what most hormonally driven teenagers would have done – screwed one another for the best part of seven to eight minutes – they spent the night sometimes sleeping, often talking while trying to maintain some semblance of both touching and distance, of proximity and prohibition. This, they had both decided separately without consultation with the other, was one of the best nights of their lives and would be a long-cherished memory of restraint in the face of carnal adversity.

In fact, both would forget the actual events not more than a couple of years later with Angus insisting in conversation while she was safely miles away at university that he had actually 'dipped her rotten'. Dan didn't much care for Angus as he had the air of someone who knew he would do well in life.

Dan and Caroline started dating as young innocents do – in the company of others. Money was tight for Dan as he spent all that he had on a range of music related things – records, magazines, strings for his bass guitar, hiring a practice room, going to gigs and festivals. There was a lot of month left at the end of the money and Dan didn't really have the enthusiasm to ascribe his hard-earned cash to something that wasn't centred on music. In a sense, Caroline scared him a bit as he had no real idea how to communicate with her so he thought it better to keep her at arm's length and not allow her full and open access to his faults and foibles by surrounding themselves with other like-minded people or doing things like going to gigs where the emphasis would be on listening to the band rather than trying to make conversation.

Dan struggled with starting the chat and found sustaining it an almost impossible task. He was, however, pretty good at bringing them to an end as he would often say things which led to an abrupt response from the other person who were usually somehow offended by the position he had got around to espousing. Dan was the king of the conversation cul-de-sac. He often felt that he had no real control over what he was saying, and he would very often need to listen to himself talking to find out what his point was – as if he were eavesdropping in on his own thoughts to establish what the bloody hell he was saying and work out how best to avoid making a complete tit of himself. There were times when he would say something controversial for no apparent reason, perhaps to appear a contrarian par excellence, an agent provocateur of parley, a warrior of words – all just to get a response out of people and to provoke a reaction. Any reaction would do as it served to remind others that he existed.

In the January of 1997, Dan asked Caroline to marry him and six short months later they were husband and wife. This was during the period that his band was falling apart for various reasons, and so Dan saw this as a sign that it was time to commit to something, and someone, else. There were no photos in the house of the wedding day and even though Molly would occasionally ask her dad about it she knew very little other than 'some people were there' and 'it was a decent day'. In fact, there were no photos of Molly's mum at all in the house, at least none that Molly could ever find and she had taken a very methodical, almost forensic style approach to her searching.

For Dan, the hardest part now was just how pure and innocent it all felt. How easy. How much in love they were, or at least how much in love he was. It was, without question, a natural progression in his life that rarely needed questioning. It was the simplest of decisions to move forward in his life with Caroline; he was smitten. What a fool he had been.

Molly often imagined the scene where Dan exorcised the house of all photographic evidence that Caroline had ever played a significant role in his life. Occasionally, he was calm as the scenario played itself out in Molly's mind. He would simply collect the remaining traces of Caroline, including favourite coffee cup, a few items of clothing, photographs, hairbands, post-it notes on the fridge and whatever else was lying around and pile them in a corner ready to put in the rubbish. He was humming but with a serious facial expression, like a calm master criminal who was ensuring that the scene of whatever crime had been committed was left unblemished. This was Molly's preferred vision of events. She knew, however, that this was probably unlikely.

Other times, her vision involved Dan throwing the items on to a huge bonfire, tears streaming down his face as he was seen through the flames which made his face wobble a little due to the heat of the fire, a cool technique of camera placement in films to suggest an unnerved moment of disquiet. Molly often imagined things like scenes in films, taking into account not just the action as it unfolded but also things like the camera angle, movement and its meaning along with the accompanying non-diegetic soundtrack. This took the edge off the emotional rawness and realisation that this was an important moment in her father's life.

By imagining such events as unfolding on screen rather than in real life, whatever that meant, there was a sense of emotional disconnect which helped to dampen the rawness of living, as if the shout of 'Cut' would be able to dispel all sense of feeling. Life was like method acting but without the whispered sense of motivation or direction from others who would prove to be worth listening to, and no prompt hidden away to help when you got stuck for your lines.

No doubt the active expulsion of the traces of Caroline's existence in the house had not happened as soon as she had walked out of the door. Molly could not remember a time when there were any photographs of Caroline on the wall, and so therefore trying to figure out when they may have disappeared was a pointless intellectual exercise. There must have been a period when Dan thought, hoped, prayed that Caroline would come back, and as a result he would vow to change, to work harder on being a good man, or to no longer place spoons the wrong way up on the draining board, or to stop his habit of leaving trip hazards such as clothes, books or magazines on the stairs, or to always place the toilet roll in Caroline's preferred way, or to squeeze the toothpaste from a more consistent place on the tube or whatever it was that Caroline needed from him, and they could go on being a family together.

If Dan got rid of all evidence of her ever living there, then that would perhaps ruin any chances of reconciliation if she ever were to return only to see empty space where visions of her once belonged.

How long, then, was the gap in time between the door closing behind Caroline for the last time and Dan realising that she wasn't ever coming back? Was it a case that when that moment came he lost all hope, or was it a feeling of relief? Had he even reached that point, that moment of unnerving lucidity? Maybe he wasn't as tense anymore from constantly thinking, expecting even, that he would hear her key in the door to end all of this. Maybe he was glad she had gone. Maybe that.

Molly always viewed Dan as quite a placid, static individual. She rarely saw bursts of emotion from him and he took everything pretty much in his stride. He had moments of being outwardly anxious and Molly recognised these as centring on his worries about people's perceptions of how he was coping with raising his child alone, or at least that was what she interpreted as the cause of his occasional lip biting, non-verbal mood swings. Molly noticed Dan's nervousness as being more pronounced when he was out and still.

In queues he seemed particularly edgy and would constantly be scanning and planning and observing everybody and every detail in as subtle a way as possible, but in a manner that made Molly think that he was trying to store as much of the minute, mundane detail in case an extraordinary event happened which would need him to recount the day to the authorities. When Molly was with Dan in queues, usually at the Post Office or in a shop, she would notice how he became increasingly mobile, hopping from one leg to the other rather than standing on both legs at the same time like a normal human being. His eyes would be darting around, never fixing on one thing for too long, and he would begin fiddling with the letter/parcel/object in his hand.

All of these signs would have gone entirely unnoticed by the casual observer, Molly thought, but she was a little more than that.

She wondered if he had always been like this or whether this side to his personality came as a result of the wounds that Caroline had inflicted upon him. Maybe his exterior projection of calm was perceived by Caroline as emotional detachment and apathy and was one of the main reasons, if not *the* reason, why she wanted out. *But if she pissed off because of him, then why not take me with her?*

The memories in Molly's head of her mother's face were increasingly distorted and blurred with time and her own reluctance to more regularly utilise them. She recognised how the features in her mother's image were often a composite of others who were in her everyday existence. Molly felt that her mother was a ghost although not one that was likely to haunt her on a regular basis, if ever. But, similar to spirit apparitions, thoughts of her mother would seep into Molly's mind unexpectedly, and certainly uninvited. Molly tried to be dispassionate about her mother, but this was often a hard position to sustain as, try as she might, there always a little flicker of heartache, coupled with a degree of annoyance, involved.

Molly was particularly aggrieved at the fact that this woman was unlikely to ever age, as memories do not have the ability to accurately keep up with the decaying effects of chronology.

On April 9th 2008, unexpectedly and uncompromisingly, Molly was left without a mother. Caroline had gone, and apparently nobody knew where. Molly felt that some people must have known where Caroline was but as far as Molly was concerned, nobody had told Dan, or he didn't try to look for her hard enough or wasn't all that bothered about looking. Perhaps Molly had searched for photos of her mother for longer than Dan had tried to locate Caroline herself.

Molly knew so little about her mother's withdrawal from her life - this was the one topic of conversation that was rarely welcome in the house. The unspoken agreement she had with Dan about this subject reminded Molly of a joke she had heard somewhere or other at some point – a man buys an elephant for his best pal. The grateful recipient says 'Thanks, I'll keep it right here in this room.' 'Please, don't mention it' replies the friend. Caroline was the behemoth (no longer) in the room. Perhaps Dan knew exactly where she was and why she left. Maybe one day Molly would know, too.

Molly would not allow herself to feel like some semi-orphaned sympathy case. She had Dan, and Molly knew that he unquestionably tried his best to be everything that he could be for her. She could not remember ever seeing him not smile at her, though as she got older she started to more fully appreciate that Caroline leaving left two people to deal with the situation. It is all too easy as a kid to think that you are the only one affected by a situation, and that others' feelings are not as pronounced, justified or acute as your own. For many years this was how Molly felt, that this had all just happened to her, and to her alone. She did not have the maturity or the wherewithal to consider Dan and how this must have hurt him deeply, how this was surely seen as a judgment on him by others.

As the years passed, occasional lapses into hating Dan for being worthy of leaving were phased out of Molly's thoughts and she started to realise that there was an unseen tidal wave of negative emotions that she had not been privy to or, as she suspected with the passing of years, she had been protected from.

With each passing year, Molly felt that the loss of her mother was easier to cope with, but she also developed a more acute awareness at the pain that Dan must have gone through, and this was not a trade off that she felt comfortable with.

* * * * *

Molly's favourite words were what she called 'warm words' – those that possessed semantic ideas of comfort and happiness. Words such as home, bed, snug and hug were warm words for Molly. Obviously, for most people the word family would also be considered as having a certain charm and positive connotation to it and Molly felt the same while also knowing that the jigsaw of her family was missing a vital piece. In this analogy, Molly saw Caroline as taking up a space in the middle of the puzzle rather than the corners or the edges.

Molly was a very methodical jigsaw maker, always amassing the four corners first before gathering all of the edge pieces together. Once correctly in place, the frame was set and sturdy, and it was just the detail that needed filling in. Caroline was a totem for pieces in the middle that, even though they were missing, didn't impact the full picture as much as they might because the main pictorial representation within the boundaries of the jigsaw was clear; it just so happened that it was apparent but not whole.

Since she left, Caroline had not, to Molly's knowledge, sent a birthday or Christmas card. No notes. Nothing. 'Family' relates to a whole being in whatever shape or combination of people that may take, as far as Molly was concerned, not a disturbed and disrupted one. Molly never felt that her familial circle could ever be considered dysfunctional just because the two of them, Dan and Molly, did not fit into conventional ideas of the family unit. *Screw conventionality*. That traditional nuclear family of a smug, emotionally neutered mum and dad and their 2.4 children was being challenged in society nowadays and Molly didn't feel that cultural pressure was the reason for feeling that her family was somehow broken, it was just the fact that without the closure of knowing whether her mother was even alive she could not help but think there was something left unresolved even though she told herself time and time and time again that she didn't *need* to know.

Dan was all the family she needed, of this there could be no doubt, and Molly felt a sense of shame in her own emotional state that there still sometimes existed a nagging sense, despite her attempts to vanquish them, that she just wanted to know what the hell had happened. Yet this position changed on a week by week basis and Molly was pained by what she saw as her inconsistent nature on this matter when, in relation to all other things, she prided herself on her assuredness and stability.

The unknowingness of the situation was, Molly often felt, perhaps better than the certainty of facts. She was at least aware that this emptiness could be construed by others as genuine angst, and would therefore add credence to her potential life as an artist. It gave her a back story although she would forever make it clear in all of the future plush magazine interviews that she was likely to give that her work was not a reaction to her family situation, more an analysis of the human spirit in moments of hardship. Something like that, anyway.

There were times, quite a number of times in fact, when Molly would lie awake in her bed blaming Caroline for everything. Then, on other occasions, she would stare at a ceiling that the dark did not allow her to see blaming Dan for everything, although in such instances this feeling was usually actively eradicated with some haste. Despite not feeling that her family was fully formed, despite her usual concerns about her father's loneliness, despite wondering how her life would have been different with a more prominent female role model, despite all of these things, Molly rarely, if ever, missed her mother. In fact, the absence of her mother made her develop her own personality rather than cultivating such a thing in the shadow of another. Or at least that was how Molly had trained her thought processes to accept the situation and to adopt a sense of self from the wreckage of Caroline's exit.

Molly did not presume that people cared enough about her own feelings about this scenario to feel let down by the fact that since her mother left other family members had not referred to her in some way – 'Oh, you look just like your mother when you pull that face' or 'That's your mother coming out in you when you say that' or other such phrases.

The absence of her mother's physical and emotional influence was felt but not mourned. Molly knew full well that she was a chimera, a hybrid of the genetic consequence of Dan and Caroline but there was also a sense of freedom that her same-sex parent was in a land far away or wherever she was, as she could not present a mirror of femininity which Molly could reflect or reject. Molly felt empowered when she thought about this as she felt that her own sense of self was developing autonomously, not in the face of a dominant female presence. She could not be a copy of somebody she did not know.

Not long after her mother left, Molly convinced herself that she would one day bump in to her and it would all be revealed that Caroline had to leave in the interests of national security. This was easier than thinking that her mother couldn't stand the sight of her.

As the years went by, Molly reconciled in herself a sense of resignation that she herself was not the influencing factor in her mother's disappearing act but that it was all down to Dan, the man who was not only left to pick up the pieces of his own life but the man who also seemed to have sworn a vow of silence in the face of early questions from his daughter. Now, on reflection, Molly felt that her social awkwardness which eventually led to her anxiety issues probably stemmed from the fact that she did not know the answer to the one burning question which she demanded of herself be pushed to the most remote places of her mind where it would remain buried probably until her last breath.

Caroline was her Rosebud, and there would be a cut at the end of the film of Molly's life to a slow zoom on an open funeral pyre as Caroline's face was contorted and blistered by the engulfing flames that would soon tear her to ash. Molly loved that film. But best ever? Probably not.

As the years went by, Molly stopped worrying about where her mother might be and started unwittingly projecting ideas of what she was like now. She didn't want to, it was a form or purgatory that she put herself through to relieve whatever mundanity she was experiencing at the time. The where was superseded by the who.

Had she changed since leaving, and if so, how? What bands did she listen to, which books had she recently read, what were her views on same sex marriage….? The list went on and on and on and as the list went on and on and on the list became more achingly dull. But, Molly reasoned, as you get to know a person better you probably become intensely bored by that person's opinions, mannerisms and eventually their inevitable shortcomings – time to move on when that happens. If you adore them, one day you'll bore them.

Molly enjoyed these questions but would often disconnect Caroline from her position as 'mother'; she was just a person that Molly had lost contact with and it was just her curious nature that led to her thinking of this woman, not her emotional psyche. Whenever these thoughts idly wandered through her mind, though, Molly felt a slight visceral twinge in her gut that she found difficult to place or describe. It was as if her belly were being flipped in every direction, like being on a demented, four-dimensional rollercoaster that had no driver at the wheel. This was adrenaline, Molly thought, a natural response as a fight or flight mechanism that was needed for people to decide which paths were dangerous and which were benign. Thoughts of Caroline were becoming increasingly less traumatic for Molly, but they were never without a degree of harm.

Molly worried about Dan in an almost proactively obsessive way. She felt a need to develop a sense of concern for his well-being as in that way at least somebody was projecting adult concerns in his direction. Theirs was not a relationship where they could sit in the same room for hours on end pursuing their own activities or talking endlessly about everything and nothing. Molly tried to play the role of protector by regularly asking Dan how his day at work had been and she almost always received the nonchalant, ritualistic reply of 'Alright, but it's over now' which was a hell of a way to shut down any subsequent lines of investigation.

Molly wanted to be able to look deep into his eyes to see all of the pain that was present there - the recurring echoes of a failed marriage, the frustration of his increasingly lonely lifestyle as a decreasing circle of friends seemed to be ever waning, the moderate but regular alcohol consumption which perhaps meant that he couldn't even make a success of being a drunk, and his erratic sleep patterns which Molly was aware of due to the regular noises of the late night shuffling of furniture downstairs all added to the profile of Dan as an individual with a sense of tense restlessness, a gnawing sense of rejection and worthlessness that came with being left with a child to look after. Molly couldn't look too intensely for fear of finding out too much. A sense of mystery was better than naked truths that led to disappointment in someone's character - especially with a parent.

The worry for Dan served as a useful vessel of deflection away from her own issues, of this Molly was sure and thankful. Somehow, Molly felt that her father was aware that he was being observed as a source of investigative interest for her analytical microscope wherein the hypothesis was that everyone is as screwed up as the next.

Dan worked as some sort of team leader for a charity. A lot of his work was office based but occasionally Molly knew that he worked on the streets asking for people's time when he really wanted their money. As he rarely ventured a sensible response to Molly about the events of his day, she was entirely unaware of whether he was actually any good at his job or not. She felt sure he hated the work but then pretty much everybody seemed to hate theirs, so this did not stand him out from others. Dan was no good at mundane things such as jobs, cleaning, cooking, gardening, active listening etc.

He had cocooned himself in a world of films, music, comics ('Actually, Molly, they're graphic novels, thanks'), burning sarcasm and other forms of seemingly mindless entertainment. This, Molly reasoned, allowed him to focus less on his own worries and to propel himself into the lives of (more interesting) others. A form of diversion. An escape from himself. An escape from all of this *being*.

The burning, crippling sensation that Dan felt as a result of his daughter not knowing the reason for the departure of her mother was palpable. He felt, in fact he *knew*, that on the day when Molly's ignorance was addressed, he would have to face up to the fact that daddy's little girl wasn't a girl anymore.

He vowed to do so when he felt that Molly was emotionally intelligent enough to be able to handle the information. He also appreciated the fact that when the time was right he would wait a little longer.

When Dan reflected on his own life he realised that mistakes had been made yet he was quietly proud of how he had managed to raise an intelligent, though admittedly troubled daughter. Perhaps she was no more troubled than other kids her own age in the same way that nobody else's headache is worse than yours. He knew that he had changed beyond all recognition and that the fire in his eyes had been dimmed many years before Caroline had actually gone. His poor diet, sedentary lifestyle and smoking had all contributed to a diminishing of the things that had once, many years ago, made him attractive.

He knew he had to quit smoking, but he simply didn't have the drive to do so and could not find a justifiable reason for giving up the one thing in his life that was undeniably his. In a life such as his, Dan knew that there were very few desires in life that could be satiated almost immediately, and for that reason he was thankful to tobacco. When Dan wanted a cigarette, that momentarily became the sole purpose of his existence, the need for the next puff was temporarily at the front and centre of his very being until he had the opportunity to satisfy his craving. What else in life, particularly in Dan's life, could be so immediately remedied?

When he craved a cigarette rather than merely fancying one, his essence was solely focused on putting that sweet cylinder in his mouth and lighting the flame that would burn bright in his heart's desire. Dan could not think of anything else in life that he had sufficient control over to want it so badly and that he would be able to serve this yearning with immediate, gratifying effect. In this way, smoking cigarettes, despite the negatives that he was all too aware of, performed a role of allowing him to feel a degree of control in his life that, in the harsh reality that clarity provides, he knew was entirely lacking. He had, briefly, thought about vaping but had hated himself for the entire duration of the thought as such a thing was not reasonable for a man of his age.

He was in the netherworld with regards to change – he could not alter his appearance nor his lifestyle choices without looking desperately sad. Not that there would be anyone to notice such alterations, but that was neither here nor there.

Dan was nothing but a reasonable man, perhaps too reasonable at times. He had mood swings the same as everyone else but the sharp intensity of being solely responsible for Molly's well-being weighed on him like nothing else had before or ever could in the future. If it takes a village to raise a child, then he, and he alone, would be her village. Nobody else could be entrusted with something so precious as culpability for Molly. Dan knew that the deep-seated betrayal that Caroline had put him through, and his inability to articulate his feelings anywhere other than in his own head, cut a scar in him that ran deeper than simply not trusting people anymore. Dan had said for many years that the only thing that he had ever really done that got him into trouble was thinking. Now it was the actions of another.

He tore himself apart in trying to work out what he could have done differently in order to allow another scenario to play out. Regret, pain, pity, agony, loneliness, anger, despair – these were just a small number of the sensations that were so pronounced for Dan and led to him undergoing what he called an 'emotional castration'. He was numbed by the whole sequence of events so much so that he never wanted to feel again.

There was a certain comfort in feeling sad, he thought, but there was even more consolation in knowing that nobody could hurt him again as his defences were well and truly up. He had changed his lifestyle patterns, becoming a social hermit. Over time, he systematically, and through a quite conscious process, dropped out of his various friendship groups as he knew that the point would come in the future when some of them would start to entice Dan into another relationship. Time would not be allowed to heal these wounds, as Dan was a little too comfortable wallowing in them. This was the self-fulfilling prophecy of his maudlin teenage song lyrics coming home to roost.

There would be no malice in the attempts of his friends to try to matchmake, quite the opposite in fact, yet Dan felt that this would be the cruellest, most vicious thing that anyone could do to him.

Perhaps there was one act which would be more barbarous and that would be for someone to allow Dan to fall for them. He knew that such things always ended in tears, and that they always would, so he wasn't going to fall for that old trick again. He had more than enough on his hands with Molly and felt that somebody else trying to wave their attempts at influence at his child would not make for comfortable viewing for anyone. He would focus on Molly and that would bring him enough satisfaction. Dan often felt that he had lived a privileged life when compared to others on the planet and so a little bruising to his heart in comparison to the physical suffering of others was very little to worry about and perhaps now was the time when he had to sacrifice some of the pleasures he had previously taken from life in order to focus on what really mattered.

Dan often worried that the position of no longer seeking female attention made him something of a misogynist as he would not have wanted anyone to think that Caroline had made him think that all women were the same. It wasn't the fault of his potential future never-going-to-happen-anyway lovers; he was the constant in any relationship that he could get involved in. He was the element that would make it all fall apart.

He could only ever disappoint anyone as he had failed to do anything other than be a let-down to those closest to him thus far. He had never felt close to his parents who substituted genuine affection with financial incentives. His siblings rarely contacted him and were always seen as being a cognitively conjoined pair who, unintentionally or otherwise, ostracised their older brother. And Molly would likely seek emancipation from him soon enough. That day probably wasn't too far away.

There were waves of feeling which ebbed and flowed and Dan was rarely in control of the worst lows which he never saw coming. The feelings of isolation that he had every day of his post-Caroline existence were not too bad, but there were occasions when he often felt that he had reached the pits of despair while continuing to be required to wear a (barely visible) smile. Dan enjoyed his own company and only ever got sad about it on those rare occasions when he heard a noise in the house and for the briefest of moments thought that Caroline was home, like some sort of sonic flashback to a romanticised ideal of the past.

Although such moments were infrequent, the feeling would stay with him for quite some time. Days, weeks, and on one occasion, months.

He would be angry with himself for the lapse which allowed her to creep back into his thoughts and he would be annoyed that the events of the last however many years since she left were seemingly not sufficient to warrant his emotional firewall recognising the presence of her malware. When these thoughts came, Dan needed a reboot.

The most startling example of Caroline's capacity to enter his cognition was one morning maybe twenty-six or twenty-seven months after she had gone. Dan stirred from an unsettled night's sleep and felt her hand gently stroking his hair; he could feel her breath on him as she whispered in his ear that everything was going to be alright. It was then obvious, for a split second, that he had simply woken from a very realistic nightmare of abandonment and loss, and that Caroline was lying next to him while he had played out his worst fears in his night-time visions. The sense of relief was palpable and washed through him in an instant. On opening his eyes, he realised that the bed was cold, and he was more alone than when he had fallen asleep. His brain was never happier than when fooling him into brief spells of contentment.

Sleep was no longer a friend to Dan. In his dreams, Caroline was physically the same as when she had left, yet Dan transposed the years of her absence to create a torpid, hateful, twisted aura around her dream-state presence. He figured this was because, no matter how hard he may have tried, he still felt a form of physical attraction to Caroline despite undeniably and deeply hating her. It was the omnipotent sense of poison that he felt for this woman that denied him safe, comforted and restful sleep. The fact that he would not, that he could not, open up about his feelings to anyone else meant that this destructive, cathartic, overwhelming, and justified seething simply ate away at his very being until he even questioned his own ability to resist the urge to kill her if she ever darkened his doorstep again.

All of these feelings were tied up with an aching sense of self-pity, wrapped in a worry that Molly's future children would suffer due to their mother's emotional stuntedness in the face of her own poor experience of an inadequate and restricted family life. Recriminations, doubt, hopelessness, loneliness, self-hatred, and a desire for reconciliation regardless of everything else meant that sleep was never a guaranteed visitor.

Dan knew that his focus needed to be solely on Molly, the one good thing in his life, and he changed his work, his aspirations and his social life to always ensure she never felt any form of abandonment from him. He ended up working in a job he hated to pay the mortgage for a house he could ill afford to appease for the actions of another. Dan always knew that he had a martyr complex, but this is not how he thought it would play out.

He would worry about every element of Molly's day and how things would inevitably reflect back on him. When he packed her lunch for school, he would ensure there was enough variety from day to day to make certain that other kids did not go home and say that Molly was not being sufficiently well looked after by her broken father.

He would spend time each day attempting to remove every

last bit of fluff from her school clothes and every speck of dirt from her shoes to make the school gate community of hell as bearable for him as possible. He wanted to make people realise he had all of this under control and that they had no need to worry, pry or sneer.

The grinding routine of the school drop-off was to run the gauntlet of looks and half smiles that always set off the day in a poor way and he wished, more than anything else in the morning, to avoid it if he could. But run it he did.

He had never felt more judged than by people who were far too busy with their own wretched lives to worry about the dad who stood quietly on his own, ensuring no eye contact would be made with others which could then possibly lead to a conversation. Dan felt no desire to engage with these other people, not because of who they were but because of who he was. He felt that he had nothing to offer in conversation with these people who he saw as nothing more than parents of children that his daughter shared space with.

His introversion was almost certainly seen by others as an air of arrogant aloofness and although he was averse to anyone thinking this of him he was not able to control his actions sufficiently to alter this. He was quietly relieved when Molly told him she thought it best to discontinue her formal education at school.

His petrification in the face of others presented many obstacles for Dan. Engagement with Molly's teachers was never a problem because all they wanted was a quick 'hello' or any other form of acknowledgement of existence and nothing else. In fact, they probably heaved a sigh of relief when parents chose not to stand and chat.

The other parents, however, only ever seemed to have their minds set on asking leading questions in an attempt to gauge whose child was academically or socially dominant. Comparisons were forever being made in the conversations that he overheard in the playground which served as the meeting point to pick up the kids from school. Parents would conflate, exaggerate, provide alibis and sympathise with other parents in a manner which made him feel that all that was happening was a fairly obvious ritual of establishing a hierarchy of performance and behaviour for their offspring in relation to their peers via incessant chatter.

Dan wanted no part of it for himself or for Molly. He knew that she was top in the class at everything expect PE. Everyone knew it. It didn't need saying.

When Caroline left and people eventually found out about it, Dan was met with nothing but kindness and concern, but this was not enough to assuage him of the idea that one dark day the Social Services would come knocking on his door after receiving some credible calls of concern from a range of anonymous people about the well-being of his daughter. Dan was so preoccupied with how other people saw his situation and how he was coping in their perception that he had little time to take in the vast scope of what had happened to him, but he felt that maybe he knew deep down that this was how things with Caroline were always going to end. There are no winners or losers in romantic relationships, just endlessly disappointed participants with the intellectual engagement of an exhausted, dying hamster in a wheel.

Dan had become a sexual Sisyphus.

Every year, around but never actually on her birthday, Dan

wrote Molly a letter that he stored away under his socks and pants in the top drawer of his wardrobe. In this assembled-at-home case of MDF lay the truth, written in Dan's all too often scruffy and rushed handwriting in whatever colour he could find, that he would one day either leave for her to find or give as some sort of rites of passage into adulthood at an as yet unspecified age.

He initially wrote his letters in a manner that suggested that by the time she read his words, he would be dead. There was, he felt, a certain degree of romance to this – the doomed father who had spent his life protecting his daughter from the reality of her past while sacrificing his own happiness. There was also, Dan was assured, a sense of absolute pretension about the whole affair. The letters could never truly be heartfelt and honest as there was a knowledge in their writing that this was an attempt to vanquish himself of any form of responsibility or wrongdoing in the thing that had most shredded his daughter's state of mind.

Dan first started writing letters to Molly three days before her second birthday as a way to fully express his feelings towards her as an appeasement and act of self-forgiveness to his approach to fatherhood in the early stages of Molly's life.

The initial few months of beaming pride at being a dad were soon usurped with crushing worries about his child's future, the possibility of her being kidnapped or hit by a speeding car played over in his mind on a constant rotation of greatest hits catastrophising. Rather than enjoy the moment for what it was, Dan often slumped into irrational, irregular but inescapable fits of what most would call depression but what he termed as simply an elongated foul mood. He knew he had what many others craved, yet found it increasingly difficult to find any sustained enjoyment in his life. He was too wrapped up in worrying about future possibilities that his calm, rational self knew were entirely unlikely, but why ruin the constant pain of life with passing contentment that would only make loss more difficult?

He would pay for every day that he enjoyed himself when this all came tumbling down around him. Nobody reclined the car seat when they sensed a crash ahead.

He felt that perhaps he had cut the umbilical cord at Molly's birth too well and it had somehow acted more like a sprung coil as she had already slipped away from him in her first few months to be a constant adornment to Caroline's hip, breast or focus. His letters were attempts to reconcile his feelings with how he should have felt, and he wrote at length about the admiration he felt for Caroline and how seeing her with Molly was the essence of his being, the most joyous aspect of his life and the thing that he most gave thanks for. He burnt that particular letter six months after Caroline left and it was a few more years before he could bear to continue with this annual letter writing routine.

Molly and Dan, entirely by mutual consent, had agreed to go a whole year without looking things up on the internet. They would often hide behind their phone screens in the evening and ignore each other that way rather than the more traditional sense of placing thoughts and introspection as a barrier to engaged interaction.

They reached the conclusion, independently of each other but simultaneously, that their intellectual development was being held back by the immediate access to facts that was at their fingertips at any given minute on any given day. Debate, discussion, contradiction, the nurturing of ideas – these were all aspects that were gone (or at least going) due to the omnipotent presence and allure of the world wide web in daily life.

The population were flies - weak, feeble and unsuspecting - to the powerful spiders of the internet's oligarchs. Internet users, like flies, can be duped despite the illusion of three-hundred-and-sixty-degree vision. Why else was it called the web?

Dan would often say that discussions, disagreements and quizzes in pubs were dead as a result of phones that were smarter than the owners who kept buying the latest model for no apparent benefit to anyone other than the shareholders of these corporations who now had more wealth than many countries combined. Molly felt this was an interesting position to take as she could hardly remember the last time he went to a pub.

Molly didn't mind removing herself from the social media sites she had signed up to. She had created an echo chamber of people who shared similar views in the things that mattered – music, politics, feminism, films – so as to avoid the real world and she was sure that all sixteen of her followers on Instagram would hardly notice her digital demise. She would not miss the occasional forays onto news sites where she could engage in ridiculously one-sided debates with crypto- and not-so-crypto-fascists whose only recourse to argument was to call her a snowflake for caring. Molly thought it strange that they should choose that particular term as a way of homogenising people.

There was, Molly felt, just too much communication these days, whereas Dan felt that there was no longer any lasting power in saying goodbye as time and distance were not an obstacle to contact. Peace and quiet was lost to the din of opinion, to raucous rhetoric and the glaring mundanity of people's lives. Dan didn't really care what he ate so could not muster sufficient interest in the often resplendently photographed nourishment of others.

Social media also emboldened ideologies and values and offered people a platform to air them, safe in the knowledge that they were unlikely to ever be held accountable for their dubious views. The world was becoming increasingly both connected and divided. Word limitations on social media meant that people were required to express the nuances of their very being in only a few characters, and therefore arguments tended to be more and more about soundbites of information, often with no context. The digital age was ironically creating a more binary set of users.

Molly was reminded of one of Dan's favourite sayings, 'Just because you are talking that doesn't mean you are saying anything', whenever she thought of how she should be missing social media. She often craved the ability to check facts from reliable sources, but she didn't react in anything other than a neutral way when it came to thinking about the mind-numbing hours spent trawling through page after page after page of the pixelated projections of happiness that people implored the world to see. *If,* Molly thought, *all of these nights out are so great then why do they stop every few minutes to take photos of it? Why can't they just be in the moment?*

Such thoughts made Molly feel simultaneously superior but also disconnected from the kind of life that everyone around her seemed to be choosing to live, as if she didn't belong in this time or with those people.

Maybe she just wasn't welcome with those people. She wouldn't want to be welcome, anyway. Their skin was too shiny and seemed to be unnatural tones for humans, and their photographs were awful. Why did these copper tanned people insist on pointing at one another, sticking their tongues out and be constantly leaning towards the centre of the image as if some sort of vortex or personality vacuum was in the middle of the frame and this was pulling their physical form to the middle while sucking out every last vestige of individuality that they may possibly have ever possessed? People are strange when you're a stranger.

CHAPTER 3

School

Molly's decision to drop out of school when she was fourteen was supported by her doctor, her father and, eventually, by her teachers who promised to send work for her to complete at home, though they rarely ever did.

For her part, Molly understood that she could no longer cope with the increasingly benign impact that this increasingly banal environment was having on the development of her mind. The routine nature of the day and the expected lines of intellectual enquiry were overly formulaic, simplistic even, and it was apparent that this educational arena tried to stifle students' tangential curiosity if it had the temerity to not fit into the planned flow of the lesson.

Everything seemed rush. Targets were set. The joy was sucked out of learning by dead-eyed individuals who all seemed to be at their wits' end.

People were taught to compete, not cooperate, to comply rather than question. If this was a preparation ground for the working world then the working well could go to hell.

School was, Molly reasoned, all well and good for the unthinking masses that were happy to be dehumanised in an attempt to create an army of unquestioning drones for the capitalist industrial machinery's workforce, but it wasn't really for her. With hindsight, the final spark to her decision to discontinue her schooling was when Molly watched the first fifty-six minutes (she could last no longer) of an old film called 'Metropolis'.

It was in the repetitive rhythmic actions and slumped postures of the workers in a film almost a hundred years old that she recognised and grasped the banality of workplace labour. Strange that something so old would seem so pressingly relevant.

One day, Molly thought, the world will be entirely automated and then humans will see the folly of their previous occupations. But then what would they do? All that would be left would be to watch one another - ceaseless cycles of talent shows, sports, surveillance imagery and twitching neighbourhood curtains as replacements for time spent in mind-numbing and inhumane work. Humans are weird.

Why, in the second decade of the twenty-first century, were identifiers of capability of apparent workplace suitability solely measured against the ability to remember things? Not apply them, argue for or against them, but simply to recall them?

Molly felt that she was becoming increasingly confrontational with regards her view of the dysfunctional society that she was growing up in. As she got older, things seemed to stop making sense until everything was confused and there seemed no reason to most things. There were, she had come to realise, no happy endings in life but there could possibly be a time when things weren't to be driven by survival instincts.

The number of people becoming homeless seemed to be rising rapidly, all while the rich at the top got even richer. Molly didn't know why the wealth of a nation wasn't measured against the happiness of the people who lived there rather than hanging on ideas of material gain where your ownership meant somebody else had to go without.

This was a topic of conversation that annoyed Molly whenever it came up with her peers as they all seemed to share the idea that the super-rich deserved their wealth. They seemed entirely unaware that nobody needed billions of pounds or dollars or whatever. And they all seemed to believe the lie that one day that could be them. The phantom of meritocracy was painful to see.

The anxiety that Molly felt in school had the same visceral effect that she felt on trains and boats. Whenever she used these modes of transport her heart rate increased, her palms became clammy and she found it hard to swallow as her mouth had a dryness to it that all the liquid in the world couldn't have fixed. She refused to bow to the pressure of her anxiety and continued to travel by these means as and when appropriate, but it was really only trains that she took these days, and even then it was simply because the prize of momentary escape from her home town was worth the pain of the journey.

Molly's attempts to rationalise the irrational led her to think that her feelings towards these vehicles centred on her inability to look forward to see her direction clearly, and this is how she connected this feeling to her formal education – she was not in control and could not map her own route as she saw fit. If she was going to crash, she wanted it to be under her control and due to her own inadequacies rather than the ineptitudes of others.

The teachers and support staff at school tried their best to help, to cajole and then, when those tactics failed, to unwittingly intimidate Molly into staying. They only saw success as a few letters on a certificate by means of measuring and validating someone's intellect, and they didn't really value individual cognitive progression that could not so easily be assessed and data tracked.

In Molly, they saw someone who would be able to achieve letters with stars attached which would validate their own teaching abilities in the face of ever-increasing reluctance from the other students to play the academic game. The detachment Molly felt to these people meant she had no desire to sacrifice her own sense of personal freedom to help them achieve better statistical evidence of their abilities in the classroom. Whenever they spoke to her, it was obvious that their central, perhaps their only concern was in the grades that she could walk away with.

Her well-being, they assured her, would no doubt improve with some educational certificates.

Molly didn't hate school or education in general, but she hated how it made her feel. The only truly brutal aspect of her school was its architecture. In all honesty she was mildly fond of the place and never felt threatened, disturbed or challenged – the latter being the main issue as she wanted some form of intellectual stimulation that the structures of the curriculum denied her.

She just felt out of place there in the same way she often felt out of time elsewhere. There was nothing tangible that she could point to as a reason for 'dropping out' (or 'switching up' as she preferred to call it) other than a sense of innate frustration at getting nowhere, a boredom borne out of the perpetual grind of having to endure the teachers' increasingly floundering attempts at inserting relatively useless knowledge into the inactive minds of the unwilling.

Her school was selective, and she could remember that it was quite a big deal when she passed the test to go there, but it was the home of the differently clever rather than a hotbed of learning.

Friends were few and far between, yet enemies were entirely absent. When she first mentioned to her dad that she wanted to switch up, Dan reasoned that there must have been a root cause that she was not vocalising and he took it upon himself to speak with her Form Tutor to find out who was bullying her.

Miss Dent found his questions worrying as she had not noticed any particular changes in Molly's behaviour, a sure sign of psychological intimidation. Dan reasoned that this old spinster had no real understanding of the kids of today and wouldn't be able to spot a bully if they cut her hair. His frustration at not being able to control all aspects of Molly's life to ensure a happy childhood moved to the forefront of his mind for the first time in many years and his lack of control over this particular situation brought back feelings he hadn't experienced fully for some time.

A father's job, he argued to himself, was to protect without smothering. He had done all he could at home to develop an environment of honest and open communication and so he was at a complete loss as to understand why Molly had not raised these non-existent issues of bullying with him.

The truth was that there were no fractious relationships in school. No looks in the corridor, no hateful words uttered in the lunch queue, no notes passed around class or comments in online group chats that resulted in scornful and unjustified judgement upon her. She was simply bored of the routine that this environment enculturated and, for her, encapsulated. The mundanity of wake-'learn'-sleep-repeat had reached a sustained peak in Year 9, just before her fourteenth birthday, when all she could see in front of her were years of irrelevant study in order to fall into an even more irrelevant career.

She didn't want to become a part of the machine as she felt that it was bleeding to death from the inside out.

As an artist, Molly had no interest in learning how *not* to express herself which seemed to be the key concern of her Year 9 Art teacher who perceived the subject as a tick-box criterion of homogenous 'articulation' rather than free will and experimentation. Molly felt that this teacher had good reason to think as such as this was merely a tactic of self-preservation to ensure good exam grades and therefore continued employment, yet there was something markedly wrong about a teacher who taught a subject such as this in a repetitive, formulaic and lifeless manner.

Molly could understand this approach in something like Physics or Maths, boring subjects with 'correct' answers, yet the beauty of potential expression was being sucked out of all of her classmates in Art and Molly had no desire to see this continue. Lunchtimes with the other teacher in this subject were much more fruitful whereas Miss Lynch was just a grade-chaser.

There was an awakening – a pretentious term, no doubt, but one that Molly nonetheless felt to be most appropriate – when she read her dad's books that were scattered around the house. Sociology, cultural anthropology, even issues of economics led her to question her place in the world and how things had got so entirely futile. These were not subjects that her school included in their Key Stage 3 and 4 programmes and Molly felt that this was a sure sign that the educational establishment did not wish to engender curious minds in conflict with the status quo.

Despite some of the teaching staffs' best intentions, the school was a hotbed of cultural neutering, steadily but assuredly castrating the ability to think and restricting students' needs for intellectual exploration. Issues were presented as black and white, as right or wrong, when Molly knew that things were a lot more complicated than that in reality. Perhaps this was why people always made it clear that their best days were their school days as they were covered in an unnatural blanket of simplicity where the complexities of real-world issues were hidden from sight.

It was as a result of these thoughts that Molly's cognitive resistance to the school began to manifest itself physically. The classroom walls started to bend in on her as she sat dutifully taking notes, the teacher's voice often becoming more distant while their visual form loomed ever larger over her. The teacher's voice would fade into the background with an echo attached to it which Molly reasoned was symbolic of the space in her brain in which she was actively choosing to place this person – towards the back.

She felt stifled, closed in and a slow sense of impending panic started in her belly.

On such occasions, she wanted the release of an anxiety attack to draw everyone's attention to her. Molly felt that if she were to suffer an attack of this nature then she would happily endure it in the knowledge that her feelings had peaked and that this would all be over soon, a fleeting feeling of disorientation before 'normality' resumed.

However, this somatic peak was never experienced and in its place was a dull, throbbing ache of numb discomfort as her senses seemed to play tricks on her for an extended period of time. As a result, Molly was unable to alert anyone's attention to her increasing sense of claustrophobia and fear. The pit of her stomach felt on fire, her hands vibrated rather than shook, her feet twitched as if ready to run while in the knowledge that her legs would not have the strength to carry her out of the room and past the school gates.

Pins and needles slowly enveloped her hands and feet, a tingling that at once made her aware of her extremities while assuring herself that the visceral prickles were unlikely to lead to an out of body experience. Molly felt that her inner being had become smaller within her physical form – her brain shrunk within the newly confined space of a diminished skull which dislocated her auditory, and altered her visual, senses. The nerves in her body moved further away from her skin which resulted in the tingles, and the essence of her heart moved inward from its muscular walls which led to observed but unobtrusive palpitations.

All elements combined made Molly feel as if she were fading into the background. Her breathing became shallower, more rapid and more desperate but always with sufficient self-control so as not to alert Susie Ellis next to her as to what was going on. It was only ever in the classroom that she experienced these feelings and it was at times like these that Molly was grateful for sitting next to the wall at the back of the room as this limited the potential witnesses to her struggles to retain her composure.

Thoughts of school rarely gave her a rush of adrenaline or an enveloping sense of dread. Initially, Molly assumed that her feelings of disquiet came from the topics covered in class, or her peers, or a general feeling of unnecessary entrapment, but as these instances became more and more regular Molly realised that in fact it was the fault of the rooms rather than anything else.

The ominously high ceilings, the impersonal magnolia of the walls and the for-some-reason locked windows combined to establish a sense of suffocation in Molly that was oppressive and liberating – liberating in the sense that it gave her cause to do something about this stifling situation that she found herself in. Molly was not immune to the romantic tragedy of the enclosing walls and the breathlessness she felt as a result, but she was incapable of dispelling these thoughts from her mind. In her own way she embraced the feelings as ones which made her more acutely aware of her own existence as a being with individual agency.

For a number of years, Molly had sat in classes with the same faces, body odours and persistent apathy from her peers (which stemmed from their sense of entitlement) that brought a familiar schema of comfort and belonging, coupled with a knowing urge for rejection and removal.

There was, for Molly, no camaraderie present but this was not borne out of a sense of disconnection from the people but the place. Explaining this to others, she knew, would prove problematic. Dan's deep-seated drive to identify the cause of her disenfranchisement led him to focus on external forces at play, rather than Molly's own views and opinions. For a while, this created a rupture in his relationship with his daughter as she felt that he simply was not listening to what she was saying.

In actual fact, he quite admired her viewpoint but decided

to position himself in a stoic, supposedly adult manner in the hope that this was merely a passing phase. In his daughter he saw a sense of intellect, reflection and bravery that was sorely lacking in his own life. He felt somewhat jealous of her ability to think things through rationally with clearly defined sense of emotional detachment. Dan saw himself as a reactor to situations, someone who never felt totally in control of his own path as life threw hurdles at him while he looked the other way.

Molly, he knew, was made of sterner stuff and this made him proud of her. Maybe one day he would be able to find the right words to tell her as much.

There was no tinge of sadness and only one regret in Molly when it was decided that she could retreat from school and be educated in preparation for her exams at home. She knew she would miss the daily contact with those who sat in her vicinity in class (she did not view them necessarily as friends, rather than accidental acquaintances) yet this somewhat unfulfilling sense of companionship would perhaps only be felt for a week or two once the routine of school had eroded.

The sole regret that Molly felt at this time was the sense of unease she experienced when, for the sake of the appropriate paperwork, she succumbed to presenting her issues with school as being in relation to her mental health rather than a well thought through, considered and fair assessment of this form of education which she saw as offering no benefits to her personally.

Without using this approach, Molly may well have been stuck in that environment. If she had simply taken the stance of being a school refuser it may have been that Dan would have found himself in trouble over this situation, a factor that

Molly wished to avoid if at all possible.

There was, however, an injustice in this situation which Molly felt as she was not allowed a platform to actually express her views which, had she been given the chance to voice her opinions to teachers and people from the local educational authority, Molly felt sure that they would have listened with sympathetic ears and that they would have seen sense in what she had said and then tried to turn her suggestions into reality. This was her sole disappointment in this scenario, and she felt that as a result of not being asked then others like her would suffer the same fate. She didn't simply want to leave without giving a full and reasoned explanation; she wanted to look into the eyes of those she was walking away from and tell them exactly why she was off. Then they would know. But she was never given the chance to do so.

There had been good times at school, of course there had, but Molly did an effective job of not bringing these to the forefront of her mind once she had left.

Her first days at both secondary and primary school were eternally etched into her memory for opposing reasons. She went to primary school just after turning four years old and her first day (or, at least the portion of it she could recall) was traumatic.

Molly could not remember much about her life prior to this point, only snippets of images which felt disjointed and most likely not true memories but a collage of recollection from previously seen photographs here and there.

The walk or drive to school had completely gone from her mind, as had the parent who dropped her off. She could not accurately say whether it had been Dan or Caroline who had been with her that morning – perhaps both, although that seemed unlikely for some reason.

The first part of the memory that Molly could hand-on-heart say was true was when she started screaming and crying for the hazy figure on the other side of the frosted glass window as it walked away. Her left forearm was being held by a Teaching Assistant, while the other children looked on in that expressionless yet enquiring manner that children of that age have - all snot, furrowed brows and gaping mouths.

Molly could no longer remember the name or the face of the Teaching Assistant, but she can recall her pink v neck jumper and silver link chain wristwatch. She spoke words which were now lost in time and space, yet Molly knew they were intended to soothe her emotional state. They only served to enrage her further.

Through the streaming tears, Molly could see the figure on the other side of the door get smaller and smaller as they moved slowly (painfully slowly) down the corridor towards the office that served as the exit.

There was, Molly thought, a slight pause in the movement of this figure just as they were about to turn right and out of eyesight. At the same point, Molly was at the end of an exhausting scream which sapped all of her energy, but when she saw the movement of this figure come to a halt she breathed deeply for one last effort and tried to scream her lungs out. On doing so, the indistinct frame at the end of the corridor swiftly turned right and out of the door.

Often, Molly would think of this day and would add and amend parts of the memory, depending on how she was feeling. When she was lonely, it was Dan that she pictured dropping her off, when she felt more content then she replaced her father with an apparition in the shape of a mother and the manner that she was left in the classroom that day only further served to add to the idea that Caroline had no heart.

Abandonment issues were at the heart of Molly's very being, she knew that, and this was just another illustration of the searing pain that accompanied such feelings.

The first day at secondary school was markedly different. Molly had walked in on her own which was, for her, a sign of real maturity as it placed responsibility for her own safety solely in her hands. She knew a few of the other kids from her primary school had been placed in this new incubator of intelligence and Molly felt positive that she would remain friends with them while also being affable enough to make new friendship groups. This was the reason that Molly had chosen to walk in to school that morning on her own rather than bend to the all too obvious trap of going in with allies.

She would be making a statement to the rest of the school that she was open to new experiences, new people and new topics of conversation as she moved into this more adult environment.

Molly had thought long and hard the night before about whether or not she should walk to school while reading a book – this would show her intelligence, studiousness and also highlight her physical motor skills. An hour and a half went by with Molly wrestling in her mind about which book she should be seen to be engaging with before she gave up on that idea as a bad one. She reasoned that it would perhaps make her seem aloof and therefore unapproachable as others may read this signal as a barrier that she was putting up.

So there would be no book, which then made Molly question

which facial expression she should utilise while on her walk. Too smiley would invite accusations from others of being one-dimensional and not necessarily deeply intelligent. Too frowny would scare potential friends away.

This was a minefield which kept Molly awake until around 2.30am while she tossed around ideas of how to present herself while simultaneously arguing with herself that nobody cared as they were all experiencing the same sets of self-doubt.

Molly wished that she didn't have to think too much about being herself and simply did what felt natural. Truth was, very little did feel natural to her. Human interaction was uncomfortable because she was at the mercy of others and the almost infinite possibilities that afforded. She could not control their thoughts, actions or responses in the same way she had authority over her own introspection and it was often the case that she got upset when people responded in a way she had not pre-empted.

The walk in to school was uneventful, to the point where it had almost entirely gone from Molly's working memory banks. She often recalled how she felt that first time going into this huge, brown building with children who were much older than she was and almost twice her height. An overwhelming sense of pride enveloped her, and her gait unwittingly developed a slight bounce as she moved into the confines of the school for the first time.

There was a sense in Molly that she was now in the big time and that this place would afford her the opportunity to talk to, hang out with and be accepted by the older kids who would enjoy her enquiring mind and her sharp wit.

It was only at that point that she realised she had no idea

where she was going as she had no preordained route once inside the school. She had seen Jenny, Josh and Alfie from her previous school in the playground and so maybe they knew. But she couldn't turn around and go back out there now.

Molly decided just to keep walking until she saw somebody that she could ask.

There were notices on boards that some of the children were looking at, but Molly didn't feel comfortable enough to stop in case she realised that the information written had no relevance to her which would surely rouse the suspicions of the other kids that perhaps this one wasn't as clever as she was trying to project.

Teachers scuttled through the corridor, darting from one room to the next and occasionally acknowledging the presence of a colleague with a raised eyebrow, yet Molly did not see them engage with any of the students, so read this to mean that the kids at this school were expected to be more autonomous and mature in their actions, an aspect which Molly would have to assimilate with quickly.

No doubt, she thought, she had been given the information on which room to go to and who her Form Tutor was but she had been so preoccupied the night before by playing with ideas of the personality that she wished to present to her new classmates that she forgot to pay heed to the important information that would have served to ensure she did not feel lost.

The labyrinthian corridors, repetitively styled rooms and red coloured doors combined to make Molly feel that she was in a cheap cartoon where the illustrators used the same backgrounds over and over and over due to budgetary constraints as the dog and his drug buddy ran after the old guy from the fairground who had covered himself in a bedsheet. It was always Mr Johnson from the fairground.

Molly resigned herself to the fact that as she could not find any office where a sympathetic member of the admin team would no doubt take pity on her, she would have to ask another student. But who?

One of the really old ones might not have time for this shit on the first day back and this would then tarnish their perception of Molly, making it more unlikely that she would be able to engage on an equal footing with people from this year group at a later date.

Molly had seen enough films and TV shows to know that girls who stood in groups in school corridors were bad news and therefore she couldn't ask them for fear of being press-ganged into taking up membership in their clique. Molly knew so little about hair and make-up and boys that it would prove to be a fruitless relationship and, more importantly, she had no interest in learning about hair and make-up and boys. Not just now but ever.

Molly reasoned that if she asked one of the older boys of the school for help then that may give off the wrong impression about her and anyway, they all seemed far too busy jumping all over each other in some form of homoerotic ritual which allowed them to enjoy physical contact with one another in the face of masculinity's ideas of emotional distance and isolation.

Maybe I should just ask anyone, someone Molly thought, as she started to feel the tense excitement of her first day subside into a momentary lapse toward a smothered blanket-coma of self-doubt coupled with the dizzying effects of the norepinephrine that was tangible in her body.

Towards the end of the corridor, standing the other side of the water fountain, was a girl who looked a couple of years older than Molly. She had her hands in her blazer pockets with her thumbs on the outside, and she leant against the wall with her right knee bent so that her foot could be placed on the wall, level with her other knee.

Molly thought she had all the arrogance and practiced cool of teenagers from some of the 1950s American films she had seen, so Molly decided that she was as good a person as any to ask. In the seconds that separated her first sighting of the girl and placing herself in front of her, Molly struggled to decide upon how to initiate the conversation and which form of salutation would be best.

'Hey!' Molly winced at her choice. 'Erm…sorry but I have no idea where I am going. You're not new here or anything are you? It's just that I could do with some help and everyone else seems… sort of seems to know where they are going and…' Molly stopped when she saw the girl sigh with an exaggerated downward slope of her shoulders that also seemingly dragged her gaze away from towards the ceiling as if the weight of her shoulders forced her eyes down.

'What?'

'Sorry…I'm not sure where my classroom is and…'

'Sure. It's down that way' the girl replied and pointed down a corridor that was just to the right right from where she stood.

'Okay. Erm…cheers.'

'Yep, no worries.'

Molly went in the instructed direction and felt a sudden sense of deflation as she was hoping for a little more engagement with the first person she spoke to at her new school.

Nevermind, she thought, the rules of this place would soon be observed and learnt.

'Molly!' a voice called out from behind her. 'Where are you going?' It was Alex Jennings, a lad who lived around the corner from Molly and went to her last school but, to Molly's mind, had never spoken to her before. 'This way.' Molly rolled her eyes to Alex as if to suggest that she was useless although for many years to come this gesture was read by Alex as an involuntary and negative non-verbal comment on his presence in her class.

Although he never raised this point with her, or indeed with anybody else, it was a moment that stayed with him for a long time and which helped reinforce his own sense of worthlessness and self-pity that he struggled to express.

At the time, however, Alex hardly registered this moment and simply showed Molly the room that was to be her Form Room for the next year. On the door was the number 16 and the name Mr Cooke which Molly recalled from the letter she read and had partially forgotten. The teacher was not there at this point and so Molly had no idea where to sit until she saw that someone, most likely Mr Cooke, had put a plan of the room's seating arrangements on the whiteboard with names indicated on the numerous squares which referenced the desks.

At primary school, Molly had always been on a shared table with at least three other kids but here she had her own desk. Adult, indeed.

There was a strangely subdued feeling in the room. Most of the kids, Molly assumed, did not know one another but she at least expected that clusters of acquaintance would form between those who had previously spent time in the same classrooms when at the junior level and that noise would be generated due to their incessant babble about their holidays or haircuts or how their parents told them that they would soon fit into their new school clothes. Instead, the other students seemed jittery, fearful that their expectations of 'big school' were inevitably to be met with immense disappointment as their inability to adequately reinvent their personality during the summer break would soon tell. They were alike in both their uniform and their trepidation.

At this point, Mr Cooke was just a name on a door and Molly was surprised that she could not remember him from her transition days when she came to visit the school at the arse-end of her time at primary school.

Molly took her seat which was the third row from the right, second from the front. While she waited, rather than look around the room at the other students as if to appear needy, Molly looked at the board and tried to work out the order that Mr Cooke had used in placing the students, but there appeared to be none. The pupils were not organised in any alphabetical order (surnames or first names), were not gendered sequentially and did not appear, at least to Molly, that those from the same previous school had been positioned next to one another.

Mr Cooke was a randomiser, then. This suited Molly, as it seemed to suggest a fair man who believed in the flow of things rather than structural determination. Once this thought had settled in her mind, Molly looked to her right towards the door and waited with excited anticipation.

Since leaving school, Molly had not formed as many lasting memories about humans and their varying interactions as her life had become one of increasingly self-imposed isolation. The daily, initially inconsequential, utterances of others would often resonate with Molly for one reason or another and stay with her for some time.

She would have liked to have been a person in possession of the confidence and the raconteur skills to be able to convey these instances as she was sure they would be popular with others, but she would not be able to find the right words to communicate the moment and would only muddle the story with minor details that would distract the listener. With hindsight, Molly felt that one of the main reasons that she could recall so many small happenings from school was that she was rarely directly involved in the stories in an active manner, she was merely a silent observer on the periphery of the events as she attempted to better understand why it was that people were driven to perform in certain ways.

One such story centred on the menstrual cycle. Molly had, of course, known about periods for quite some time before hers began, as other girls had spoken about them regularly around the age of eight or nine in that way that children do when they wish to convince someone they know more than they do.

Molly knew that her father would be uncomfortable talking to her about these things at such a young age, so she played a joke on him instead as a way of reassuring him that his then nine-year-old daughter was more innocent than she was. She approached him one day and said 'Dad, what is a menstrual cycle?' Molly could see in his widening eyes that he was searching for the right phrase to answer while simultaneously being hopeful of nipping the conversation in the bud at the earliest opportunity.

'It's something that girls have,' Dan replied. Molly knew that this was likely to be the kind of reply he would offer and so rather than embarrass him further she went for the comedy reply she had prepared.

'Oh,' she said, 'so it's a bike with a basket at the front, then?' She knew that by playing dumb she would be able to settle Dan's worries about his little girl growing up too fast.

Max Delaney, however, had no such excuse for his brilliant piece of inept fuck-wittery. It was in a Year 8 science class where he made the comment that resulted in him forever being referred to as Tampax Delaney (a joke which didn't entirely work but was close enough to the subject matter to raise a smirk or two).

The teacher, Miss Jarman, was teaching a disinterested and hormonal group of twelve-yea-olds about the intricacies of the menstrual cycle, when she noticed that Delaney was staring at the board in a manner which suggested to both the trained and the untrained eye that he had no clue as to what was going on.

'Max, what's wrong? Why aren't you writing on your worksheet?' Miss Jarman asked in that snappy manner that only science teachers seemed to possess. Tampax (he was now only seconds away from being christened this in the mind of Rav Shastri who coined the sorrowful sobriquet) stumbled out the immortal words 'What is all of this about, Miss?' The rest of the conversation would, she was sure, stay with Molly for eternity:

'What is all of what about, Max?'

'This. All of this. This stuff about eggs and blood and ovations.'

'It's the menstrual cycle, Mr Delaney. What exactly do you not understand?'

'Are you saying that this happens in women?'

'Yes, Max. Women after puberty and before the menopause.'

'No…'

'What do you mean?'

'I don't believe it,' (laughter from the class)

'Quiet! Max is right to raise points he does not understand. You should always ask for clarification. Go on, Max.'

'Are you saying that this happens to my mum *every month*?'

'Twenty-eight days, Max,' shouted someone from towards the back of the room.

'Thank you,' Miss Jarman responded.

'But…' Max was really struggling now and his speech was decreasing with larger gaps between the words 'I… no, I… my mum?'

Molly could not quite remember if Tampax Delaney had tears in his eyes at this point. She had turned herself around in the chair to see him two rows back, but he was on the other side of the room so it was difficult to be able to judge the moisture levels of his eyes with any degree of certainty. His voice was certainly trembling in that way that suggests the imminent arrival of what Molly termed 'wet regret' which also made it clear that he wasn't joking.

In that wilful way that children mock one another without remorse, this moment was recalled more often than not each day for some time or, at least how Molly remembered it, until Max's mother died when he had just turned fifteen. There was then a silent consensus amongst Molly's peers that this was no longer a reasonable subject to bring up in conversation and so the mocking abated, but the name stuck.

Molly enjoyed some of the disclosures of human inadequacy that she witnessed, but they often marred her learning as they were more memorable than the subject topics. This was more often than not down to the teachers' delivery – the excited and vibrant nature of the students' assertions compared to the listless apathy of the teacher's. What a shame, Molly thought, that those who had enjoyed these areas of intellectual investigation so much in their earlier lives that they wanted to spend their working life imparting the information to enrich the lives of others were so beaten by the system that they were more than likely to turn others off these areas.

Like a bloated Elvis going through the motions in Las Vegas towards his death, the faces of the majority of Molly's teachers at secondary school were unnervingly the same with a steely cold, glassy deadness in the eyes that even a zombie would be alarmed at.

The cordial inconsequence of the teachers troubled Molly, as did a number of things they said which she challenged without second thought. She had been told on several occasions by a number of staff to 'dial down the feminism' and to not believe that 'everything is about the patriarchy' but it was Mr Shah, a Physics teacher, who most offended Molly.

He once said, in a PSHE lesson that he was covering for the hapless but friendly Mrs Cowdrey, that she was known amongst the teaching staff as a 'powerful girl'. He had meant this as a compliment and by way of showing the class that although he had not taught them until this point he did have some prior knowledge of them.

Had Mr Shah been more observant he would have noticed Molly's fists clenching so hard that the knuckles went white. She could feel herself starting to shake a little, one of those minute convulsions that you are almost certain that nobody else notices, and then she heard herself say at a volume higher than intended, 'What is that supposed to mean?'

Mr Shah was already halfway through his next sentence and his obvious alarm at Molly's question seemed a little overplayed.

'I am sorry, what did you say?' he asked, his voice developing a more genuinely sympathetic tone towards its end. He took off the glasses that seemed forever glued to the tip of his nose and moved towards Molly's side of the room. He attempted to act in a manner that would put her at ease, but at the time she read his actions as an attempt to loom over her desk and intimidate her further.

By now, the contradictory voices inside Molly were working overtime and the inner turmoil did nothing to make her think about holding back. 'How dare you!' she said. There was a slight quiver in her voice that she was ashamed about as it made her feel the others in the room thought that perhaps she was not in control of her emotions.

'Why say I'm a powerful girl? Why put 'girl' in that phrase? Why not just a powerful person or a powerful student or just powerful or…? Are you saying…are you saying that my sense of power is only relative to me being a girl and therefore that my sense of power is remarkable because I am a girl or that my power is drawn from me being a girl or that me being powerful is only in relation to the fact that I am also a girl and so you could say that out of the girls I may be powerful but out of the class I am not but out of the girls I am? How would you like it if I judged your ability as a teacher just against the other Indian teachers in the school or any other ethnic minority? Huh?'

It was that last line that resulted in Molly being sent to the Headmaster as Mr Shah complained that she had been racist.

'Molly, I…' Mr Shah attempted to interject but thought better of it as he could see she had more to say.

'Not only,' Molly continued 'do I have to put up with these micro-aggressions about expected gender behaviour every time I turn on the TV, watch a film or open a magazine, but now I have to put up with being patronised and put in my place at school, too. Is that what you are telling me? My value in this school is only in relation to being a girl rather than having some stupid flaccid piece of skin protruding outward from between my legs like a… like a… a homeless slug, is that right? You want me to be grateful because I am seen as a powerful girl but what do you mean by that? I would have thought I could get more solidarity from you, someone who is probably aware of how white male privilege works more than most in this school unless you have been blinded to it to suit your own lifestyle choices,' (perhaps it was this line, in fact, that made Mr Shah send her to the Head).

Molly barely paused for breath and her speech patterns were becoming faster paced but were not increasing in pitch, a fact that Molly felt very proud of later when she went over and over and over this monologue in her head for her own edification and dissection.

Mr Shah ended this interaction by saying 'Are you done?'

Molly added 'I have to put up with being a girl all the time without any support from culture, men or other girls who are so caught up in the web of patriarchy that they are told that to really be a girl you need to shop and bitch about each other to be divided and opposed rather than strong and unified and all because of weak masculinity trying to keep women in their place. It isn't about being in the kitchen anymore, it's about women learning to hate themselves by consuming the vitriolic and poisonous ideas in magazines with article after article telling them how to change so the woman's place now is a place of deep-seated self-hatred and reductive stereotypes of behaviour which is to be small, pretty and lacking in opinion and worth. And this culture's infantilization of women is just weird. Adult women are often called 'girls' when they are far from it and the complete removal of pubic hair to replicate the vagina of a ten-year-old is just obscene, let alone the sexualisation of school uniform which pushes a form of paedophilia into mainstream sensibilities while simultaneously suggesting that women over a certain age are worthy of nothing more than a sexual scrapheap.'

With the benefit of hindsight and time to contemplate this exchange, that is what she *would* have said, but in actuality after Mr Shah had enquired whether she was done, she simply shrugged, lowered her chin a little further to her chest and hated herself just a little more than usual for not having what Dan would have called the 'brass neck' to make her stand.

Molly would relive this confrontation in her mind over and over and over again, replaying it each time with a slightly different response to Mr Shah's last comment from her imagined self as a means of rehearsing her lines to steady herself for the next time these words would be needed. It most likely wouldn't be too far off so she decided she should prepare as best she could. She would need to remember to take a deep breath before starting the outburst as men were very good at talking over women and she noticed this trend was more apparent as she got older. She wanted to be loud, to take up space, and be not just heard but understood.

The decision to leave school was, from Molly's point of view, the most sensible thing in the world. She hadn't quite understood the intricacies involved and how this supposedly affected other people's lives, though. She wrongly assumed once she was afforded the opportunity to present a cogent argument to those who mattered the issue would be settled swiftly with a minimum of fuss. Reasons needed to be given, and Molly spent a lot of time covering every single base of any potential discussion she had with any teachers to ensure that she would be fully equipped to deal with any questions or scenarios that they might throw at her.

Despite the pretence of upheaval that Dan presented to Molly's teachers, he carried on as normal once she was officially seen as being home schooled. He trusted Molly implicitly with being home alone and she had enough about her to do the work that was required of her to pass her GCSE exams. Whether she would actually feel the compulsion to sit the exams was another matter entirely, however.

She knew that there was a game called the curriculum that she had to play and she did her best to convince herself that she was sufficiently inspired by its content to cover the work, but this seemed a hollow victory in the face of her intellectual thirst which was not satiated via the right-wrong, yes-no dichotomies of this level of education.

Like actors reciting lines they did not fully comprehend, Molly felt that knowledge gained via repetition showed a lack of humanity. This was a monkey see, monkey do form of drilling, the lowest common denominator of intellectual delivery. She had voiced this concern several times and was told to hush down. How inspiring.

The new routine that Molly found herself following was a strange one at first, and Molly worried that cabin fever would take hold. She decided that she should keep her alarm clock set to 7.25 for fear of losing the will to wake up and wasting every day. Molly often thought that sleep was a waste of her time as books didn't get read, films didn't get watched, and thoughts didn't go through an active process of deconstruction while asleep. Molly was never more tired than on waking so there seemed little point in seeing sleep as some sort of relief, if anything it only added to her issues.

At school, much though she hated the fact, the day was controlled by the rigidity of the timetable. She knew where she needed to be and what she was going to do once she got there.

At home, this was not the case. She needed to find her own schedule and was determined in keeping to it as best she could. She was worried about the nonchalant, apathetic teenager in her coming to the surface and wreaking havoc although she knew this was unlikely, but she would worry about it all the same. It was good to worry about things that were not so obviously going to happen as there would then be a sense of achievement when the thing didn't occur, as she could convince herself that its non-appearance was due to the constant fretting that took place to subdue these acts.

Twisted logic, perhaps, but there was a degree of satisfaction that could be achieved when you knowingly talked yourself into a position you knew to be nonsensical.

Molly did not miss the company of her fellow students as she replaced their chatter with the thoughts of the thinkers in the books she read. She had an unerring habit of needing to read books in the voice of the author, or in a close approximation to how she thought they would speak. Jane Austen was softly spoken but with a barb to her tone that surprised Molly,

Shakespeare had an interesting twang to his accent which Molly could not rightly place, whereas Dostoyevsky just sounded like a poor comic's use of stereotypes.

This practice made Molly feel more connected to the author and the inflections in their voice often made some of the subtler inferences stand out with more clarity. However hard she tried, though, she could not benefit from this approach on the three occasions she attempted to read 'A Brief History of Time', a book she knew would forever go unfinished.

For the first couple of weeks of not attending school, there was a feeling of both release and confinement. The constant background noise of school had gone and in its place was an often-suffocating silence that was interspersed with the intrusive sound of people talking as they walked past the house.

Molly was often able to pick out the details of the conversations of those who walked by outside, and soon it became a fixation of hers as she needed to know that those in her vicinity, even for the briefest period of time, were not plotting against her.

She would often worry that every car she heard at night was carrying someone with ill intent toward her, and that they would either soon be banging hard on the door or, worse, driving the car straight into the house. She wasn't sure who it was that might have such malevolent regard toward her, or what she had done to bring about such feelings in others, but Molly always felt it was better to brace herself for every eventuality as opposed to walking blindfolded through life.

The same level of tranquillity that often kept her awake at night was present in the house during the weekday, an aspect of her new life that Molly was not expecting, and she was therefore not mentally prepared to develop a coping mechanism for it. She was now immersed in an anechoic chamber of her own making and she was not sure she would ever fully get used to it. If she focused enough she could hear her pulse, and if she put just a little more effort in she was sure that it was possible for her to feel the inside of the skin on her forehead above her left eye touching her skull.

Reminders of the mechanisms of her own body merely acted as a prompt to the idea of her own mortality and how, one day, these feelings and thoughts would slip away from her for the last time and she would be gone.

Once she had started at secondary school, Molly couldn't recall a time when she thought of Dan during the day, she was too busy, but she now found herself worrying about him more. This, she thought, was most likely because there were constant reminders of his absence during the day. She couldn't reconcile herself with the idea that she missed him, she just felt more aware of the space that he would have filled with his presence. She needed to ensure that she spoke to him more. It didn't matter what about, they just needed to have better channels of communication.

The eight or so hours between Dan leaving for work and arriving back home often resulted in Molly not speaking at all in that time. There was no need to verbalise although she now realised how much she missed having her voice heard. She wasn't particularly a fan of talking as such, but she needed to be able to express herself to others so that those others would benefit from her reasoning.

Molly was convinced that few others thought in the same way as she did and therefore despite her own sense of messianic contriteness, there was an urge in her to, perhaps indirectly, influence others into thought. There seemed so little thinking these days, just remembering and dumbing things down to globules of meme-sized understanding of issues.

At home, there was nobody to actively bounce ideas off, nobody to react to and nobody to vociferously disagree with. Molly felt that this was perhaps suppressing her emotions and so, as an experiment that lasted no more than three excruciating days, she vowed to watch some daytime television. Here, she saw the contemporary equivalent of the Victorian freak-show playing out in front of her eyes as the poor, uneducated and hapless in appearance were wheeled out to detail their misfortune for the pleasure of those who were just above the socio-economic level of the wretched soul being prodded with the metaphorical stick of base level journalistic enquiry.

Laughter, Molly had read, often comes as the result of relief at not being in the situation that is being observed and reacted to; that our sniggering comes from the realisation that we, too, could fall flat on our face on the ice or the rope on the swing in the woods could snap plunging us into a nearby stream etc. etc. etc.

On the screen in front of her, Molly gawped and gasped at the revelatory nature of the most private details of these people's lives who seemed happy to have their fifteen minutes of infamy. It was hard to watch on occasion, but it appealed to Molly's macabre side more than shows about people's houses or making small sums of money through selling shit old things.

The television host in this arena of intimate and condescending violation was expert at pandering to the needs of the baying crowd in the studio, raising his voice where necessary, putting his arm around the perceived victims at others. Positions of crowd allegiance were often switched at the behest of the ring-leader of this unkind spectacle without their knowledge. The show worked on the Barabbas Effect and Molly felt this would make a more honest title for the programme, rather than the egotistical nature of the eponymous label.

Fodder for the masses was such an elitist term, Molly thought, but it fits so well for this 'entertainment'.

Once or twice, but no more, Molly agreed with what the host said which was enough for her to turn the television off. She decided to read some essays by Theodor Adorno instead. School related work could wait for now.

CHAPTER 4

Doing girlhood

'I AM NOT A FEMIN – I – I – IST!' screamed the peroxide blonde riot grrrl grunger from the stereo. One of Dan's favourite bands had been made considerably more famous when their singer married a guy from a much more celebrated, but not quite as good, band.

He shot himself in the head a few years later and she was Yoko Ono-ed and vilified in popular discourse as strong women tend to be. He also began to be credited for her career which seemed weird as her band's best album was recorded before the two had even met. Molly often saw people younger than her wearing his band's t-shirt, but she could not recall once seeing anyone in a Hole shirt in the street. Dan had an old one in his wardrobe, she was sure of it.

Molly considered this shrieked line from the album and realised that it was being delivered by a character within the narrative of the song rather than representing the true feelings of the singer. She must have listened to this song a million times, maybe more, but it was only on this occasion that she noticed the words 'she said' before the denial of feminist values. How could she have missed that obvious part of the song over the years since she first heard this masterpiece?

A clear sense of relief began to swell in Molly as she came to fully appreciate her error as the singer was relaying the views of another. This feeling was also mixed with annoyance at her own musical appreciation skills which were now confirmed as being suitably lacking enough to not notice important elements of a lyric. Molly reasoned that the writer had put a lot of effort in and so it was only fair that the listener did the same. This was the same thinking behind her hatred of the spines of books being broken rather than looked after.

Molly loved this band – it was something that Dan had passed down to her and it made her feel an unashamed, though fleeting, pride in their relationship.

He had not been overly persuasive in his methods of playing cultural gatekeeper of the aural hand-me-downs and he had even played along and engaged in the music that she chose to gorge on when she was an oh-so-grown-up eight-year-old who could sing along to whatever she pleased. Dan was secretly delighted, though, when Molly got to about eleven and began delving into his record collection as he assumed that she would grow up knowledgeable of the greatest body of recorded music that his financial position could afford.

Molly initially just thumbed through the LPs and singles for the artwork and photography but then her attention moved more to the lyrics as she realised that they possibly reflected somewhat on Dan. By listening to the music that he had cherished for more than twenty years, she felt as though she were opening a window into his personality that would have been otherwise eternally closed to her. Music, she knew, was at the very centre of Dan's being and he seemingly lived in the past enough for her to surmise that his emotional maturity had not sufficiently developed beyond the state it was in over a quarter of a century ago.

One of the things that Molly had realised about growing up was that your worries came with you; things weren't easier as you got older, there was just an assumption that you were okay as you grew more disconnected from people in your day-to-day existence. Less connection with others meant less opportunity to engage at a level deeper than small talk about the weather or something equally as basic, banal, inane, potentially platitudinous, perennially predictable and uninspired. Being an adult, Molly had begun to realise, was pretty shitty.

What, Molly thought, was it to be a feminist or, in this case, to not be a feminist. Why would someone choose *not* to be a feminist?

She had read enough to know that there were different forms of feminism which all got a little complicated for her at times. There was, however, a kind of monolithic representation of this concept in the media, or at least in the things she noticed. When feminism came up in television or radio shows, or in newspaper articles, or online discussions, she noticed that many of the men seemed to take umbrage with the notion, as if they were somehow being attacked and that their positions were in jeopardy. Maybe they were.

Maybe they were hearing one thing and translating it another way to suit their own narrative. From what Molly had read, she couldn't remember any of the writers championing the idea of castrating men or putting them in cages or sailing them off to an island where they could either kill each other or just masturbate themselves to dust or cry themselves to ash. Most of the writing seemed to centre on justifying the *need* for a feminist discourse and most of the pages in books were given over to every day examples of sexism that were so commonplace that they were taken for granted as unproblematic.

One of Molly's favourite examples that she would wheel out from time to time to the sighs and moans of others was about television newsreaders. The book she read it in, she couldn't remember exactly which one but she somehow connected it to Virginia Woolf although she knew it had nothing to do with her, based its case studies on American television and so Molly thought it would be interesting to see if the British broadcasters dealt with the issue in a similar way. They did.

The book used television newsreaders as examples of every day subtle micro-sexism and how professionals of different genders are expected to perform their sense of self differently due to gender labels. It was argued that news programmes often had two presenters, male and female. The male would pretty much always be older than the woman and would invariably speak first. She was secondary in speaking role, younger, and more glamourous.

There was no pressure exerted on him to look good. He had an air of authority about him; she would have if she were allowed first dibs at talking and wasn't presented in a manner that was something akin to his attractive deputy or whatever. It made Molly think of the magician and his grinning, leotard clad, arms waving, long gloved and feather hat wearing younger female assistant who was there merely as a form of visual distraction while the man put in the real effort and got all of the reward.

This pushed the idea of what the book termed 'the third shift', where women and men nowadays had more equal responsibilities in terms of the first two shifts – in the workplace and chores or childcare. The third shift was seen to be exclusively for women, though, and centred on the need for them to look good, a pressure not exerted on men in the same way. Molly felt this was right but was perhaps changing a little since the book had been written a long time ago and she knew enough to know that ideas of gender and identity moved with the times now and then.

Molly felt that this was a persuasive example of how small, how seemingly insignificant things can be seen to perpetuate ideas of women being unequal in society. Not many others that she spoke to about this agreed with her. She had never raised this topic with Dan, but she knew he would agree as she was gaining this knowledge from the books he owned.

A disturbing trend that Molly noticed in Hollywood films was one of younger women falling for much older men, and she saw this as the playing out of male fantasies rather than instinctual female desire. *What was it about younger women that so appealed to men?* she thought, and she did not like the conclusion that she drew. The men would always pursue the woman to the point of exhaustion, too. Women were seen as the hunted, the prey who would eventually fall victim to the wily, patient predator.

Molly's interest in visual arts meant that she would examine, analyse and interpret every element of the album covers in Dan's collection as this was the way that he had explained how music consumption had changed as kids these days no longer considered the art in the way the artist intended.

Things such as song order, album cover art, liner notes and lyric sheets were all fading into obsolescence, disregarded by today's youth who Dan argued were much more interested in the immediacy of sound rather than the underlying sonic architecture. On looking through the album cover where this singer screamed about not being a feminist, she noticed for maybe the 300th time that the singer for this band had chosen a photo of herself on the inner sleeve which was (perhaps unintentionally) sexually provocative. She wore small, tight stripy shorts in the shot and Molly's eyes were always drawn towards the crotch, despite feeling a sense of a more than mild violation.

Not only was her gaze always attracted to this part of the image, but from as far back as she could remember Molly genuinely felt that Prominent Vulva would be a brilliant name for a punk band.

Was there, then, a connection between singing about issues of feminism and this particular photo? Was Molly thinking too much about this or was the singer so pronounced in the way that she wanted to articulate her own sense of self that even the smallest details like this were considered and intentional?

The photo felt seared into Molly's consciousness because it always raised so many, often contradictory, thoughts and this was the whole bloody point of art, right? Art raises questions more than it offers answers. Molly thought so, anyway.

Was the singer simply wearing a pair of comfortable shorts and a photographer just happened to take a candid shot that she approved for the artwork, or was she being displayed like the gargoyles of old as somehow overly aggressive and therefore lacking female sensuality? What did that phrase mean, anyway? Was she in control of this image or were her record company like the stonemasons of the olden days who painstakingly chipped away to create vulvic rock? And if she was in control, would she ever be given full credit for being so?

Who was the photo for?

How can still images offer different meanings from time to time?

Why was Molly transfixed by the idea of the hidden messages in things that were maybe never intended in the first place?

Molly often thought that women who chose to present themselves as sexual entities were not anti-feminist as long as it was their choice to project themselves in the manner in which they selected.

It seemed like an almost pointless task for Molly to define sexiness or attractiveness as everyone had their own particular likes, dislikes, quirks and peculiarities and so there seemed little to be achieved by definitively defining 'sexy'. There was, of course, the stereotypical and impossible to achieve image of the big breasted, flat stomached, small waisted, sexually provocative virgin that was ubiquitous in advertising, but she knew enough about boys to know that although this was an aspiration, they themselves were too weak and scared to be able to hold down a relationship with such an imagined woman and they were also not so stupid as to know that this image hadn't been digitally manipulated.

Strong women were often sexy women, Molly thought, but this didn't sit well with some men, maybe most men.

Sex was an interesting cultural phenomenon that amused Molly no end. She perceived herself as wanting no part of this particularly shabby business as it held no allure nor function for her. Others of the same age were increasingly and annoyingly more vociferous about their sexual awakenings whereas she was on the other end of the libidinal spectrum and was mentally putting in the warm bedding for her sexual animal to go into indefinite hibernation.

As Molly's mind skipped from one set of questions to the next, she always reminded herself that a couple of years before, when she had first started taking an interest in Dan's past and his musical preferences, she had become so transfixed by the image of the singer's shorts that she decided that this made her a lesbian.

In many ways, Molly thought, this was a shame as she had not expected it but then, as she got older, she realised that nobody expected it as there was little space in society to explore all options. As a child, hour upon hour upon hour was given over to watching television and films where inhumanly thin princesses would marry their princes, so it would only seem natural to young children watching that they should follow suit. Monogamous heterosexuality was almost made compulsory by the cultural landscape that surrounds us all. Molly's asexuality, she believed at the time, would not be overly hindered by her occasional lapses into consciously restricted sapphic fantasies.

Molly wondered if any of the princesses in the tales she was told ever had the (mis)fortune to stare at their hand long enough to allow it to raise questions of death and decay? Did the Little Mermaid look at her hand and think 'Oh, the water has made it wrinkly already. I am closer to death. My story will soon be over. Perhaps I should not have given my voice in exchange for the attentions of a mere man rather than a merman? I am full or remorse, I am weak and bowed not just by the pressures of the sea but by the vigorous certitudes of heterosexual normativity'?

Probably not, but you never know.

Lesbianism was often a fraught terrain for Molly as she was more comfortable with the idea of going through life as some sort of asexual hermit who only had her own thoughts to torture her rather than commit to a life of shamefully grinding her body parts against unwitting sexual 'partners' who would then expect some form of conversation and chit chat at the very least either side of the physical stuff.

However disappointed she felt at the time about having a burgeoning sexuality and preference, she was also more explicitly aware that her fear of human contact meant that she would most likely stay pure and virginal until her dying day. Could someone call themselves a lesbian if they had never even so much as kissed another girl? Was a lesbian defined by their being or their doing? You can call yourself a driver if you have passed the test but don't own a car so surely the same rules apply here – but Molly had no intention of even casually sitting the theory test.

She was not disappointed by the idea that she may be a lesbian, more with the idea of there existing within her the possibility of a desire towards human contact which surprised her. There would be no shame in any sexuality that she felt within, just shock at such feelings existing at all when her tendency towards isolationism *in extremis* would be tested.

This singer's crotch had provoked a discussion inside Molly that she wanted her own art to produce. Not so much questions of sexuality, but taking a simple image and allowing people to perceive it in whatever manner they wished. Not that Molly was intending to show people her work but the point sort of remained the same. Viva le vulva, and all that.

Even the name of the singer's band was sexually explicit in the crudest of ways, but Dan had told her that it was more about existential angst rather than a euphemistic term. Molly didn't believe him.

This band had introduced Molly to a scene that she knew as Riot Grrrl, though she was always unsure about the number of Rs required in the second word of the term. This was an early 1990s thing that was around the same time Dan was playing music regularly. Riot Grrrl was usually female fronted aggressive punk rock which argued for stronger rights for women, gender equality and all the obvious but ignored stuff.

Molly noted how quaint and somewhat ancient the scene now felt in an age of non-binary identities, gender fluidity and ever-increasing inclusivity and the rejection of pre-ordained, meaningless labels. The right to confront issues of inequality were clearly not new and Molly felt that maybe her perception of this scene as being somewhat twee was linked to the advances made as a result of such actions. A lot of these bands played with issues of female identity but not all through the use of photographs that showed an outline of vulvas through clothing.

There was a certain sense of asexual shabbiness from the women in this scene that appealed to Molly – DM boots, ripped tights and jeans and dirty dresses were commonplace and celebrated strong women through female forms, not just trying to assimilate to male or masculine ideas of identity. There was a problematic sense to some aspects of the dress code of their grunger allies, though, which Molly often tussled with and that was to do with the 'baby doll' style clothes that were often worn.

Some of the bands would wear *Alice in Wonderland* style dresses, often with rips as if they were the celebrated survivors of sexual assault. Maybe that was the whole point, that their clothes were illustrative of the struggles of women in male dominated society. They dressed to appease and appeal, but their actions showed resistance to those in the audience who understood. Maybe it was just girls wearing dresses who went on tour and ended up with messy, ripped clothes as a result of their shenanigans which probably involved quite a lot of drinking and drugs although the thought of drugs always scared Molly to the point of not wanting to think of her cultural heroes being weak enough to hide behind the veil of numbness that drugs afforded. Alcohol, she remembered hearing once from somewhere, wasn't a drug, it was a drink.

Was Molly, as a girl, free to wear dresses in such a manner if she chose to do so or had the time gone where people would identify her as a listener of music like this as opposed to simply being seen as some sort of potential case for Social Services?

Molly questioned whether an aggressive celebration of femininity is more powerful than a dilution of girldom? Do dresses worn in a particular manner shout 'I AM a feminist' in ways that perhaps choosing to wear jeans, or dungarees or no make-up can't? Surely it is just better to wear what you want to wear and wear it how you want it to be worn – that was Molly's idea of feminism: choice.

She remembered that when she was younger and obsessed by princesses, Dan had tried to reason with her that women who relied on men to rescue them were real but really weren't worth the bother. Molly couldn't quite recall whether this was before or after her mother had left the family home so maybe Dan was just voicing his anger and frustration. Molly knew that he worried about her, and always had.

It was maybe a part of her condition that she had got from him (despite the fact that she felt her issues were hers alone and were not influenced by others, genetic or cultural or otherwise). With hindsight, Molly realised that Dan had tried to inform her about things such as glass ceilings and female struggle from the youngest age without trying to make it seem impossible to overcome.

One memory that often circled in her head when she least expected it was to do with dolls and dresses and how boys were stopped from playing with them when they were younger whereas girls had more choice available by dint of being a girl.

'Do you not think,' Dan would say, 'that it's silly that boys aren't usually allowed to wear what they want whereas you can wear trousers, skirts, dresses, shorts, whatever you feel like?'

Molly enjoyed wearing skirts when she was younger as they swished around her when she pirouetted. Dancing was so much better with a skirt to swirl around your body to take attention from your disgustingly thin legs. The same effect was not possible from trousers or shorts and so there was a certain sense of sadness that came over her when she was younger when she considered the fact that this feeling she had, the sheer joy of a ballooned skirt, was denied to boys for no good reason.

Maybe this was why the boys in the playground seemed to find it difficult to control their actions and would just run round and round and round until they almost made themselves sick – they lacked the control of a simple circle turn which would bring about a pleasing skirt swish and so this lack of equal clothing rights would forever burden them with an emptiness that would never be filled, no matter how much they ran, kicked each other or tried to secure dominance over one another by other means. Boys, Molly concluded, were a bloody mystery that she had neither the inclination nor the time to solve.

When Molly contemplated her place in the world, her function and purpose, she rarely considered her genitals as being of any significance. She did, however, appreciate that this was an important marker for society. She had no idea why, however.

Her reading had led her to develop an understanding of men's fear of the hidden and there were arguments she was aware of that suggested because female reproductive organs were on the inside rather than hanging out for everybody to see that this presented an issue for some men. Maybe it was in the ability to compare that society felt the penis to be a much more relevant marker of power than the hidden mysteries of the vagina – the lack, the no-thing of which there was much ado. Comparison was a key element of competition which was a crucial aspect of capitalism, whereas maybe vaginas were just a little bit more socialist.

Common phrases such as 'grow a pair' and 'ballsy' showed that society favoured male genitalia in terms of the subsequent resilience, fortitude and bravery that was brought about by having testicles, but there was also a sense for Molly that they increased the degree of masculine vulnerability as these dangling, fleshy protruding sperm-making globes were open to attack. Such undeniable jeopardy was a possible reason why, in general, boys were subjected to constant reminders to keep their emotions in check.

Molly had read about the vagina dentata – the idea that men were so scared of the unknowingness of female genitalia that they imagined they had teeth within. Typical of men, Molly thought, to make a monster out of the centre of the human universe from which life was (often) born. To Molly's mind, vaginas were like fleshy snowflakes as they were all, she assumed, different and beautiful in their own way. She liked this visual analogy until she remembered how, when she was much younger, she liked going outside when it snowed and she would stick her tongue out and feel the flakes melt on her expectant taste buds.

There was something about these two images that disturbed Molly as she maybe felt that it was her subconscious tapping into her sexuality. This sense of disquiet was also evident whenever she found herself idly tonguing the inside of her cheek as she often thought that the smooth, spongey skin tone there was probably the same as vaginal skin. Was vaginal skin even a term, or was it just skin? Vaginal skin made it sound like it somehow didn't belong on a body; it was a condition one had to go to the doctor's to have diagnosed with a skin graft the only corrective procedure currently available.

Men's seeming obsession with vaginas, Molly felt, had something to do with its hidden nature but also a hatred for the infinite possibilities of its shape and a deep misunderstanding of its functions.

Someone somewhere had no doubt previously argued that men's fear/fawning over vaginas was related to their deep-seated desire to retreat back to the warmth and safety of the womb. Misogyny, then, could be explained as a reaction to the vagina that spat out their woeful, small penised selves, and the woman whose body it was a part of. To argue that men wished to venture back into the recesses of the vagina seemed somewhat ridiculous to Molly but at least it went some way to explaining some people's preoccupation with pot-holing.

As much as her own sexual and gendered identity was

something of an enigma to her, men were more so. Molly placed categories on men, and these were:

Most men

Men in town

The former group were those she was too scared to talk to; the latter were those she was simply scared of. 'Men in town' didn't mean males in certain geographical locations more than it related to the type of man who looked to own space that she ventured into and this, Molly felt, was actually most men which confused her own sense of categorisation.

Men in town were also invariably termed men in vests by Molly and she often referred to them as The Grunts.

Her issue with these people was the marking of their area, like wolves pissing to lay out the boundary of their territory. These men would walk with their bodies swinging and their arms flailing in such a manner that they took up more of the pavement than was necessary whilst simultaneously betraying their base simian core. They sat on benches in town with their legs spread wider than seemed possible and they made noises – shouts, grunts, exaggerated laughter, disgusting coughing and spitting – which were unreasonable and were made, at least to Molly's mind, to relay a sense of power for an otherwise powerless pile of flesh and half-baked ideas who seemed entirely lacking in the ability to construct fully formed sentences.

These men were the dispossessed; they had no place in society to which they ideologically belonged. They wanted to perform their masculinity as a form of oafish brutalism, yet they had nowhere to put their gendered performance which was possibly why they had to play it out so loudly and so extravagantly in the hope that fear and wonder may be the overarching sentiment of those frail creatures left to marvel at these fine ideals of maleness. Molly termed these people men, but they were often only a little older than she was – some as young as sixteen and others in their early twenties.

Their territories seemed to be marked in the grotesqueries of sputum. She would see them gathering in their packs, maybe five or six of them standing around talking but making no actual eye contact with each other as they were often more like a bunch of meerkats with their heads swivelling from side to side in a twitchy manner.

Molly felt that they were on the look out for the police or, more likely, that they were pretending to be on the look out for the police as that would then make the others in the group feel that they had recently been involved in some daring escapade or other which would therefore, and quite inexplicably, increase their value within their particular little community of hypermasculine being and anti-social doing. Molly was of the opinion that most human interaction was a performance and you picked your role, subconsciously or otherwise, to fit not just the mood you were in but also to allow those who you were interacting with to create a picture of you in all aspects of your life – an often one-dimensional portrayal of a complex and faulty human being that had no sense of nuance about it.

Had this type of masculinity, Molly wondered, always been there or was this new?

When boys of thirteen and fourteen, maybe younger, were going down the coal pits and working in factories eighty-odd years ago were they possessed of a need to assert their masculine identities to onlookers or were they too pre-occupied in their manual labour which offered them a sense of worth and value?

In a way, this made Molly pity The Grunts as perhaps they had little say in their own actions and were simply acting out (re-acting out) this scenario based on what was denied to them by previous generations. Having said that, the life expectancy of those kids in the pits were probably much lower than this current generation so maybe that was a positive – or perhaps it just prolongs their own lack of a sufficient and adequate sense of identity and self-worth, stretching out their unrecognised acts of being top dog when everyone else saw them as runts. Molly hated them and felt for them in equal measure. She cursed her ability to overthink everything.

These men had no nuance, but they were all a nuisance as far as Molly was concerned. She had experienced their loutish behaviour and had been on the receiving end of a few taunts, wolf whistles (often at the same time for some reason) and on one occasion she had been stopped in the street by one of them who then proceeded to ask questions about where she lived and whether she would show her breasts to him, although that was not his chosen term. If there existed a sliding scale of unreasonable requests they would be at opposite ends.

Feminism, Molly felt, had much to teach these people but then so too did civilisation and the twenty-first century as they seemed so hopelessly cut adrift of all things that made society viable.

On unusually hot spring days they would be in town with their tops off, sinewy torsos on display for nobody's pleasure, sharing one can of strong lager between three or four of them. There would always be one with his hands down the front of his jogging bottoms. John from school had explained to Molly that this probably meant he had a knife as this is where they were hidden to avoid the police finding them, although Molly just assumed that they stood like this so that their group and others walking by would think they had a knife in their hand rather than just a few pubes and the inoffensive weapon of their ridiculous looking penis.

Those body parts, as far as Molly was concerned, looked like slugs in snoods and so she often wondered about the power of the phallus only really relating to erect penises as nobody could be overly impressed by an appendage that lacked life, authority or hope. Vaginas were much more optimistic. Perhaps.

Their vile spit, their volume and their physical appearance all led Molly to be afraid of these men and, moreover, of being wary of going into town in general.

This feeling was also coupled with the idea that most things in town scared her and the thing she feared most of all was bumping into somebody she knew from school so that put these men into some perspective at least. None of her friends, male or female, had ever asked Molly to show them her tits, or at least not that she could recollect and she was pretty sure that this was something that she would be able to recall, in fact it would be something she would think about every day in a ninety minute (give or take) cognitive cycle of despair and fascination.

It seemed to Molly that it was easy to be a boy, and problematic to be a girl. Boys had a limited sense of what their performance of self was allowed to be. Their clothes shops had row upon row upon row of the same items but in different sizes and slightly varied colour schemes. The variations of haircuts were also seemingly limited to the 'lad' who basically had short hair in the style of whichever current footballer was worthy of copying at any particular moment, or the 'nerd' who had had the same mother-approved haircut since their first ever secondary school photo – all straight lines with jagged edges. Lads considerably outnumbered nerds.

There were a few exceptions to these guidelines that Molly occasionally saw around her. There were the longhaired metalheads who wore the same uniform of black jeans and band t-shirt.

Molly was obsessed in a way with some of these men, particularly the indecipherable lettering on their garments that seemingly acted as an obstacle for outsiders. She liked their pretence of separation.

Then there were the cool skater kids whose jeans were baggier, and their hairstyles harked back to the 1990s with floppy curtains being de rigueur for those choosing this lifestyle. From an outsider's perspective, these lads felt little in the way of competition with regards to their external appearance, an aspect that seemed to be a key trait of being a girl.

Men looked at men, and men looked at women, but this 'look' was somehow different, controlling. Women looked at women in the same way that men looked at women and Molly wondered what was lacking in the sisterhood that they would fall into this trap without realising.

Weddings were a case in point – the men were expected to wear variations of the same form of clothing whereas Molly heard anecdotes about women being mortified if they attended the same event where someone was wearing the same outfit as them. Rather than being some sort of affirmation of style, they would see this as an attack of their supposed individuality and need to stand out. The need, therefore, was for women to stand apart when they really needed to stand together.

Molly was aware that the world was changing, and that in some ways feminism had without doubt made great strides forward and allowed women the opportunity to be more in control of their own life chances. But it often felt like two steps forward and one, sometimes three, back. There was, after all, a President of the most powerful country in the world who was, in Molly's words, a sexual predator, and in his own a 'pussy grabber'. The phrase made her feel unbearably nauseous.

In the news recently, Molly had seen a story about global warming and how this awful man was on the telly saying how he didn't feel as though humans had much role in this, and he thought that things would change back again in the future. All Molly could think of was how like Emperor Nero he was – Nero played the fiddle while Rome burned, and Trump fiddled with vaginas while the world went to hell.

Molly would often receive a hostile reaction from people when she started talking about feminism, interestingly from girls a lot of the time. She was often told to 'wind it in' as they argued that things were better now and so she needn't keep going on about it. It was boring for them.

Not only did Molly see this as a sense of their own privilege but also of their ignorance and how well trained they had become by the cultural products of the mainstream. All she had to do was point to Trump as an example of how illusory some of these so-called advances had been and that having a notorious sex pest in a position of authority took the feminist cause back twenty years or more.

Molly was used to hearing conversations about how young girls should not wear 'provocative' clothing, or that they shouldn't walk alone or in small groups in certain parts of town, or shouldn't get irresponsibly drunk, or shouldn't have sexual organs if they didn't want to be assaulted blah blah blah. *What an absolute load of abhorrent horse crap! How about changing the story to 'men shouldn't rape'?*

Molly knew very little about cases in UK courts, or courts elsewhere, of male-on-male rape but she wondered if clothing choice came up on such occasions. This was an issue that Molly wanted to look into in more detail, to know more about so that she had some really killer information to hand in the event of a conversation about this with someone who had no idea what they were talking about and just used internet memes as sources of their information about the world.

She wanted to think that rape was not about sex, it was about control, but she felt that her insufficient reading on the area made her feel uncertain about declaring this thought aloud in front of others. She wanted to read about it and use facts, case studies and statistics to back up what she thought was a pretty common-sense idea.

The idea of sexual assault as a form of power and control came to her a couple of years before when she was reading a news article about a war somewhere or other (Afghanistan? Sudan? She couldn't remember the specifics) where the soldiers had raped a number of the women of the village they had just 'secured'. This made her think of the rampaging ways of the Vikings.

Was it that these soldiers were far from home and felt sexually frustrated? No. Molly thought that the reason why this had become a form of ritual in war was more to do with power and a sense of ownership, how an army can do more than merely invade your land, they can violate your women and thereby desecrate your masculinity.

It was obvious in this instance that women were seen as property, as belonging to the defeated men, who now had to live with not only the shame of losing the war (assuming they survived, of course) but also of sleeping next to *their* woman every night who was no longer solely *theirs*. The term 'sexual assault' was a misnomer as Molly felt that there was nothing sexual about it in the slightest. These weren't easy thoughts to ponder for Molly, and she knew that her views came from the privilege of not having experienced something so shattering as this.

Molly felt uncomfortable assessing her own identity against others – femininity vs. masculinity, youth vs. age, wise vs. dumb etc. but she was intelligent enough to know that in order to really understand a thing, one must also have an appreciation of its opposite and that knowledge works by measuring these two against one another. Or something like that.

Cold as an understood and recognised concept, for instance, only existed because people had an appreciation of heat. Opposites create meaning. If there was no up, there could be no down.

Molly used the example of space to help her with this concept as there was no conceivable way in which she felt an astronaut could determine up from down when in zero gravity with nothing in her eyeline. Therefore, these relational concepts were Earth-bound, which made her feel very perceptive and intellectually engaged.

In this way, femininity only really existed in comparison (and perhaps as contrast) to masculinity but this didn't mean that girls should be compared with boys – the penis wasn't masculine in its true sense, the vagina was no more feminine than someone's eye. Being a girl was one thing, being feminine was entirely different and one was not necessarily linked with the other. Issues of gender were often focal points in Molly's thinking, as she wrestled with how and why things had gone so wildly wrong in society in terms of equality.

Molly had often engaged in conversation on matters relating to culturally prescribed identity with Dan, and from time to time with those few people who she genuinely regarded as her friends.

It was in these chats with Dan that Molly felt most connected to him – their views were similar, and he listened intently to her point whereas more often than not he had a tendency to finish her sentences for her (correctly, for the most part, but that wasn't the point).

Molly would regularly become frustrated with the conversations that she had at school (friends never came to her house, she never went to theirs and hanging out in town or in the rec was not on the agenda). If Molly needed any reminder that her ways of thinking and intellectual vocabulary were different to many peers, then she need only think of an exchange she had with Billie Cattermole while they were in Year 9.

Molly: Do you ever feel let down?

Billie: What do you mean?

Molly: You know, sort of let down by the society we live in and how far women have come in recent decades but also how much further we need to go to, you know, sort of to do anything?

Billie: What?

Molly: Do you get frustrated that you won't have the same opportunities just because you have a vagina?

Billie: Molly!! What the hell?

Molly: I'm serious, Billie. It kills me to think of glass ceilings and…

Billie: Who are they? Molly: …what?

Billie: Who are Glass Ceilings? Are they one of those weird bands you listen to?

Molly: What? No! Are you kidding me, Billie? The glass ceiling is the idea that women can't reach the top in their jobs and how men put up this…

Billie: But what has that got to do with me?

Molly: It doesn't have anything *to do* with you – it's not something you've done. I'm just asking what you think about it and what you want to do about it.

Billie: About what?

Molly: Bloody hell, Billie. What you want to do about the lack of opportunities you will have in your future career, that's what. This is like getting blood from a stone, here.

Billie: Are they another one of your bands?

Molly: What?

Billie: Blood From a Stone – they sound like something you would listen to.

Molly: Are you joking?

Billie: Yep. Good one, eh?

Molly: Yeah, good one. Well done. What a day brightener that was.

Billie: You want me to say that we should smash men in the balls and take their place in charge of things, don't you? You want me to say that we need to do something about all of this and make ourselves feel that we have a personal responsibility to change things for the benefit of all women, don't you?

Molly: That would be a start, yes.

Billie: Then you want me to stop mucking about with pretending I don't know what bands you like, and you want me to talk about moon-cups and mindfulness, don't you, sister?

Molly: You always have to take things too far, Bills. I just wanted to talk about something, that's all.

Billie: Are they new flavour crisps?

Molly: Yeah. They're horrible. Want one?

Billie: No, thanks. You didn't really sell them by saying they were horrible.

Molly: Yeah. Sorry.

Billie: No biggie. So, what do you think you want to do about this?

Molly: About what?

Billie: About not having the same opportunities as complete numbnuts like Ian Jewsbury over there?

Molly: Oh my…what is he doing?

Billie: I think he's pretending to ride an imaginary horse.

Molly: Obviously that's it. Sure. Why not, eh? Have you heard the new Prominent Vulva album?

Billie: You have got to be kidding me. Prominent What-Now?

Molly: Ha! Do you not think that would be a good name for a band?

Billie: Not really, no. Anyways…so, you think you are likely to earn less in your job than Ian over there?

Molly: Well, maybe not specifically Ian Jewsbury, but less than most men. Poor Ian has got 'minimum wage forever' written all over him. Statistics show that…

Billie: Why do women get paid less, then?

Molly: I don't know. That's my point. They do, though, and that's the issue.

Billie: There has to be a sensible reason for it, though.

Molly: There is a reason for it and it's because men are trying to keep women in their place. Feminism has made the right moves but there is still so much to do.

Billie: And who is going to do it, then?

Molly: We have to do something about it and getting angry about it is the most obvious first step.

Billie: So, it's down to just you and me, then? Sort of feminist superheroes in dungarees, no make-up and armpit hair.

Molly: Is that what you think feminists look like?

Billie: No. I just like winding you up.

Molly: Well, it isn't working.

Billie: It is, though.

Molly: And it's not just down to you and me.

Billie: I know that. Would be cool if it was, though. Imagine the views we'd get on YouTube. Billie and Molly – feminist freedom fighters!

Molly: Molly and Billie sounds better.

Billie: Bolly and Millie – ha! No, that wouldn't work.

Molly: Do you get angry thinking about it, though? That just because he has a willy that Ian bloody Jewsbury over there has better life chances than a lot of us?

Billie: I get annoyed listening to you talk about it every break time and Ian bloomin' Jewsbury is really not a great example of the point you are trying to make. And I don't like the idea of thinking of Ian Jewsbury's little sad willy, cheers.

Molly: Well, it's important to me.

Billie: His willy is important to you?

Molly: Obviously not. Unfair opportunity is important to me.

Billie: I know. And because of that it's important to me, but I can't get fired up about it the same way you do. I can't get all annoyed with what I can't control.

Molly: Yeah?

Billie: Yeah.

Molly: So why did you get upset yesterday when you forgot your coat and it rained?

Billie: That's different.

Molly: It's not. Not really. Not if you think about it.

Billie: Come on, Molly. Let's go and sit with Danny and the

others.

Molly: No, I'm okay here. You can go over.

Billie: I'm going to. Catch you in a bit, loser.

Molly: Okay. Don't forget your Maths homework is in tomorrow.

Billie: Okay, mum!

Molly felt that her feelings of isolation and separation were self-perpetuating and often came as a result of opening her mouth and saying something meaningful to the wrong audience. Although Billie was clued in, she often simply didn't wish to engage in the same conversation over and over and over again and Molly thought this was a problem as lots of people her age were not used to anything other than a culture of soundbites and memes, not meandering musing.

Disposable, not debatable.

Instant, not interesting.

These distinctions were of value for Molly as they allowed her to place a division between herself and her classmates, a separation which afforded her the opportunity to dwell in her sense of segregation, a self-imposed exile from the discursive ineptitudes of those around her. She found a sense of comfort in this pain, as it was a feeling that she had in recent years become to rely on. The sadness that she felt at simply being was all encompassing, but she had used it as a way of reassuring herself that she was alive.

There were, however, issues which she wanted to get over in the way she thought about others as it made her worry that she was becoming increasingly more snobbish. This did not sit well with her as it did not show a sense of solidarity with those around her. By consciously acting in a way that made her stand out against the crowd, was she deliberately creating a social schism which was in fact the very idea of 'them and us' that she so vociferously declared to abhor? Or was this a standard rite of passage for all people in this broken society where they were desperate to scramble around to form their own sense of identity away from what they were being told they should become?

Molly was sure that, deep down, many people her age (and younger, and older. Perhaps everyone, in fact) were struggling with what it meant to be themselves. *I don't know what being 'me' means,* she thought, *so what's to say others don't feel the same?*

She even considered on occasion that she wasn't *being* Molly but *doing* Molly as she was transmitting an idea of herself that she felt was the required display for the project of her life that satisfied her particular needs at that particular time. Or perhaps this sense of overthinking and overstating everything was exactly what Molly was like, but it did not make her feel really comfortable admitting it to herself. She wondered if other people agonised over the smallest things – what to say, what to wear, how to walk, where to look – or whether those voices in their heads were made redundant by the constant dull hum of existence, like tinnitus for the servile.

The problem with being a girl, of course, was that this label was one loaded with expectations. She had heard people talk time and time and time again about how boys and girls were 'wired differently' which confused her when she was younger. She assumed at first that the phrase related to how the urethras of boys and girls were different and that in some way this was the wiring that was being referred to.

As she got older, she learnt that many people held the view that boys and girls, particularly at young ages, acted the way they did because their brains had some sort of pre-conditioned values in them which resulted in an identifiable difference in mannerisms, temperament and attitude. Molly did not know for sure, and she was interested in reading more about this, but it instinctively felt like a load of old horse shit to her. Her future research in this area would be undertaken in a very cynical manner, though, as she was sure that research was skewed to fit the cultural ideas of the time.

It seemed to Molly as though a number of people failed to see the role they played in forming the identities of others. Parents, for instance, would still gender their child from the youngest of ages. She remembered going with Dan one year when he was going to vote in an election or something similar. The polling station was in her old school and this meant that the children had that day off, possibly the only positive thing to come out of politics for years for the younger generations.

As they walked across the playground, towards the entrance, Molly saw a woman with a boy, probably three or four years old. He was holding a worn ragdoll in his right hand and was clutching it close to his body to help this anthropomorphised fabric act as a form of comfort and consistent reassurance to him. Humans lack the same levels of static solace as dolls because their reactions to situations were all too often dependent on their own moods at that particular moment in time, Molly thought.

This rag doll, to Molly's mind, was a safety blanket for this kid. This was clear from the placement of the doll (head up, arms over the boy's arms as if it were a real baby) and how close to his heart he was holding it. The doll's face was even tilted upwards a little towards the boy, as if to suggest that regular personal communication was a part of the relationship this kid had with his companion.

'I can't believe you have brought that thing,' said the mother. 'Dolls are for girls.' *But comfort is for all*, Molly thought. The woman was hurrying the boy across the playground by holding his left wrist and being a pace or two in front of him so that his little legs were working hard to keep up. For a moment, Molly thought that this was not a loving relationship that she saw in front of her, but then she realised that this whole scene had lasted about fifteen or twenty seconds and so it would be harsh to judge these people on such a short period of time. *It must be hard for parents* Molly thought. At the same moment she squeezed Dan's hand a little tighter and he instinctively reciprocated.

This moment helped Molly to more fully understand how parents go about shaping the identities of their children while also restricting the possibilities and potentialities of that burgeoning individual.

No matter how hard she tried to actively separate herself from how she had been socialised, she knew that her familial upbringing had played a more significant role in the person she had become as opposed to the books, films and music that she wrapped her identity around. She was not so happy to acknowledge this, however, as she felt that this idea weakened her own sense of empowerment and gave her a diminished role in the formation of herself.

She felt that people could not really define their own

personality and that this was something for others to do. At least, this was true for most people as they were social animals whereas she had the social skills and drive of a sloth. A near dead sloth with muscular atrophy, at that.

By allowing others to define you, Molly thought, *you are leaving yourself open to the frailties of human language.* This was a common thought that Molly had, that life centred so much on the compromise between cognition and communication. What someone thought they could not always express, and what someone said was not always what they meant.

Molly knew that her own knowledge of language hindered her as there were a few things she could think of – sensations, tastes, feelings – which she would not have been able to verbalise successfully. Like actors playing at being drunk, there was an entirely unconvincing element to Molly when she tried to convey certain things. Words, sentence structure, tone of voice, and other methods of interaction always seemed to result in the original thought being altered to fit the method of human engagement. This made humans weak, as there was always compromise between thought and phrasing.

Language also controlled many ways in which people understand the world, Molly considered. For example, she could never quite get her head around feminine and masculine clauses in French, not because she did not understand their uses and application, just that she became increasingly preoccupied by the way in which native speakers would perceive certain inanimate objects due to the gender bias. Was there something inherently different in the mind of a speaker when they referred to a 'le' or a 'la' thing?

This interested Molly but she found that the two French

teachers that she had during her time at school either did not understand the question or were just not happy to engage in the trivialities of non-curriculum topic areas.

And speaking of masculine and feminine, what about the language of sex? Why was it that men penetrated women rather than women enveloping men? Would the world work in entirely different ways if that had been the language of intercourse over the centuries? Maybe not.

It was an interesting thought, though.

CHAPTER 5

The photo album

Molly would often catch the train in order to go to places where she knew the chances of bumping into someone she knew would be minimal. And besides, she always had a feeling that when she stayed within the ever-greying confines of her hometown she was perpetually distracted by scanning the ground for dog shit as opposed to looking up at the stars. Her town was at once too big for her while also being suffocating and small. Time outside of its bounds was almost always time well spent.

One of her favourite places to visit was Rochester. Not because of the banal tourist attractions relating to Charles Dickens, the dockyards or the imposing cathedral and castle, but for a shop that sold second hand books.

This place had the unmistakable essence of vellichor about it. Since learning the word vellichor, Molly had grown a little obsessed with it. It meant the wistfulness of the smell of second hand books and, by extension, second hand bookshops were filled with it. There was a mustiness to the odour, a sourness that stung the nostrils and was right on the olfactory border between smell and stink. Classy people liked the smell, Molly assured herself, as they understood its value and meaning.

The exterior of the shop was unremarkable, with crumbling walls covered in indiscriminate swathes of now dirty grey and green paint. The interior had a sepia tinted aura of deadness and long-forgotten knowledge and reminiscence about it and this brought out the romantic idealist in Molly.

Where the outside was an all too familiar sign of the former prosperity of the shop, with its elaborately written but now decaying sign, the inside retained a sense of reverence for the hush that the contents of the establishment necessitated.

Over its three storeys there was a whole world of outdated facts and opinions at Molly's bitten to the quick fingertips. There were maps that featured countries that no longer existed, biographies on people she assumed to be anonymous by dint of not knowing who they were, and shelf upon shelf upon shelf of identically bound books that seemed almost militaristic in their banal uniformity.

The kind man who ran the shop let people browse for hours without urging them to buy anything; it seemed as if this venture was about communion rather than commerce.

The sections that the books were divided into seemed haphazard to say the least. The bottom floor included History, Local History, Sports, Travel, Fiction and War sections, identified with handwritten signs. Molly was in awe of the way that the lettering on each sign was perfectly aligned and satisfyingly symmetrical. She took great pleasure in order and considered action.

Molly wondered how long the sign-writer (she assumed it to be the shop owner but wasn't sure) took before they got the spacing between the letters just so. This was the kind of job that would result in Molly having sleepless nights with worry as she tried to work out a method of getting it right at the first time of asking. *Whoever wrote those signs deserves their work to be noticed*, Molly thought.

There was a pleasing aesthetic quality to the work and Molly considered the possibility that if some, or just one, of the signs had been slightly askew then maybe she would not have been able to go back into the shop as she was sure that her contentment in that space would have been spoilt. There was an undisguised horror in Molly upon seeing a handwritten sign where the letters got smaller towards the end as the available space was diminishing, or the all too commonplace apostrophe where it didn't belong.

Simple things that other people would see and be forgiving of were the things that exasperated Molly to the point of distraction. She hated this aspect of her personality, but also saw the need for precision in almost everything that she did. If she wanted precision then she needed to be able to more readily accept the frustrations that accompanied that particular trait.

The second floor had Fiction, Non-Fiction, Crime Fiction and Fishing. The last floor had no signs but consisted of loads of dusty old maps, books from a variety of genres awaiting rescue through collation, and those that were damaged beyond a saleable, yet not readable, condition.

Molly often spent the longest time in this top floor with all of the other unwanted things.

Everything seemed to be brown in this room, from the curtains at the end of the room to the shelves, to the lamp and tassels of the deteriorating lampshade, to the book covers, to the parchment of the maps, to the gloomy, pleasingly suffocating atmosphere. Molly really felt as though she were stepping back in time in this room and although the dimensions of the building suggested otherwise, this room seemed significantly smaller than those on the other floors.

Despite visiting this shop at least twice a month over the last year or so Molly had no idea of the name of the man who ran the place. They knew each other by sight, hardly ever saying a word, yet Molly felt pleased when he recognised her each time and he would smile slightly before cocking his head upwards as if to indicate that he knew it was the upstairs room that she would be heading to for the next few hours or so.

She loved nothing more than blowing the dust from a book as this made her feel like a character in a film who was about to uncover the secret to all things. Most of the books had a similarity to their design with brown leather-bound covers, although some of the leather was soft and some was hard. Very few of these books had the title or the author's name on the spine, the omission of these important pieces of information only increased Molly's sense of wonder and awe in this room as if there existed a real possibility that she were just about to stumble across the long hidden writings of some alchemist, necromancer or ancient philosopher whose work would forever change her perception of this drab little world that she unwittingly found herself existing in.

Molly had been making the journey into Rochester on her own for a couple of years now, even while still at school, and there was something about the trips which made her feel as though she were on a mission where discovery was the destiny. Discovery of what, she was not so sure, but that was the point.

She was a browser, not looking to purchase anything in particular. Specifics could be bought online; the power of the casual surveyor was almost unlimited wherein the unknowing mystery of that which could catch the eye was tantalising.

Molly had overheard her dad once talking about 'digging' for vinyl records, and she assumed this meant dipping in and out of racks of records in the hope of finding a hidden gem that he didn't know he was looking for or needed, or even knew about, but on locating it he was overcome with the urge to spend good money on it. This was how Molly felt, albeit with the financial restrictions she experienced making it somewhat unlikely that she could take away all the gems she found here.

There was also less of a need for her to take items home as the length and regularity of her visits resulted in the consumption of a significant number of tomes. She particularly liked the ones that used words that she struggled to comprehend. The process of reading, rather than necessarily understanding the meaning of the text, was of as much importance to Molly.

Learning would come from absorbing as much as she could, knowledge would come from understanding some of it.

The trips to Rochester now formed a part of her routine and Molly felt that as she got older the rigidity of her routine was becoming more and more pronounced. Molly needed structure of sorts in her life, but she desired structure of her own design.

She felt a little unsettled when she became aware that Rochester's train station was to be relocated about half a mile from its current position in order to accommodate commuter trains that required more carriages than the old station could handle. It would have been easy, Molly reasoned, for her old self to simply break from this regular trip and to stop going to this town as the familiarity of the excursion was being disrupted. The move was imminent, by all accounts, which caused a ripple of shock within her.

Even though she had made this visit as much as a couple of

times a month there remained a degree of hesitation each time she arrived at the station to board the train to Rochester. She had spent countless hours managing her feelings and ensuring that all potential occurrences of the journey were accounted for.

She knew what to say to the person she needed to speak to in order to purchase her return ticket and she went through the script several times as she got nearer to the station entrance, just to ensure she had the speed and tone of delivery just right.

She preferred it when the kiosk where the tickets were sold were not staffed as she then had a legitimate reason to use the machine where she could simply punch in the relevant information for her journey, pay the money and two tickets would be produced. For someone like Molly, these ticket machines were a boon, but she could only use them if the kiosks were closed because as much as she hated human interaction, she also knew that as automation increased in society so did job insecurity. She refused, as a matter of principle, to use machines for train tickets, shopping and postage stamps.

She had never actually bought a stamp in her life, but she knew that when the time came then she would not use a machine prior to posting a letter.

As the days drew nearer to her first visit to the new station, she found herself being surprised by her feelings of excitement about it. She imagined it would be a fresh, open and almost futuristic space that the architects, the workforce and the people in the local area could be proud of. A couple of days later she realised it wasn't.

Grey was the overwhelming colour in the newly constructed station; from the waiting shelters, the concrete of the platform, the dullness of the walls, the lifelessness of the window pane frames and the listless professional characters who wore homogenised suits which reflected their neutered genuflection in the face of Mammon's omnipotence. They were, Molly thought, as castrated in their individual lives as those citizens of Communism in their state approved overalls who these money-obsessed human shells were seemingly opposed to ideologically.

These people were like the dead whose eyes remained open when they breathed their last. Instead of coins being placed on their eyes to appease the ferryman into the afterlife, the money was placed into the illusory pockets of bank accounts to appease the capitalist ideals of consumption as these people surrounded themselves with supposed luxuries to deny the fact they would one day die. The material seducing the mortal.

King Commute - delusional in the way they held back the tide of thought and self-awareness by being far too busy making money for other people to consider how their lives had turned out and that death would come as a sweet release. Molly was more than aware she would die. In fact she considered it almost every hour of her waking life, but she hoped to do something different from these people before her time came as she hoped to actually live, even just a little.

The drained colour palette of the new station was seen by Molly as an opportunity missed. Those responsible for its design had a huge blank canvas to draw upon and could have created a thing of beauty rather than this carbuncle. Instead, it simply served to reflect the extensive air of ennui that seemed to haunt almost every person that Molly saw here and so, perhaps for the majority of aimless souls who unthinkingly wandered like inconsequential ghosts on these platforms, it was a suitable hue that matched the lost state of the people here.

Molly preferred to travel by train during the busiest times of the day even though the ticket price was cheaper just half an hour later. The earlier trains were best for intently observing people while simultaneously being as unobtrusive as possible.

There were still plenty of interesting people to spy on during the times when the majority of travellers were already tucked away in their offices, meeting rooms or schools and colleges, yet it was much trickier due to there being fewer people around to watch without being seen to be doing so.

Covert observation was her modus operandi. Also, seeing just a few people at a time did not suit Molly's interest in trying to find out more about the human condition as seeing one or two people behaving in a certain way said nothing about wider groups, which was of much more specific interest to her. If she were to gain a more nuanced understanding of society, the observation of a few scattered individuals was of little value, she needed to witness the herd in action.

Trains now arrived at this multi-million pound station right in front of the city's twin assets of the cathedral and castle. These buildings were about five hundred metres from each other and so appeared as impressive icons of the historical significance of this area. Both the castle and cathedral, for Molly, symbolised wealth, power and indulgence and she couldn't help but be more drawn to the two storey flats which were at the foot of the station and ran parallel with the tracks.

Despite it making her journey to the bookshop longer than was needed, Molly enjoyed walking left out of the station in the direction of these homes.

There was a sense of unbearable irony about these small,

no doubt mentally restricting spaces and their proximity to the rail lines and the concomitant potential for escape they symbolise. So close to getting out and shaking the dust of this crummy little town from their clothes, these people were likely more psychologically hemmed in by the prohibitively expensive cost of rail travel in relation to the low paid work they likely did which resulted in them living in such housing which was neither particularly objectionable to Molly nor inviting.

The idea of a communal entrance on its own was enough to put her off ever living in such a place for two reasons – one, the inevitable need for small talk when carelessness resulted in seeing a neighbour and, two, the dirty DNA of others on the keypads and door handles was almost too much to comprehend without feeling sick.

About eighteen months after the new station had opened some blue-painted wooden barriers were in place between the busy road and these flats. Molly saw these for the first time on her last trip to Rochester on a Saturday; her penultimate week of going to school was ahead.

Molly had no idea what these barricades were for, but she felt sorry for those people living in this space behind them as these pieces of wood acted as restrictions towards the natural light of the morning sun. Over the course of four trips around three weeks apart, Molly witnessed what she perceived to be the destructive malice of the moneyed.

First, there were the wooden boards that seemed to asphyxiate the life out of those who lived in these flats. Then came the ten foot tall wire fencing which she noticed behind the wood on her second visit, before the third time walking that way made it clear that these abodes were not being renovated but destroyed, torn down in order to improve the landscape surrounding the train station to ensure that the working-classes were not visible to the tourists attracted to stopping in Rochester after sighting the imposing historical artefacts of the castle and the cathedral.

On this third post-barrier Rochester venture, Molly realised that the occupants of these buildings were no longer there. She walked slowly by, noticing the cracks in windows where stones had been thrown by passers-by. The resulting effect was that the glass remained in place yet splintered into every direction across fractured lines of unpredictability, seemingly in remembrance of those who used to live within who had been scattered who-knows-where while hoping to retain a sense of structure, regardless of the impact from external forces.

On her next visit, the builders had ripped apart the very fabric of these homes, exposing segments of the interiors after smashing down sections of the walls. This made Molly appreciate the distinction between the building which housed something like sixteen groups of people and the sense of home that each had made for themselves. This was evidenced in the variations Molly saw in the flats as she walked by their prematurely enforced decay.

The side of the first block of flats had been exposed as the process of knocking them down had started and Molly understood that each occupant lived in a couple of rooms on one floor whereas she had thought previously that their living arrangements meant that a family had an upstairs and a downstairs room but this was clearly not the case. It took the death of this living space to reveal itself.

Molly saw the top floor had bright purple wallpaper with a design of white, large flowers that entwined towards the top of the wall. Downstairs had a poorly administered magnolia paint job which seemed from the six or seven metres distance between Molly and the wall to be patchy at best. The skirting boards appeared filthy, and there were brown stains on the walls from what looked like spilt drinks.

These tiny insights into those who previously had lived, loved and loathed in these flats were tantalising for Molly. She could only remember seeing one person go in or out of these buildings, a short haired woman of about thirty-five who was wearing a green uniform which reminded Molly of something a vet would wear, or maybe a care worker of some description, yet these exposed rooms offered Molly so much in terms of making up stories of the inhabitants which only added deeper sadness to the mystery of where they now were, and whether they pined for their former homes and the people they lived next to.

As she walked to the far end of the flats she realised that the walls of this end had also been knocked through and Molly again saw the variations evident in the dwellings. Upstairs had a bright yellow colour scheme with some cartoon character transfers scattered in an almost random manner around the wall. This, she surmised, was the room of a young boy whose parents were liberal or not caring enough and therefore allowed him to place the transfers wherever it pleased him.

The brightness of the room and the seeming playfulness of the allocation of the transfers sent a shiver down Molly's spine as she realised that life was here – the energy and verve of children – whereas the other rooms she could see at the opposite end of the block had an almost eerie sense of the inevitability of hopelessness about them as if only ghosts rather than people had ever lived there. Here, though, Molly was able to picture the life of a boy, and although the room seemed quite pokey to Molly's eyes, she felt sure that the little man whose room it was would have seen it as his kingdom.

Downstairs, however, the air of decay returned as the room below seemed stagnant in comparison. It was exactly the kind of room where people died in their chairs and were left to rot for a few weeks until a neighbour complained about the smell.

There was a dankness to the room which belied the possibility of healthy human habitation. Patches of mould seeped through the paint on the walls and there were thick cobwebs hanging from the lampshade which made Molly think of Miss Havisham's despondent existence, although the previous tenant in the room she was looking into now had Stella rather than Estella for company. *You're a snob, Molly* she thought to herself. A tone of rightful chastisement making her feel a small twinge of embarrassment.

When the side of the first block of flats was demolished, Molly was reminded of the imagery of war she had seen where people were scrabbling through the rubble created by bombing.

This damage, though, seemed to be done by the oppressive, crunching fist of gentrification. Molly became aware of this as the original blue wooded barriers that were previously in place were superseded by similarly sized partitions but this time the intentions of those behind the destruction of the flats was obvious as information about forthcoming two, three and four bedroomed apartments was visible.

The people in the earlier flats had perhaps been relocated to remove the eyesore that their modernist buildings had presented to those entering the city from the new station. The newly torn down flats, in the shadow of the perennially judgemental cathedral, seemed to act as less than impressive mausoleums, a cenotaph to the invisible and the downtrodden wherein the importance of the death of this place was so insignificant that it was to be built upon. The vultures of capitalism rearing their ugly heads to displace those who offered no means of profit.

It was then that Molly remembered this road was called Corporation Street and whereas most road names often had a meaning which was lost by the passage of time, perhaps this was a much more forward-thinking piece of labelling.

The castle in many ways acted as a reminder of the decadence of death and the privilege that came as a result of human sacrifice and suffering. It was a static mechanism of warfare; every design feature was focused on defending a territorial space that didn't need defending until it was built.

Such buildings, for Molly, represented the ultimate folly of mankind – the defence of a meaningless but painstakingly constructed artefact with no other function other than to serve as a vehicle for defending that which was deemed defendable. Men laying down a marker to other men by declaring 'This is mine and you are to marvel at it, but you are not to have it'. It then only became a source of jealous plotting due to its mere existence, a symbol of power and possession that all men craved due to concerns over the magnificence of that which was within their pants.

Perhaps it was no surprise to find phallic imagery in all castles. Molly did note, however, that the most vaginal aspect of a castle was probably the most significant in terms of keeping the enemy at bay. The embrasure, the arrow slit through which archers volleyed at their foe, even had a mildly feminine name as it had a sense of embrace, and the soft sounding name put in mind ideas of comfort, safety and an almost womblike notion of idealised existence.

It was just a shame that Molly's reference to the vaginal in this instant came with the acceptance that it was the phallic arrows that were sent out from this position to harm others. Most likely as a result of her own views on men, this read to Molly as an analogy of the protective nature of the vagina as a source of stability which spat out violent actions in the name of the phallus.

Molly had read somewhere in one of the old history books in the bookshop that burning pigs had been used as a form of weapon in an attack on the castle. She remembered a good number of details about the siege such as the date (1215), and the purpose (for King John to gain control of the castle from the Archbishop of Canterbury, or maybe from some of his barons – some facts were not wholly remembered).

A two month campaign to gain entry and secure the castle included using huge catapults to throw rocks at the walls, along with trying to dig under the perimeter of the keep, all to no effect.

Forty obese pigs were subsequently used, sent toward the castle engulfed in flames, their fat exploding as they burnt. The source material from which Molly gathered this information was unclear as to whether the pigs were actually still alive or whether they had been pre-slaughtered. The thought of squealing, burning pigs running in all directions seemed less sensible as a military strategy than dead flaming mammals being flung at a wall from a catapult in the hope that they may burst, grenade style, at just the right moment.

It was, Molly conceded, an intriguing image yet she didn't really like history all that much and so she never quite knew why she read about the siege in the first place. The eviction letters that the occupants of the now-destroyed flats likely received notifying them of their need to vacate the premises must have felt like the equivalent of molten swine being aimed in their direction.

After a few more months, cranes took over in what were now building sites and dominated the skyline. There was one in each of the construction areas, trampling on the graves of those who had lived there as they went about their business.

The one closest to the station was inset from the road, towering over the builders who scurried below at their unforgiving tasks. The second, about 350 metres further down, hung over the road. Molly looked up as she passed by, feeling dwarfed by the imposing machinery.

The white metal base rose to maybe eighty metres, where the white and red cab sat. The wind that whistled past Molly made the structure seem less stable as she looked up, imagining it swaying due to the elements. She stood for a while, frozen on the path, at the somewhat reassuring thought of the crane crashing down on her and putting a speedy end to this façade of a life.

If only she hadn't looked up she would perhaps be squished without knowing her fate; the unknowing aspect of it resulting in a more satisfying end to her time on Earth. She realised that she needed to walk under the crane, not because it was the only route to the bookshop available to her, but because she had already planned her path and was not in the habit of altering her course which she had so painstakingly projected for herself as a form of imagined rehearsal, pre-empting uncertainty and ensuring that she felt confident on her first step as she had planned where she was going and who she was likely to see.

Instead of changing the habit of a lifetime, she decided to stand there and see if she could beckon the machine down.

She stood, transfixed and looking upwards, for what may have been approaching ten minutes. She refused to be put off her thought processes by those few people who walked by her, despite their occasional looks backwards to see what it was she was doing. How obvious, she thought to herself, that nobody actually took the bother to ask what she was doing. How typical of the Southern Englanders to concern themselves only momentarily with the acts of others without enquiring as to their well-being.

In her mind's eye she saw her right hand extend so that it was vertical, just a little higher than her chest. It was now a mystical gun scope as she lined her eye up and aimed her magic at the cab. In reality, however, she simply stood with her mouth open staring intently at the object of her intended destruction.

She willed the floor of the cab to come apart from its fixing, causing a ripple effect which would see the whole crane fall in on itself with a slight angle which would result in the tower falling to the left, onto the path, and making her one with the concrete in a union of death that would surely make the evening news.

She repeated the phrase 'come down, come down, come down' over and over and over in her mind, feeling the force of the words come out of her voice despite not moving a muscle. This, Molly felt, was how real powers of persuasion worked and now was as good as any to make some sort of telekinetic connection.

She felt a brief sense of warmth envelope her as she no longer became acutely aware of her surroundings. Her attention lay firmly on the attempt to topple the death bringer in front of her from its foreboding height. A faint, almost inaudible squealing noise rose in her ears, a constant high-pitched frequency which made her feel that the unknown powers inside of her were beginning to react to her wishes. This, for Molly, was a sign of progress and of an awakening in her abilities.

Time stood still and the trees behind the crane no longer seemed to bend with the wind, and the birds fell silent as they pondered the fate they were about to witness.

Molly appreciated the fact that, for a first timer, such a task was quite a trial and she was sure that she would feel a sense of euphoric exhaustion a split second before the crane landed on her. As a result, there was a moment's hesitation in her as she did not wish to tire herself out too quickly, thereby resulting in the frustration of an incomplete task. She also worried for a split second that someone was in the cab, unseen.

Images of a grieving family – a distraught wife, parents holding each other, and a bemused young child incapable of taking in the magnitude of recent events that would impact their life forevermore – flashed in Molly's mind, and there was a momentary lapse of focus which she was proud of herself for regaining.

Suddenly, her head became filled with the high tone that removed every other sensation in her body with a vibration whose origin could not precisely be located. She refocused on the cab but realised that the sound of the traffic, the trees moving and the birds calling to one another were audible again.

This, Molly realised, meant that her powers were subsiding

and her chances of securing her reputation as a powerful mover of objects would have to wait until another day. It started to rain harder, so she put her hood up and continued on her way.

* * * * * *

Molly often felt she had an obsessive personality. She fixated on the seemingly mundane while the world carried on and passed her by.

Words, gestures, eye contact, tone of voice, volume, physical space, appearance, gait – these were only a few of the things that went around and around and around her head at an ever exhausting pace as she tried to put a marker down for herself as to who she was that would serve her well for the rest of her life.

Maybe she would struggle with any sense of honest and authentic identity.

Perhaps there was no such thing as a core, immovable identity from which all choices, decisions, opinions and morals sprang from.

Maybe Molly's concept of personality being the true essence of someone was in itself a weak concept and not valid.

Perhaps identity and personality were notions that were, and always would be, in flux.

It wasn't easy for Molly to think things like this through in too much detail because she always ended up with the conclusion that such things would be considerably easier if she actually liked the person she was. Maybe she did like herself, and it was the recent years of trying to project a pained artistic persona that affected this. Perhaps sometimes she just needed a little hush from her thoughts.

As Christmas drew closer, Molly visited the bookshop again

and, as usual, went inside to lose herself in the sepia toned solitude the store offered. It had been seven weeks since she last felt strong enough to get on the train and go to Rochester and she worried that some of the mystique and musk of the shop would have been lost in that time.

'Hello,' said the owner. 'Not seen you in a while.' Molly shrugged and smiled simultaneously and went upstairs. She noticed that as she walked slowly up the steep and curved staircase there were raindrops from her coat dropping in front of her onto the brown carpet, marking her path upwards as if the drops of water were leading the way for her to obsequiously follow.

It was also at this point that Molly realised that her right trainer had a hole in it as three of her toes were soggy and there was a distinct yet not overly intrusive squelching sound when she planted her foot on the floor. Now that she had noticed the dampness in her sock, Molly knew that she would find it difficult to focus on much else.

She stood amongst the familiar surroundings and scanned the shelves for new additions or any sign of change which may signal the presence of another hardy soul since last she were there. Half of her wanted to see some disruption in the room, the other half wanted things just as they were as some signal of how deserted the room was and therefore how unique her presence was within this space. She knew that other people came and went because she had set some cunning traps for them previously. Books left open by Molly were often, but not always, closed on her next visit.

Molly had no recollection at all of another person being in the room when she was there. She felt almost sure that she must have shared this room with somebody at some point as the bookshop was very often busy with browsers seeking the same sanctuary as her, and so she put this down to just how unaware of her surroundings she was when engrossed in the dreams of escape that this room encouraged. And anyway, notions of 'busy' were relative and it wasn't as if this place had ever experienced any real consumer hustle and bustle or the throng of intellectually curious knowledge hounds.

The bows in the floors were due to the age of the building rather than as a result of any trampling horde. If the zombie apocalypse came any time soon, Molly would seek refuge in this bookshop as there was a pure safety in the knowledge that this was not a place most were familiar with. And there was a gun shop nearby, too, and that would obviously prove invaluable in such a scenario.

Molly was drawn to one particular corner of the room, the back left as she faced it after walking up the stairs. This was the dustiest, dankest and most unwelcoming aspect of the room as there were only shelves and books whereas the other corners had a chair, a lamp, some nondescript dust covered paintings on the wall amongst other attempts to normalise the space.

The corner that Molly found herself moving towards was usually the one area that she rarely ventured into due to what she perceived as its lifeless void of negativity. She didn't really believe in ghosts, but if she did then this corner would be where she would most likely consider one to dwell. There was an evident drop in the temperature in that part of the room, but this was due to the cracks in the wall that let in the cold from outside rather than from any sort of phantasmagorical eerie presence.

On this occasion, this part of the room at least gave her some respite from the pouring rain outside as it was the only section of the room where she could avoid looking out of the window. As this shop offered a temporary illusion of freedom away from the drab confinement of the real world, the move to this corner made sense on this particular day.

As a rule, Molly enjoyed walking in the rain, but she hated the aftermath of damp clothes and, for today at least, squelching feet, and so she perhaps subconsciously or unwittingly needed the refuge this corner offered. It was here that Molly first learnt about William and initiated a friendship with a dead boy.

The dim light of this region of the room broke down the colour spectrum to muted tones that homogenised all the book covers into a mass of dusty nothingness.

Molly's eyes were drawn towards one particular book which stuck out further on the shelf than its equally neglected colleagues. Its shape led Molly initially to believe it was an art pad and this led to a shock of excitement that emanated from her belly. This thrill of electricity, though rare in Molly, was one of her favourite sensations, only bested by the tummy flip experienced when a fast-moving car goes over a short-humped bridge.

The edge of the book was scrappily bound, consisting of light grey/once-white tape that had been repeatedly placed over where the broken original spine had lived out its use. The placement of the layers of tape were haphazard, a bandage rather than a binding.

The height of the spine was about ten or eleven inches and the length of the book, guessed by how far it was sticking out, was likely about fifteen inches or so. When Molly moved it from the shelf there were no markings on either the front nor the back to suggest what was inside. The front and back covers were entirely indistinguishable from one another on first inspection although Molly would later come to realise that the black cover on the front had faded a little more than the back, suggesting that in a previous life this book had been kept stored face up, so that the elements faded its surface layer.

She knelt down on one knee, the resulting pressure allowing a little more rainwater to be pushed between her toes. The carpet was stickier than Molly was comfortable with, but she now felt committed to this stance and it was too soon from the previous squelching discomfort in her trainer to move again.

When she remembered this moment later, as often she would, she replayed it with a greater sense of significance in her actions than was actually the case. Rather than blowing her cheeks out in a manner which befitted a moment of paramount importance, Molly did nothing other than yank the book from the shelf in an unceremonious manner. She had misjudged the weight of the book, resulting in the bottom corner almost knocking against the floor as she lost its balance when she moved it from its second shelf perch where it had been for who knows how long.

When Molly turned the cover over it became immediately clear that she had opened it the wrong way as she flicked through five blank pages before realising her mistake and awkwardly moving it into its correct position. She looked at what was now obviously the front cover to see if there were any indication or distinguishing features to it that would notify people of its contents. There were none. Once opened (which

Molly did swiftly and without any sense of engaged ponderance, regardless of how she would reconstruct the events later when she recalled them to herself), it was obvious that what she held in her hands was a very old photo album.

The first photograph that she saw in the album was entirely unremarkable and would have been enough for most people to place the book back on its shelf without a second thought. The writing next to the mix of grey and sepia colour image simply read *March 1912* in ornate handwriting in either silvery white or white silvery ink.

At this stage of her investigation process the writing was of no interest to Molly other than as a form of exposition, but it made Molly stare harder at the people in the image, realising that all were dead yet trapped here forever, their lives limited by lack of understanding by those with voyeuristic tendencies who were dumb enough to spend rainy days browsing through nondescript and anonymous photo albums in damp smelling second hand bookshops.

The image could not in any way, shape or form be described as being in focus, and this gave the two adults and the child staring back at Molly a ghostly aura. There were almost halos of light surrounding them due to the inevitable deterioration of the photo which came with being more than a century old.

This made Molly think that their spirits were aching and desperate to leave their bodies while the bodies still lived – a nice image, especially for someone who was adamant in her belief that there was no such thing as a soul, or auras or spirits. The family were also positioned far too far away from the camera by modern standards and although they were centred in the middle there was plenty of dead space around them. *Dead space*, Molly thought, *is all that these people are now.*

In the photo, there were three figures – a man, a woman and a young boy. *The perfect sodding family.* The man was dressed in a suit but one that was ill fitted to his wiry frame as it looked to be several sizes too big for him, particularly the trousers which went up past his waist and rested what looked like a matter of mere inches from his chest. His baggy trousers had a thick pinstripe that was matched in the jacket.

The quality of the photo made it hard to discern what type of fabric was used for the suit, or indeed what colour this magnificent oversized ensemble was. Molly had an idea that the suit's fabric was scratchy to the touch and a sort of sickly mish-mash of yellow and brown tones, the fashion equivalent of a dog's piss and shit in the snow. Still, the man looked quite proud in his suit and it was likely his Sunday best and Molly's momentary gloating was almost immediately replaced with a shameful reflection of her own sense of privilege.

Molly had, to the best of her knowledge, never been in a position where hand-me-down clothes were a necessity, but then she couldn't think who the person would be who would have donated the clothes as there were no cousins that she knew of around the same age as her. She did enjoy shopping – browsing more than purchasing, Molly didn't fully understand which of these were the most important and defining aspect of shopping – in charity shops but this was mostly due to a combination of the stunning lack of decent clothes in High Street shops coupled with the fact that High Street shops were, as their collective noun would suggest, in the centre of town and were therefore best avoided.

The woman in the photo was dressed in a black coat that was

buttoned all the way from bottom to top, suggesting a chill in the air that was obviously not felt by her husband whose clothes suggested something more akin to a balmy spring evening.

Her clothing was juxtaposed further by the shorts and shirt that her son was wearing. He was also dressed in scruffy knee length socks which were strewn around his shins through lack of care of appearance.

His mother was wearing a wide brimmed hat, the like of which Molly had never seen before. It was similar in elaborate style to the ostentatious curvature of the flappy hats that Molly associated with old kings, Charles II or someone like that, but with a flat, limp top which was skewed to one side. It looked for all the world to Molly as though this was some sort of hat hybrid, the painstakingly designed and haphazardly realised bastard offspring of a Restoration era monarch and a 1920s dandy.

This woman was either 400 years out of date or just a few years ahead of her time. Either way, the image made it look as though here was a woman for whom appearance was thoroughly important.

Molly felt a peculiar sensation, as if a shiver ran down her spine and squeezed her skull at the same time, when she met the outward gaze of the woman. The photograph's deterioration over the years made it difficult to be able to read the woman's expression with any degree of real clarity. Her husband, tall and almost smug looking next to her, portrayed a sense of family togetherness and pride.

The mother, on the other hand, looked a little sheepish. Molly reasoned that this had more to do with the gender politics (or the lack of gender politics, more like) in that era.

Perhaps a woman being seen to be overly exuberant, filled with personality and energy, and anything other than passive and demure was frowned upon in that era and therefore she was simply fulfilling her role as the dutiful wife.

Molly also considered the fact that photography in 1912, particularly for people of the social class that these three seemingly belonged to, was quite a new phenomenon and therefore she had not practiced her photo-face in the same way that girls of the twenty-first century could. Molly thought it would be so cringey in the future when the grandchildren of today's teenagers look back at the vast number of images of their respective grandmas scattered all over social media and realise that at one point they all had an almost permanent duck faced pout glued to the front of their faces.

There was a vulgarity in the photographs that Molly saw on social media that she could not reconcile with the positives of increasing personal liberty and freedom that women enjoyed in contemporaneous society. There was a gracefulness in the women she had previously seen in old photos, but she knew that this moment of seeming tranquillity came with the price of a lifetime of servitude and a relinquishing of choice.

Molly's response to the woman's stare took her aback, and she needed a minute or two of looking elsewhere, anywhere, before she regained the strength to compete in another stare-out competition that spanned a century. There was a frustration in Molly that the photo didn't have more pixels, or whatever the relevant term for old style photographs was, as she realised it was the inability to clearly see into this woman's eyes that caused her brief moment of alarm.

For one thing, the left eye of the woman was obscured by

an unfortunately positioned crease in the photo, but this only exacerbated the situation further rather than being simply prohibitive to Molly's attempts at ocular investigation. The right eye had no such obstructions yet still could not be assessed fully due to the standard of the image. Molly also noticed as she stared more intently at the woman that there was a thumb-print mark just under her chin which made Molly feel that the intimacy of this moment was now somewhat tainted. It also reinforced the 'til now suppressed notion that this image was not hers to pass scrutiny on.

This thumb mark may well have been from a loved one of this family, yet Molly had the impression that the blemish must have been created by someone really pressing into the photograph rather than by a casual turning of the page. Molly pictured the son of the young boy in the photo looking at the image just after his father's death and therefore the ineradicable mark was a representation of the degree of grief felt by the person who left it there.

Molly then realised that this image was one of death, not life. She quickly moved on to the second page.

After a few minutes of further perusal, she began to develop a better sense of who these people were. Although only a date was written next to the first photo, names and locations, along with fairly loose dates (often the year or the month and year), were often next to others. The two adults were always just referred to as 'mum' and 'father' in the notes, but Molly learnt that the young boy's name was William.

There were, in total, twenty seven photos in the album. The first page contained one image, and there were two each on the next thirteen pages that followed. There were maybe seven or eight pages at the back of the album that were blank, with empty charcoal black pages as a symbol of an unfinished document of family life or as an overly ambitious project to document the fleeting happiness of the mundane.

On the first empty page there were four white corner stickers which were the same as the ones used on other photos to keep them in place, perhaps because someone had planned to add to this collection or maybe that one image had been taken out before Molly got her hands on the album. When Molly turned this page slightly towards the light she could see that the paper between these corner marks was a little faded, and so she was happy to surmise that there had originally been another photo here which had since been removed.

She thought for a while about why this might be, and although she considered a range of options, the one that she was happiest with was that the last person to peruse this album before her simply did not like the fact that this image stood alone and therefore she believed that they had a compulsion with order and structure that she knew all too well herself. Over time, Molly would often come to think about this missing photograph as perhaps hiding some great and shameful family secret for reasons that she would never know but would have fun speculating on all the same.

Of the numerous photos included in the album, every single one raised a question for Molly, and she felt that as there was no way of knowing the intent, cause and consequence of each captured image she would be forever haunted by the ghost of not knowing that enveloped her now.

A boy's name and some carefully staged photos were not enough to allow Molly the chance to get to know these people in the manner that she all of a sudden wanted to – the urge to do so was evidently swelling in her exponentially with each passing second. She flicked through the album from beginning to end twice, inexplicably including the empty pages both times, before fully taking notice of the etching inscribed next to the third to last photo. It read '*Last photograph of William and father together – May 1915*'.

Reading this, Molly felt a little dizzy as she considered that the delay between taking and receiving photos was quite considerable in those days, as opposed to the instant, disposable and despicably egocentric snapshots of today. Maybe the photograph was developed and delivered after the death of William's father so that this image would be a treasured item for years to come. Perhaps the photo had already been placed in the album when the father was still alive, and Molly looked for signs of this in the ink of the writing next to the image.

Maybe he hadn't died but this was the most obvious and satisfying reason she could conjure up at this point.

She thought that perhaps the date, as with all of the other images, had been inserted when the person putting the album together put the photographs into chronological order and maybe added the significant comment afterwards. Molly held the album to the light and moved it around so that the angle between paper and eye altered. In this way, she believed that she would be able to perceive a difference in the ink used which may suggest that they had been written at different times. No variation of tone or colour were evident and so Molly concluded that the photo, maybe the whole album, was put in position after the father had died or gone away. No, died.

The dizziness that Molly experienced subsided as quickly

as it came, the intensity of the feeling only heightened by its brief grip on her. Other things remained a puzzle to her, such as the almost nonchalant dating of the photo.

The irregularity of the timing of the photos suggested that the camera being put in front of these people was a far from common occurrence and so the relative lack of information, and precise dating, annoyed Molly. Perhaps, she thought, the exact date not being written down suggested something about when the album was put together; perhaps the collating of the images was a considerable time after the events had passed and was therefore not a portfolio of every image taken of these people but of a carefully constructed list of memories that somebody desired to keep.

This meant that somewhere there were potentially a stack of other images that Molly could explore to discover more about these people. She could feel a developing obsession arising and a need to know more.

This image, the last of William with his father, showed the two of them playing together – a nice projection compared to the others in the photo album which were too staged for Molly's liking. There was a sense of static in most of the other photos, a degree of sterility and an absence of warmth but, more than likely, perhaps this said more about the nascent technology of the time and less about the familial relationships.

It appeared that this more playful photo was taken at home, although dad was still in a shirt, tie and waistcoat which were all properly fastened. The scene included dad's chair which was central to the image, what looked like a table with a half full ashtray to the right of the chair, and to the left just a wall with one framed picture on it, the content of which was too hard to discern due to the quality of the photo and so, as hard as Molly tried to look, it just appeared to be a framed blur. The emptiness of the frame within the photo began to match the blank expression on father's face which became increasingly nonplussed the longer Molly stared at it.

The more she studied the photograph, the more she realised that the man's face was not as full of joy as she had at first perceived. In fact, she almost started to believe that his expression had changed since she had first looked at it, as though his pretence in keeping up appearances of a happy home life were waning. Molly thought it was weird how her initial reading of the photo was a positive one and how that had changed in the last few seconds. There began to be something quite unsettling about the image in front of her that she found difficult to define.

William was on the right side of the photo, just under the ambiguous image in the frame, and was wearing boxing gloves. Although his body was facing his father's, his head was twisted over his left shoulder so that his cheeky grin was evident for all to see. There was a certain degree of glee in his eyes which was lacking from all the other photos in the album and this sense of happiness was probably helped due to the fact that this photo was the best in terms of image quality of the two subject's faces, thereby bringing a sense of life and joy which was lacking from the other twenty six images.

William was holding his left hand up in front of his chin in a crude form of facial defence, upholding the pretence that he was fighting his father, mimicking the stance he had either been taught by his dad or from older boys in the street. There was no evidence of these older boys in the photo album, or actually of the street they lived on, but Molly was already forming an image of William playing with the older boys with little by way of adult supervision, all flat caps and dad's braces and hitting things with sticks.

His right arm was extended, and the glove lay on his father's left cheek, but it was held in such a way that Molly felt it was knowingly placed there for the photo rather than the camera operator capturing a moment of unexpected impact. Of course, she had no way of knowing for sure, but in her mind's eye the two of them stood still for this image a little longer than they had hoped, and Molly imagined that William had felt the strain in his right arm as he was being told to keep it there for 'just one more second'.

Before her self-imposed exile from the internet, Molly often found herself inexplicably and aimlessly looking through the photos of strangers on nights out. The poses sometimes seemed as though they were held for just a little too long which was often highlighted in the waning smiles of one or two in the entourage. In the photograph currently in front of her, Molly started to feel that there just seemed to be something not quite as candid, or fun, about the image as at first appeared.

There was a look in dad's eyes that she only noticed after a minute or two's contemplation of the photo. He was looking directly into the camera, not at his son, but there now seemed to be a degree of anger, or at least annoyance, in the blankness of his stare.

His lips were turned up a little into the faintest of semi-smiles, but Molly was reminded of the bared teeth of a gnarly dog rather than the warm affection of a loving father. Towards whom his irritation was directed she could not say. Perhaps it was mother somewhere out of shot of the camera who vexed him, perhaps this playfight with William had interrupted his usual routine, or maybe it was simply the length of time that the photographer took to capture the moment that resulted in a loss of enthusiasm for the scene. Whatever it was, it added a more chilling element to the photograph.

Molly also noticed that dad's left hand had a grip on William's right forearm as he threw the play-punch and the more she looked, getting her eyes closer to the surface of the photo, the more Molly interpreted the hold as being overly physical.

The grainy image suggested a ripple in William's arm either side of dad's hand, suggesting an unnecessarily firm grasp on the boy that would have likely caused William pain. It was this newfound sense of mystery that made Molly realise that she needed to take this album home with her. She also felt a little uncomfortable referring to this man as 'dad' when all of the references to him in the photo album were of the much more formal 'father'.

A sense of guilt entered her consciousness when she realised that she had maybe assumed a form of relationship between man and child here that she had with Dan, one of comfort and unquestionable safety. For the most fleeting of moments, she appreciated how good she had it.

Molly looked at a few books either side of where the photo album was previously entombed to see if any related to her newly discovered treasure. She knew that none would, but she looked all the same. In fact, had there existed any form of further documentation about this family then the mystique of the discovery would have vanished in an instant.

After a quick perusal and finding nothing, Molly grasped the photo album to her chest and hastily walked down the stairs of the shop. Her unusually fast pace was dictated by the conflict in her mind about leaving the shop with this smattering of social history. If she walked at her normal speed, the common-sense side of her personality would likely win, and she would end up placing the photo album back on the shelf as her leisurely perambulation would have afforded her more time to think about the invasive nature of taking this document of family life home for further analysis. If she ran, which is exactly what Molly wanted to do, then she knew that she took the very real risk of running straight out into the street without paying the kind man who ran the place. As she moved she noticed that her wet foot had dried significantly, though not fully.

When she got to the bottom of the stairs, she felt somewhat out of breath. A fear flashed across her mind about how exactly she should go about asking to proceed with this, the unlikeliest of transactions.

There was no price-tag and, in fact, there was nothing to say that she didn't hold in her hand a much treasured personal heirloom of the shop owner. It was then that Molly realised that her quivering breathing was not to do with her level of physical fitness but the all too familiar anxiety that began to swell inside her. She had not envisaged purchasing anything on her visit and so she had not run through all of the numerous potential conversations that would be needed if she were to pass as normal.

Spontaneity was not a skill she possessed, nor one she wished to possess, as such a trait was, she felt, for those lacking the ability to consider, construct and organise.

She wanted to leave the shop with the photo album, of that

Molly was entirely sure. In fact, at this very moment Molly wanted this artefact more than anything that she had ever wished for, but she knew it came with the price of required and unprepared conversation and this petrified her. She quickly raced through thoughts to try to establish which words could be linked together best to convey her desire to purchase the object without inviting the shopkeeper to make supplementary comment that would undoubtedly put her off balance and under pressure to hold a cognitively unscripted conversation.

Molly knew that the ever-increasing *thump-thump-thump* emanating from her chest was by now clearly audible to everyone on the ground floor of the shop – all three of them. The weight of the photo album in her arms became more pronounced in line with the sweat on her palms and the newfound weakness in her knees as the conundrum of how to open a dialogue with the shopkeeper overwhelmed her thoughts. *Would it actually be possible,* Molly thought, *to just turn this into a monologue or maybe just a mute exchange of goods and money and no eye contact or smiles?* Molly was conflicted as she needed the photo album, with as little fuss as possible, without being rude.

All of Molly's last-minute preparation came to nothing as the shopkeeper didn't give her the chance to initiate the conversation that she had only just this second pictured. Panic rose in her straightaway when he first spoke to her, so much so that the exchange passed in a daze. The shopkeeper appeared out of focus and both his words and Molly's own sounded to her as if they were spoken underwater. It was almost an out-of-body experience except rather than leaving her body, Molly just felt her senses sinking into her physical form a little more.

Her body became the spikes of a hedgehog while her

emotions retreated by curling into a ball where the soft parts would stay in relative safety while the outward form took the brunt of the hit that was conversation.

As she left the shop after the whirr of the transaction, Molly had an inkling that her life was about to change. She wondered how much she had paid for the weighty document of historical insignificance. She would look in her pockets later to see how much money she had left from the £12.55 that she had when she entered the shop. Now wasn't the time for such banality.

CHAPTER 6

A trip out

Molly had a fear of the tooth fairy when she was a little girl. In fact, she was scared of anybody or anything that had the potential to enter her room without not just her permission but, more importantly, her waking knowledge of their presence.

Secrecy led to distress. She had a deep-seated hatred of Father Christmas for a few years that she couldn't talk to anyone about, too.

There was an intrusiveness to the tooth fairy that Molly did not like. This invasion of personal space was initiated by Dan who put the tooth under her pillow without Molly having any recourse to deny the tooth fairy access to the much-needed minerals that were sourced from her fallen fangs. Molly knew that these fairies were grateful for the opportunity to recycle the tooth to help their village, but the recompense of ten, twenty, or sometimes fifty pence was not sufficient to make Molly feel that this transaction, and the worry that came with it, was wholly justified.

Molly remembered these feelings when she first placed the photo album under her pillow. She knew that Dan was unlikely to ever look here as he rarely ventured into her room at all these days, finally respecting her need for privacy and her own sanctuary. There would, of course, be no harm done if he actually did flick through the album as no doubt he would find nothing of interest therein and carry on with his day, yet Molly still felt a need within her to keep the object safe and confidential. The placing of the book in this space, Molly reasoned, was perhaps as a result of a subconscious urge to connect more with the photo album, even in her sleep.

The size of the collected photos made her uncomfortable when she slept, but she had made this decision, taking into account this possibility, and so was not inclined to change her mind now.

For a relatively short but intense period of time, the photo album afforded Molly an insight into other people's lives who were long-dead, and it was the last thing she thought about at night and the first thing she thought about in the morning. It also served the purpose of giving Molly cause to reflect on those elements of human interaction which cannot be captured in a still image, and she became increasingly engrossed with the subjects in each frame. The simplistic, superficial and mundane imagery in the photos were replaced in Molly's mind by elaboration and extrapolation as she wanted to get to know William and his family better.

Molly was sure that she had not asked the shopkeeper, during the hazy nature of the exchange of goods and cash, if he knew anything about the people in the photos, a fact which pained her now. She had worked out from the money in her pocket when she got back on the train that she paid £5. Maybe it was less than that and she simply hadn't waited for the change.

How, she wanted to know, had he come into possession of this set of once no doubt treasured family memories? Did he have some connection to the family who were forever frozen in fixed poses? If so, who would sell such an album and, perhaps more to the point, who would buy it from them? These were questions that Molly wanted answers to, but she no longer felt inclined to go back to the shop now that its previously unknown purpose had been served. She had always felt weirdly drawn to the place, now she knew why.

Her questions could arouse suspicions in the bookseller that perhaps the album contained important information rather than simply being a load of forgotten, dusty old images of nobody in particular. And what, in fact, would Molly's opinion be of this man had he actually had some connection with William and his family? Would this affect how she viewed him and her time there and the warm feelings she gained from the place? Were they, in fact, *his* family?

If he did know of them then he would be an easy source for answers to the questions that Molly felt swirling around her head about these people, questions which she did not take any thrill out of having anything other than imagined answers for.

The time previously spent thinking about the shop, getting ready to go to the shop with all of the required mental preparation and rehearsal that it entailed, and travelling to the shop, was now spent in solitary examination of the photo album. Molly decided that perhaps she would actually still visit the bookshop from time to time as she now believed that if she suddenly stopped going this may cause worry in the owner who may believe that she had died. This was the most natural conclusion as to her whereabouts, Molly thought, as likely it would answer all of his questions about how she was able to be in his shop during school time and that he would therefore deduce that this poor, lonely girl had been terminally ill which was why she was not at school, and the cessation of her browsing signalled the end of her days.

It was these small selfless acts, to ensure that she did not cause another living being any form of unnecessary distress, that made Molly proud of the woman she was becoming. Better, she thought, to ween someone off her presence than to simply stop going with all the brief yet still tangible emotions that her absence would stir in them. Or maybe he wouldn't give her a second thought, too wrapped up as he often was in his own reading to notice the comings and goings of inconsequential people in his refuge. *How nice it must be*, Molly thought, *to be so lost in a world of books as that man.*

Her days were now spent with a preoccupation towards William. There wasn't a surname anywhere in the handwritten inscriptions that accompanied the photographs, and this proved to be frustrating as it did not allow her to know even the most basic of things about the boy. However, over time, Molly began to view this lack of knowledge as a blessing as it at least stopped her from being able to trace a family tree or to look for a gravestone in the cemeteries that surrounded Dungeness. Molly knew this to be the town where he lived as it was mentioned on a couple of occasions in the photo album, along with an address that she swore to herself she would not try to locate.

One of the photos had William sitting on his mother's lap with the inscription 'March 1917 – At home. Church Road, Dungeness'. In this photo, William was seated in an uncomfortable manner and his mother appeared to be holding both of his arms as if she were commanding them to make him wave at the camera.

As was now her way, Molly decided not to take this first

interpretation as meaningful and instead looked for alternative readings in the image. Perhaps William's posture meant that he was not sitting in an intolerable manner, simply that the photo was taken at the very split second that he decided he had had enough of posing for the photographer and wanted to get up from his mother's lap.

A third look left Molly with the feeling that he was not getting up, nor was he physically uncomfortable in his posture, but that his face, although lacking precise detail, suggested that he was of the opinion that a boy his age no longer belonged on the lap of another. This led to him taking up an awkward position on his mother, perhaps as if teaching her a lesson that his time as her little boy was over.

The absence of a family name in the album forced Molly's hand. She initially felt that she should go to some sort of central registry of births and marriages and deaths in order to find out more about these people but she neither knew where one was in the local area, nor what she would ask for when she got there.

Her mind raced with possible conversations that she would have with the registrar, all perfectly played out in real time in her head. She invented numerous fictional back stories about her involvement with the family in case these were the things that needed to be answered before being allowed access to such records by some jobsworth clerk who hated their job and the people they had to deal with on a daily basis.

As it was, Molly reflected that it was perhaps better not to know such details as these would have been no more than mere facts and would not have allowed her to actually get to know these people any better. She could use the information gathered to track down relatives fairly easily, but then what?

Would she have the courage to actually speak to these people? What good would it do if she did? Again, Molly reasoned that all she would achieve from such a venture would be the accrual of more knowledge but not of the personal kind that she was after. Knowing what someone did was not the same as knowing who someone was, a thought that Molly found all too familiar.

The decrepit quality of the photographs, coupled with their mish-mash of black and white and sepia tones, created an emotional distance between Molly and William that she hated. Dungeness wasn't too far away, but the teen years of the previous century were. Molly felt that black and white photographs somehow deadened the eyes of the subject and that what she reasoned to be the long exposure time needed in those days resulted in stoic, lifeless expressions on bored subjects.

These factors sucked the energy out of the people in the photographs but there was likely also some cultural aspect to it as well. The capturing of moments of real life was not as disposable then as they had become nowadays, and when things are not so easily dispensed with they are often treated with a little more reverence. This is why most of the expressions that Molly had seen in old photos were akin to police mugshots – sombre, refined and overly poised.

The spiritual dissonance that Molly felt only made her resolve stronger to find some connection between her and this ghost boy that would somehow explain her fixation that was growing ever stronger by the day.

Was he a long lost relative? Was he her guardian angel?

Of course he wasn't, Molly reasoned to herself. She generally had no time for thoughts like these and so felt a little ashamed that this had even crossed her mind. Worse still was the next unstoppable thought that invaded her conscious mind – what if she did somehow find out details about him and discovered that he had died on the very same day that she was born? This would explain the weird connection she felt with him. Maybe there was some element of William which was reborn in her. *Good god, Molly - enough!*

Despite being staunchly in denial about such things, there was a very small part of Molly that was excited and intrigued by this idea, even if she thought it to be total nonsense. It may not have been likely, but the idea was fun all the same although it unsettled her a little to think that she had generated these thought processes in the first place.

What if she were to discover things about the world and the universe which went against her beliefs? Which would she doubt hardest – her beliefs or her methods of research?

Molly played with the idea, in only a half-serious manner, that she was the reincarnated soul of William Cardew (a surname she assigned him as it sounded 'old'). She didn't like the idea that metempsychosis meant that a person's previous life, and their 'soul' played a significant role in their contemporary existence – she felt too empowered as a person to feel that strings were being pulled elsewhere on her behalf by some sort of spiritual echo.

For a short period of time, the notion that there was some aspect of William in her own essence brought with it a degree of comfort as the gaps in her persona that Molly felt would have been filled with a mother present, even partially present, were plugged for a while.

In some ways, Molly felt less exposed when she considered this, less incomplete and less fractured and frantic. Better to have the imagined personality of a dead boy fill that void than the character traits of a woman who would happily walk out on her family.

Such flights of fancy did little to assuage her fears and only served as respite from the fact that the only thing that really connected herself and William was that they were non-living nobodies. *Anyway*, Molly thought, *the very idea of reincarnation is flawed as there are more people alive today than ever before so where did their souls come from, or are there some people with no souls or some people with souls that are new to this reincarnation lark? Is there an inexhaustible supply of souls floating around somewhere who have been waiting thousands of years to be called to action for the first time like some sort of ethereal tag-team wrestling match?*

Molly decided that if she were to get to know and to feel something about William then she would probably have to go to Dungeness to see the things he would have seen, to smell the same odours and to feel the same air on her skin. All Molly knew about the place was that there was a nuclear power station there and a pebble beach that she was sure she had been to many years ago with Dan. Maybe with Caroline, too. If she were there, she certainly didn't do anything sufficiently memorable to warrant a space as a mental souvenir in Molly's head.

Molly used a map to find out how far away it was – about thirty-five miles. She called the local bus company to ask how long it would take by that mode of transport and was told by a man on the 'phone who clearly did not want to talk to her that she would need to combine bus and train journeys and that she was looking at a total time of just under three hours to get there and the same amount of time back. This threw

Molly a little as she assumed it would be no less than an hour.

She wanted to ask Dan to drive her down some day but what reason would she give? She would need to think of a sound basis for why she wanted to go there that didn't give the game away about the photo album and her weird sense of adventure, even though she knew that Dan was unlikely to ask and would simply work out a way to make it happen for her. It didn't matter that Molly knew she wouldn't be asked, she would prepare the lines anyway, just in case.

Another issue she had with asking Dan was that it was almost certainly too far for him to just drop her off and come to collect her later at a predetermined time, so he would inevitably want to hang out with her when the aim of the trip was to be alone with just the photo album and thoughts of William and an air of detection about her.

Hurry up and invent teleportation, boffins! she thought. *How hard could it be to reconstitute someone at a cellular level and to transport those cells across space and distance and perfectly and instantly reassemble them at a specified destination?* It would need to be instant, Molly reasoned, otherwise there would be a short period of time when the person being teleported didn't exist which could legally be defined as temporary murder. Even if the person arrived at the designated location in perfect shape, it would be difficult to work out whether they were really themselves or just a perfect copy, a synthetic simulacrum, as the process involved to get them there would surely require their cells to be somehow mapped and copied elsewhere. Maybe that is why teleportation didn't exist at this moment in history, for ethical rather than scientific reasons.

She decided to ask Dan for a lift.

Eight days later they were in the car on their way.

*****

Twenty, maybe thirty minutes into the journey, Molly saw a road sign for Lydd Airport which took her by surprise. She didn't know that Kent had an airport, and she was perplexed that such a barren place as Lydd would have one. She knew very little about Lydd in all honesty, but it just didn't sound like the sort of place where an airport belonged.

She wondered about the types of journeys that people took from Lydd airport and whether anyone got to their destination and admitted the place from which they departed.

'There's an airport?' Molly said with a confused combination of both statement and question in the tone of her voice. 'It's not big,' Dan said. 'Mostly cargo flights. I think, anyway'. Molly's thoughts of a bustling, international hub of travellers, smugglers and stowaways quickly evaporated and was replaced instead with images of unmarked crates being moved into luggage holds with no questions asked by apathetic security teams and pilots who could only dream of working in less lugubrious locations than here. Anywhere but here.

The sky was grey and empty. No birds, aircraft or stray forms of litter were to be seen to break the beautiful monotony of the scene. Molly had never been in a plane although almost all her friends had.

Even though her grandparents lived abroad, on the odd occasions when Dan and Molly would visit them they found ways of getting there that circumnavigated Dan's phobia of being hurtled through the air in a tin can full of strangers and their bodily emissions. Molly could count the number of times that she and her father had visited his parents on three fingers; the index finger was the time that Dan drove down in one long caffeine fuelled go bar a few toilet breaks which seemingly irked him, the middle finger was when they endured several horrendous train journeys, and the ring finger was a repeat of the first trip but, thankfully, with proper rest breaks.

Dan had explained his reasons for not wanting to fly to Molly who was wildly disinterested at the time, but since developing a more acute sense of her own anxiety she wanted to learn more about his take on things although she knew it would be impossible, or at least highly unlikely, that she would ever be able to bring this topic of conversation up with him without looking weird.

As Molly looked upwards out of the car window, she became transfixed with the idea of people moving, and then with people's thoughts moving with them. When she was younger, Molly would look up and see aeroplanes above her without knowing where the passengers were going. Off on holiday? Very likely. Away for business? For some, of course.

She often felt that aeroplanes represented a form of escape and success. Escape as people were able to use this mode of transport to remove themselves from the mundanity of their everyday lives and success as either these same people had saved enough or could afford to leave their routine behind for a short period of time.

However, there was always a thought in Molly that amongst the overexcited holidaymakers putting up with a million 'are we there yet?' questions from their kids and the nervous business tossers spending the time going over the lines of deceit and manipulation that would form the basis of their presentations, there were others who were travelling for reasons that they would prefer not to – for funerals, or to be by the side of loved ones on their deaths beds or other such unavoidable yet imperceptibly sad things.

How must those people have felt amongst the hubbub and enthusiasm of those un-self-aware annoyances amongst them? With those thoughts, Molly could no longer experience the same sense of excitement as her peers when a plane flew overhead. They were no longer perceived as winged cylinders of varying forms of triumphalism.

Molly thought that there had, for centuries, been wonder in human eyes when casting their gaze upwards – at the moon, at birds, at flying machines – and this lack of awe in Molly only left her feeling slightly numb yet a little superior to most (a feeling which she felt and acknowledged, yet suppressed so as not to feel overly complicit in her own separation from most other people).

How many people could be carried in a plane? Molly had no idea and her self-imposed ban from looking up such things on the internet hurt most when the prized knowledge was entirely useless and would be of no particular consequence to anyone else. Regardless, Molly tried to settle on a figure which she felt took into consideration the range of aircraft from big commercial flights which were the domains of package holiday types to smaller, more exclusive services for film stars and the like.

She settled on an average number of 250 people per aircraft as this seemed both a reasonable guess but also a fairly easy number to multiply which would help her mental arithmetic.

So, if there were 250 in each place, how many planes were in the sky at any one time? She knew that the airports near

London – Heathrow and Gatwick – were two of the busiest in the world with flights leaving every few minutes. She would need, obviously, to factor in much smaller airports (although perhaps such places as Lydd could be considered negligible in terms of passenger numbers for her hypothesis).

So, say Heathrow had a flight leave every five minutes, that would be 20 an hour and so 20 multiplied by 250 would be (times by two and add the zero on the end) 5,000. So, from one London airport there were 5,000 people in the sky so double that for Gatwick – 10,000 – and add in slightly fewer for Stansted – 14,000.

Then there were airports in places like Glasgow (Was there? Molly wasn't sure but felt that there likely was) and a few other provincial locations. So, for argument's sake, add another 6,000 people which rounds things up to 20,000 people. But then if there were 20,000 people who had just taken off that would mean as many who were just about to land and the same again who were mid-flight.

So, 60,000 people were in the air from UK airports. But it would need to be more than that due to length of flights for those in mid-air – add another 20,000 to be safe. That brings the total to 80,000. Now for the rest of the world.

America would need a lot more than that, maybe treble the figure. Loads of internal flights there. This, Molly reasoned, would make up more of the number than international flights. She had read somewhere that only 10% of Americans had passports so factoring in flights between American cities was important.

Some rudimentary guesswork resulted in a total figure from America of 140,000 people. So, 220,000 total from the UK and the USA. 30,000 from Canada makes 250,000. Then add the same figure for Russia, South and Central America and mainland Europe. Molly was now sitting on a total figure of 340,000.

The Asian market would be huge, she thought. China would be well over 60,000 (call it a round 60,000 for ease, though) whereas India and Pakistan and that area would likely add at least 40,000. That made 440,000 in all. Australia and New Zealand probably added about 15,000 which left only Africa left to factor in while the figure totalled 455,000. Africa was a tricky one.

If she offered a relatively low figure in this exercise would that suggest she was in some way a racist? She knew that Africa was not the famine riddled, war torn stricken and morally corrupt place that suited the Western media's projection, yet its airways were likely less busy than London and America. It didn't matter to Molly that she knew she would never talk to anyone about these thoughts, she didn't want to label herself as a racist who thought that Africa was less 'advanced' than her own geographical region.

It was a tricky one and so she decided to settle on the same figure as India, which made a global total of 495,000. Probably best to add another 5,000 for places like Japan and Iceland. 500,000 total.

500,000 divided by 250 is 2,000 which seemed like too few aircraft in the skies. Double the figure, then. Then minus 5% as that was probably the amount of people who cancelled their flights and for seats not sold. Molly had watched enough Hollywood films to know that if you were a protagonist in a rom-com and you had to travel across the country to be with your newly realised one true love then a ticket could always be bought to almost any destination after some potentially delaying cajoling or miscommunication at the sales desk, so therefore flights were not always sold out.

Bloody hell – 5% of one million was...50,000? Sounded about right. So, a total figure for people who were not actually on the Earth at any given moment was about 950,000 people. Molly excused herself the pun that this figure now seemed a little high. Chop a few off. Take it to 900,000 people. Her starting figure of 250 people on average in each plane was likely off a little. She was now happy with the total figure but assumed fewer people in more planes.

What would become of these 900,000 if they were in the air when some sort of disaster struck? If, during their flight, the first nuclear missile was launched from one side of the world to the next, or the blessed global zombie apocalypse struck, what would the pilot be expected to do?

Perhaps there was hope in these people as they could lead humanity to a new dawn once the fools beneath them had pressed their buttons and sent off their rockets to melt parts of the planet and the people who were nearby, or eaten one another depending on the scenario on that particular day. Whole countries wiped out, their landscapes, people and plant-life gone in an instant while the hope for continued human population lay in the hands of the kind of people who purchased cheap sombreros and straw donkeys on their seven-night break in Majorca. *We are screwed either way,* thought Molly.

She wondered whether there were more people at sea at any one time than in the air, not including those people who were jumping at any one point which would be an interesting yet frustrating calculation.

Oil rigs, cruise ships, merchant navy, scuba divers, surfers and pirates probably added up to a few tens of thousands of people when all factored in, but this was a mathematical problem that would have to be worked on another day, saved for another journey when a wandering mind allowed Molly to take her thoughts away from herself. And besides, Molly knew that she would only wind herself up if she started to think of the term 'underwater' which she had never understood, nor never been sufficiently brave to raise it with anyone. Only if the surface was considered to be the definition of water could deep sea divers or fish or whatever be termed as being 'underwater' – they were, in fact, IN the water. Why could others not realise this?

The road to Dungeness seemed to have an inordinate amount of telephone wires for an area that looked so under-populated. Also of note for Molly was the fact that she did not see any birds sitting on the wires.

She had once been told in a History lesson that birds no longer sang at Auschwitz and Molly seemed to be collecting what could best be described as unsubstantiated anecdotal evidence that no birds perched on the Romney Marshes either. She understood how the inaccuracies of the first statement were used in a morbid poetic sense to highlight the horrors of concentration camps that were so indelibly ingrained in the British psyche (despite the fact that the British army invented the idea of concentration camps over forty years before the Nazis, a point that Molly had raised in class with Miss Hudson only to be quickly shut down for not following the line of the agenda that the teacher had set upon); a horror so invasive that generations of local wildlife acknowledge the acts via silent contemplation.

No perching birds on the Romney Marsh was a more difficult phenomenon to explain but perhaps it had something to do with how busy the telephone wires were. Molly assumed that when a call was made, the wires came to life and most likely buzzed with an electric charge that either startled the birds or gave them a warm vibrating sensation that was pleasing. The thought of smiling birds on throbbing wires gratified Molly somewhat and so she stuck with this angle. The absence of birds on the wires, then, was down to the fact that few, if any, of the wires were active enough to offer anything to the birds.

'Looks like rain,' Dan said, breaking Molly's thought processes. Dan was not, however, looking upwards but to the side where a group of thirteen cows were all sitting together in a huddle. 'You know what they say about…' he continued. 'Yeah, I know that old wives' tale' Molly interrupted. And with that, the conversation ended.

Molly wanted to ask questions about why cows might tend to lie down if they felt rain was coming but the moment had gone. She knew that people said that cows wanted to protect dry patches of grass underneath them, but what made them aware that rain was coming? Natural instinct? Weather intelligence? Molly felt sure that she could recollect someone (although she could not say who) tell her that it was small midges in the grass that actually made the cows sit down. It was these midges that sensed the coming rain and therefore flew up from the ground in order to save themselves from an impending death by drowning.

This migration tickled the cows' udders and so to stop this

irritation they would simply lay down to prevent their sensitive bovine body parts being stimulated. This seemed as sensible an explanation as any, although the source of this information (maybe Molly read it somewhere) could not be recalled and therefore verified. She would somehow look into this more when she got home.

The silence in the car was stifling, yet Molly was aware that this was an occurrence of her own doing. She simply felt that she did not possess the necessary social tools to initiate a conversation, nor the inherent interest in people to sustain one. There were, of course, a million and one questions that she wanted to ask her father, but it was precisely because he was her father that she failed to be able to start any such interactions.

Once she had finished her daydreaming, she turned towards Dan without looking towards his eyes. Her focus settled on his plump bottom lip and stubbled chin.

She had learnt many years ago that when someone is facing you then you are afforded the opportunity to stare at their nose when talking as this will give the illusion of eye contact, that most redundant of social etiquettes in an age of text messages, emails and face-time wherein the contact is with a webcam. Side on, however, was a different story as there was something quite strange about peripheral vision that often made it more obvious where someone was looking.

Dan knew that Molly was not looking into his eyes, and she knew that he knew. She moved her head back to its previous position without saying a word.

- How much longer will we be? Just ask him where we are and how much longer we will be, idiot!

- Why did she just look at my chin?

The persistent hum of the engine, the occasional bumps into potholes in the road, and the insistent indie jingle-jangle of the compilation CD that Dan had made specifically for the journey in the hope it may act as a spur to chat were all drowned out by the white noise in Molly's mind, a piercing high pitched sine wave of remorse shadowing her own social ineptitude and inadequacy. It was some years earlier when Molly realised that her body was helping to protect her.

The internal sounds were subconsciously produced to allow the external noises to evaporate into the ether, brushed aside with no attention given as a means of ensuring a sense of emotional equilibrium, sensorial status quo and neutrality.

Conversations, for Molly, were problematic but she was grateful that she appreciated this difficulty. If there was one thing that Molly felt encouraged by, it was the fact that she knew her own weaknesses. Sometimes she was too aware of her shortcomings.

Molly knew what to say in dialogue with someone, how best to phrase her thoughts, what tone of voice to use, how to use open questions to allow for an elaboration of the point made by the responder blah blah blah, but she could not actually move her mouth and expel the appropriate frequencies through her vocal chords to allow this to happen.

She did not feel that she was entirely socially inept, just simply not interested enough in other people to bother. The effort of the initial question was nothing in comparison with the required attempt at sustaining a facial expression that suggested she was both listening and that she cared. The cognitive power needed to contort her face into an appropriate position so as to suggest a sense of active listening while remembering to also include other non-verbal forms of communication such as head nods, eyebrow raises or other such mundane elements of interaction, was too much for Molly to bear.

She was envious of those who had a natural inclination towards giving half a shit about the circumstances, stories and views of others.

The opportunity was there now, glaringly there, for Molly to engage in conversation with Dan. The words were formed perfectly in her head and she had even mentally worked through a few of his most likely replies so as to prepare a supplementary response, thereby suggesting a sense of competence in this most tricky of human endeavours. Yet the words simply clawed around the inside of her throat like sick kittens in a hessian sack, unwilling to venture out into the unknown yet obviously safe environment outside of that which they had become comfortable.

How much longer, do you think? or *Who is this singing?* or *What food did you bring?* were all entirely useful, relevant questions that she had considered asking and all had the advantage for Molly of needing nothing more from her than a simple *'Okay'* in response which she felt she could manage.

Questions one and three were completely redundant as she could likely work out the answer to the first by herself and she couldn't care less about finding out about the third. She was a little too jittery to eat.

The second question, though, was not just out of the developing need in Molly to try to talk to her dad, she actually did want to know who was on the CD as she neither recognised the song nor the singer. The guitars were high pitched with loads of reverb, what was probably a drum machine clattered away in the background with no subtlety and a woman exhaled what to Molly's ears sounded like childish gibberish. Molly liked it and was frustrated in herself that she lacked the ability in successfully enquiring as to the identity of the singer or band. She could look through Dan's records next time he was out and find the answer that way. Investigation was often more satisfying than interaction, anyway.

As Molly thought about how she hated small talk, her mind began to frantically list all of the other things she hated. She first attempted to do so in alphabetical order for a while, but she soon found that hate was such a strong emotion that it was tricky to calmly use a classification process to be ordered and structured with her thinking. Rather than fight the sporadic nature of her thought processes, she submitted to the will of her subconscious and forgot about trying to create an alphabetical taxonomy of loathing.

A number of her pet peeves centred around food and drink. Or, to be more exact, how some people ate and drank.

Crisp packets, Molly thought, very clearly had an identifiable top and bottom so it made her angry to see people eating crisps upside down. She knew that this was just something other people wouldn't consider as problematic, or probably even notice, and that just made her all the more irritated by the idiocy of others.

Molly knew there was no rational reason to get upset by people doing this, but this list wasn't about logical reactions but the purest, basest levels of aversion to the habits of humans. The notion of opening a packet of crisps incorrectly and the nonchalant manner in which people would then walk confidently through the streets, eating them without any sense of remorse was almost the very definition of anathema for Molly. She started to wonder what she would do if she ever found herself eating crisps which she had inadvertently opened upside down, but after a brief moment of contemplation she concluded that she simply would never be that clueless to have to worry about it ever happening to her. Molly decided to excuse the visually impaired from her bile in this instance.

Chompers were next on the list. Those people who ate with their mouths open but also smacked their lips together and moved their tongue around their mouth loudly so that others could hear their attempts at dislodging food which had got stuck to the back of their teeth or the roof of their pallet. Chompers were at their disgusting worst when eating toffees or other chewy confectionaries.

Molly had once witnessed the Chief Chomper in action on a train. She could not remember where she was going but the vivid memory of this man and particularly the sounds that he made would haunt her until the day she died. In fact, she was certain that her last dying regret would be not slapping this Chomper across his stupid face when she had the chance.

Chief Chomper got on the train and occupied a table seat that was designed for more than just one self-righteous business prick to use. He was, Molly guessed, around forty, with neat short hair that had outbreaks of grey towards his shirt collar – three eruptions of dullness which made Molly think of large puncture wounds in the back of his head which were put there as the standard procedure for lobotomising the life, passion and joy out of people whose sole purpose seemed to be making money for others.

His shirt was white with thin blue stripes that were about

an inch and a half apart, his three-piece suit was the greyest of grey tones possible and he had polished black shoes on. He leant on the table and retrieved a bag of chocolates from his left jacket pocket. Molly pretended to read the book she had in her hands, but he was so entirely engrossed in the bag of chocolates that she felt he wouldn't notice if she moved across the aisle of the train and sat opposite him with a fixed stare.

He placed his forefinger and thumb into the bag and pulled out a round, nobbly chocolate treat. It looked like he then held it up to the light, moving the sweet several inches higher than when it first left the bag. This pose was held for maybe four or five seconds and was followed by the hand's movement towards the man's pursed lips, his mouth swiftly opening with the same immediate action as a Venus flytrap.

That was, Molly thought, an unnecessarily extravagant process of getting chocolate from one place to another and it had the air of someone inspecting a diamond. The most annoying aspect of Molly's voyeurism was yet to come.

The lip smacking seemed to start almost immediately as his mouth and ruddy cheeks sashayed for all they were worth as the chocolate was devoured. His lips hardly ever stayed closed together, Molly was reminded of a cement mixer incessantly churning and when she was at home and told Dan about it he said he was reminded of Corrie Haim in a film called 'The Lost Boys'. Molly hadn't seen this particular film and so the cultural reference fell flat. It wasn't long after this time that Molly decided that conversations with Dan were often fruitless.

Her train seat started to feel more constricted than ever and Molly started to manifest a mental rehearsal of a guttural scream as a means of telling this man just what he was putting her through. She could envisage the moment which was due any second when she would let go a stream of consciousness tirade that would once and forever make this man question his eating habits and would allow everyone else in his future-vicinity the chance to be near him without suffering in the same way that Molly had endured.

The anger had nowhere else to go but to realise itself in a volley of expletives and righteous vitriol. If only she had the nerve to do so.

The chomping ceased for just a short while, a fleeting respite of relative solace but this tranquillity was soon disturbed by some faint grunting noises which then turned into slow, but loud, exhaling from the man. This was, Molly thought, all as a result of a fragment of the chocolate finding its way into the darkest nooks and crannies of his teeth and she imagined his engorged wet tongue darting in and out of the crevice in order to work out the mangled morsel.

In her mind's eye, she pictured the wobbling tongue of a coughing parrot, all pointy, grey and spasming in a seeming involuntary manner. The volume of his breathing made Molly realise that he was, for some reason, holding his breath as he nudged the confectionary with his tongue, like a pig snuffling for truffles. *Please. Just. Stop.* Molly felt this thought so prominently that for a second or two she was confused about whether or not she had actually said it aloud. Seemingly, she hadn't.

The businessman just took another chocolate out, held it to the light and the whole ritual was played through again almost as a perfect action replay of the first time.

There was nothing and nobody that Molly hated more at that precise moment and she wished, more than anything else, that she could tell this man just what she thought of him. She never would, and she knew that he would forever stay in her mind while she had hardly registered in his. This moment was the very opposite of the 'meet cute' in films. Molly felt it was unfair that she would think about this man from time to time and be increasingly repulsed by his actions while she remained a non-entity to him.

The level of hatred that Molly felt for Chief Chomper was only ever challenged, though not beaten, by one other person in an event that predated her encounter with CC.

Of course, Molly did not assume to think that war mongers, murderers, disaster capitalists and general wrongdoers were in any way, shape or form better than these people, but Molly had no first-hand experience of their bad habits to really raise her ire and although every ounce of her body hated those people, what they did and what they stood for, she felt that the more vicarious nature of these emotions did not serve the purposes of this exercise at all well.

On an entirely different day from her encounter with Chief Chomper, on a different train most likely going to a different destination, Molly had to endure the presence of a nurse who was not content to stop sucking the straw in her carton of a long-finished drink until she had removed all of the silver lining from its inside.

Molly could not recall at exactly what point in the proceedings of this woman's extraction routine she started to really take notice and be ground down by its incessantness, but it lasted a formidably long time once her attention to it had been raised.

The woman, perhaps around thirty, was in a light purple uniform with a watch on the breast pocket which was upside down and it was this item in particular that made Molly conclude she was a nurse rather than a care worker. The juice in the carton had been finished, of that there could be no doubt. The nurse, however, was determined to savour the lingering taste while unwittingly antagonising Molly to the point where she briefly toyed with the idea of murder.

This woman should have known better than to behave like that, and thirty was enough of an age for anyone to appreciate how to behave in a sensible and moral manner, all things considered.

The noise she made as she tried to draw up every last drop of juice to her dumb mouth was hard to describe. Part dentist's suction device, part asthmatic dog licking a puddle, part the sound made by fingernails down a blackboard like that man in that film about the big fish that was in fact all about men's fear of the vagina, part the audio one would no doubt hear if a mosquito had the ability to burrow its way into your inner ear while buzzing away merrily, with just a dash of what it probably sounds like in slow motion when an egg comes out of a chicken – this woman knew how to wind Molly up beyond all belief.

The duration of each slurp increased in direct correlation to the reduction in time of the rest breaks needed to catch her stupid breath back.

Molly's Annoyance Scale Level was turned all the way up to 11 by this point. Annoyance Scale Level 4 was stable, commonplace feelings of antipathy towards people and this was the point at which she lived her normal day-to-day life and infrequent interactions. Annoyance Scale Level 8 was not uncommon and was piqued when people spoke to her first. Level 11, however, had not been breached until this point.

Molly thought that this was the most vexed she had ever been in her life.

Five stops went by before the nurse alighted the train. At each station prior to her departure, Molly squeezed her hands tightly in a fist by way of restraining her frustration at the nurse staying and slurping. She thought of all the patients that this woman had to deal with each day and how much they probably hated her. The prolonging of life by a Slurper was no life at all.

As each station name was called out over the train's speakers, Molly looked directly at the nurse and willed her out of her seat. *Get up, get up, get up, get up get up, get up, get up…shit.*

Molly glanced around the train carriage for an ally in annoyance, but the eight other passengers in clear site had no interest in the activities of this woman. Five had headphones on, two were talking to each other and one was dozing. All that Molly needed at that moment was some sort of affirmation that this woman was irritating someone else.

The five wearing headphones and therefore trapped in the sounds of music or audiobooks or podcasts or plain spoken instruction to 'breathe in, breathe out, breathe in, breathe out, breathe in, breathe out' were ignorant of their triumph that day - they were winners in life due to their ability to seal themselves away fleetingly from the world around them and not engage in the irritating noises of the dinosaurs around them.

Despite this, Molly was not tempted to use headphones as she liked to endure the sound of the world as it allowed her to seethe, a feeling in which she found contentment and a certain degree of stability. Also, the conversations she heard allowed her to more fully understand the human condition without the recourse to interact.

Her favourite eavesdropping moment was also her most shocking. Favourite because it allowed her to understand how different people have varied ideas of shame, and most shocking because of how loud the speaker was rather than just what was said. The eavesdropping incident occurred when Molly was about thirteen and she was sitting alone in a train carriage when three girls, maybe four or five or six years older, got on and sat just in front of her, two dark haired girls on one double seat and a mousey blonde who positioned herself across the aisle. From Molly's position, she could see the girls' heads moving but was unable to make out which one was talking at any given moment.

Molly always felt a certain sense of unkind snobbery about her opinions of others but when she first heard these girls use the phrase 'and he goes…' rather than 'he said…' she knew that she was unlikely to overhear anything overly intellectual in nature. What she heard was less of a conversation, more of a protracted monologue from one of this unholy trinity.

It centred on a text conversation or some other form of social media communication, some aspect of life for people her age that Molly felt nothing but disassociation from. The girl spoke almost without taking a breath and not once did she react to the occasional attempted interjections of her travelling companions:

So, Paul was round the other day on, like Tuesday or Wednesday or whatever. Anyways, so he goes 'I'm gonna have to leave soon' and I'm all like 'Why?' and he goes 'Need to see a man' and I goes 'Where? Who?' and he goes 'It's nothing to do with you, just leave it' and so he gets his coat and just goes. So, I'm all like *what the f***?* about this and I'm getting angry now, like in a rage about it, but I can't say why, I just am. Just the way I am, innit? So, I'm just minding my own f***ing business when my phone goes a bit later and it's her, innit? You know, that ginger what started on us that time in The Tap. Anyway, so somehow she's gotten hold of my number and she's all smarmy and up in my grill and that and I just want to bun her off. And her message goes 'Paul has just been round to see me'. And that's it. Just that. Nothing else. And so now I'm all like *what the f*** is she on about*? So I goes 'Who dis?' even though I know which scraggy little bitch it is and then she goes 'Don't play dumb, it's Jen'. And so I goes 'Who the f*** is Paul?' and then she goes 'LOL. Don't play games. Paul has just been round here' and so now I'm steaming mad and I'm going to kill someone and so I go 'So what? Why you telling me?' and then she goes 'Cos I just sucked his c***, is why' and then I goes 'Well, joke's on you then cos five minutes before he left me he had his c*** deep in my a***, so…' and then that's it, I don't get no reply from her again or nothing. Paul says he didn't anyway so she's a lying f***ing whore who's getting glassed next time.'

Every time Molly recounted the conversation her increasing ability to more proficiently internally bleep out the coarsest aspects of this exquisite monologue gave her a weird sense of pride.

At that moment on the train, Molly felt in close proximity to the absolute opposite of human being from her own self that she felt she would ever encounter. The speed at which the girl spoke made Molly short of breath and she realised halfway through listening that there was a tension in her own legs that she did not fully understand. Perhaps it was a result of the topic of conversation, maybe it was a natural instinct in her that saw these people as a challenge and her subconscious was telling her legs to get ready to run in case they turned their attentions towards Molly.

At the time of overhearing this diatribe, Molly was yet to devise her Annoyance Scale but with hindsight this semen-focused sermon would have been around Level 6 or 7.

The suction power of Slurpy Nurse made it feel as though the air pressure was dropping in the carriage. Now that she knew her fellow passengers would not form a pool of sympathy and allegiance with her discomfort, Molly was clear in her own mind that she could not speak out to this woman about what she was doing for fear of looking (a) nosey, (b) racist and (c) anti-NHS.

If she started screaming at the woman, she would look like the aggressor as the others in the vicinity would not have the correct contextual information to know why this justified onslaught of venom was occurring. Molly remained quiet, fists clenched to the point where she felt her fingernails would penetrate her own palms, the stigmata of enforced silent censure.

Molly enjoyed the subtle sense of disquiet that mild annoyance brought with it as it reminded her that she was alive, although she genuinely disliked going above Level 7 on the Annoyance Scale as she felt that every minute in this zone took five minutes to recover back to the starting position of about Level 4. So, a fifteen-minute period of high intensity annoyance would take about an hour and a quarter before Molly was retracted back to her more natural state. She was not the kind of person who could merely brush off a scenario of vexatious reaction as though it meant nothing.

Molly ran the situation over and over and over again in her mind until every angle was covered so as to ensure there was no doubt that she was right to respond in the manner in which she did.

The importance of running the rule over things time and time and time again should not, Molly felt, be underestimated as her perception of an event, and her response to it, could not be fully comprehended in that moment and therefore detailed, repeated analysis was a necessity. With reflection, Molly could better decode her own reciprocation in an attempt to get to know herself a little better – not to then actively alter her emotions as a result (she felt it best that these were almost instinctual rather than coldly intellectualised like a machine) but to try to simply be more comfortable in being Molly, a task that she had found difficult for so many years now.

Molly's mind returned to the car as Dan parked.

* * * * * *

The beach was perfect. The sky, the sea and the pebbles were all subtly different shades of grey, the three states of matter almost indistinguishable from one another, as though they existed in a perfect unity of numb sterility.

The undulation of the landscape made it so that when looking out to sea when standing by the road where Dan was parked, the edge of the beach merged with the sea which in turn blended into the sky – the horizon was almost imperceptible, particularly as there seemed to be a distant fog which made the distinction even more difficult.

Molly had a sense of grey-blindness, a term she felt that

maybe she coined at that moment. The vista in front of her was a mesh of neutered tonality, a patchwork blanket of barren comfort. For the briefest of moments, before she pushed the thought aside, Molly remembered the grey atmosphere of the new train station in Rochester, but this view was different as it was nature making its statement, one of a pleasing melancholy that only suited people with a certain temperament.

For a moment, Molly imagined that she was the lead actor in one of those Nordi noir series that Dan had binged on recently. The opening credits would have long static camera shots of this desolate location, in a muted colour tone, before the protagonist is first revealed with her back to the audience, like an enigma. She is wearing a big winter coat on, her hair swirling in the wind and her hands placed firmly in the gratefully received warmth of the deep coat pockets.

In the background, a neo-classical string piece would begin to rise, all dramatic tones and pensive pauses to highlight the intense bleakness of what is to come. The camera would then sweep around her, 360 degrees just a little below eye level, to show her thoughtful face with a worried expression as she looked out to sea for the answer to whatever mystery was currently at the forefront of the programme's narrative.

In television shows and films, but not books, Molly had noticed that lead characters were often helped by staring at something for a while to either show a sense of deep thought or a sense of societal rejection. Mirrors were also good at showing this, probably because of the obvious metaphor of the sense of reflection going on.

Molly had stared at herself in the mirror on several occasions, always looking to the bridge of the nose to fool her own reflection that eye contact was being made, and each time she failed to feel any sense of inner mindfulness or clarity. She once even took herself to the creek to throw small rocks into the water in the hope that she might catch sight of her own face in the ripples, an analogy for her broken ideals and heartbreak. She had seen this image in so many music videos and black and white French films, yet none seemed to raise any particular set of emotion in real life.

The attempt to see her own face in the ripples only annoyed her as it was obvious to her when she got there that the angle of the water and the pebble throw was not conducive to seeing her face unless she stood right over the water which would be pointless and childlike and reminded her of the story of the dog staring at its own reflection and being jealous of the other dog's bone. The irritation felt at this instance came less from the actuality of the situation and more from the fact that she should have thought all of this through before even attempting to look poetically sad for the attention of the make-believe camera that would often follow her around from about the age of eight.

Molly considered this as some sort of recompense for not having had imaginary friends as a child which was a relief in some ways as she convinced herself that they would have undoubtedly bullied her.

She sat down and looked out to sea for a while before scouring the beach for interestingly shaped pebbles. It was at this point that she felt sorry that she had not paid more attention in Geography lessons as there emerged in Molly some questions about how each pebble came to be in that particular place at that particular moment. What stories could these pebbles tell? Did they feel alone, cut off from the larger rock from which they came? What kind of voice would a pebble have, or would it communicate in some other way?

A brown stone, rounded at its oval edges, caught Molly's eye for no particular reason. It had a slightly mottled effect to the right side with an indentation towards its top, two elements which made it entirely unique. Molly then moved the stone around in her hand, taking in all of its different contours and varied hues of brown before realising that her initial assertion that the slight discolouration was on the right and the indentation to the top were her misguided attempts to categorise and define, and that this pebble in fact had no left or right side, no top or bottom, only in relation to the beholder.

Rocks obviously had tops and bottoms as they were static entities and so such linguistic markers were fine. Plants, flowers, humans, animals – all of these things could be said to have ups, downs and sides. *Are pebbles*, Molly thought, *the only things on Earth that defied such categorisation*? There then followed a stream of thoughts that Molly became increasingly ashamed of as they were ideas that she was sure others of her age would likely consider, whereas she wanted to be above that.

She wondered what the advantages were in being a pebble and compared them to being human. Pebbles were, by and large, left alone to do very little, until the sea would come and take them for a bit of displacement. This would inevitably lead to falling into a totally new group of pebbles that would allow you to completely reinvent your own sense of identity.

There was probably a fair bit of buffeting by the sea before you settled into the next semi-stationary place so there was a constant sense of modification over time (but what was time to a pebble?) that would reshape your body bit by bit. There would be no pain, no fear, no requirement to engage with others around you if you got bored of them – it was, in many ways, a perfect existence as far as Molly was concerned.

The only advantage of being a human that Molly could think of at that moment was that people were not quantified in terms of how porous they were.

Molly looked left and right and tried to judge how far the coastline in front of her was. She thought perhaps a few miles. A few miles of no people, only a scattering of gulls here and there for company. The birds were hovering above the sea in a wind that was hardly perceptible at ground level but was clearly strong enough to ensure that there was a requirement for an occasional wing flutter to sustain a static position in the air.

Molly wondered if they were looking down into the shallow part of the sea that hugged the pebbles in order to spy a fish or three which would then be mercilessly swooped upon and devoured. After ten or so minutes of observing these creatures, she did not see any plummet to the water for their prey and so she thought maybe they were simply enjoying the view. *What*, Molly thought, *was the natural diet of seagulls before the invention of bins and chip shops?*

About 600 metres to Molly's right was a small boat on the beach, no more than fifteen metres in length. It was clearly no longer seaworthy. The paint had peeled off, revealing the now grey timber frames that had seen better days. There were holes, tears and decaying parts to the hull of this vessel, and it seemed to Molly to be the perfect adornment to this landscape.

There was a sense of abandonment to this object which seemed apt for the environment as she could not think of another place in her own country which looked like that which she saw in front of her. She had never been to Iceland, but she thought Dungeness was more in keeping with the barren greyness that she associated with that country.

There were fishing huts to the back of the beach where she sat, a few cars dotted around here and there but no sign of any forms of human life were visible. For a short while, she imagined that this is what it must feel like for the survivors in the zombie apocalypse. All of the usual places were still there but were now bereft of any life that would try to make small talk. The end of the world's requirement to outwit the undead would be an easier and more rewarding task than engaging in inconsequential chatter with the barely living.

Molly wondered whether the people who lived in the nearby huts saw the landed boat as an eyesore or some sort of memento of the location.

She knew about the hut where the artist had lived who had the same surname as her old science teacher and how that cottage had become a sort of accidental tourist site in Dungeness. Outside that cottage was another, much smaller, boat that had obviously been placed there for artistic merit, or at least that was what Molly assumed. Molly wanted to walk in the artist's garden but she knew that he had died quite a few years before and so she didn't know if anyone lived there now and if there were occupants then maybe they wouldn't welcome her presence.

Perhaps the artist's partner was still there, and her mawkish gawping would act as some sort of trigger for painful memories to return to him.

When Molly had first mentioned to Dan that she wanted to visit Dungeness, he had become quite animated about how much he loved the work of Derek Jarman, the artist whose cottage she was scared to go near.

'When I was at school I really liked the idea of him,' Dan said. 'What does that mean?' asked Molly. 'You know, when you think you should like something because people who you look up to like that person and so you try to get into it and eventually maybe you genuinely do get into it but it is hard work to begin with as you just think you are missing some sort of obvious thing, like a vital ingredient or something that others can see but you don't have the intelligence to understand or access.' Molly instantly thought of the first hundred times she listened to Dan's vinyl copy of 'Trout Mask Replica' and understood exactly what he meant while appreciating his honesty of how you sometimes have to try harder than others at being cool.

Dan told Molly that Derek Jarman had been a filmmaker, a painter, sculptor, writer and gay rights activist. They watched his film 'Jubilee' together on VHS, with Dan doing a particularly bad job at doing a director's commentary at what he perceived to be significant moments during the film which Molly's restricted cultural competence would benefit from by having these things mansplained to her in a way in which she was sure someone had not imposed upon Dan when he first saw the film.

He did go abruptly quiet, and for quite a while, when a female character made a sexual innuendo about a guy's penis. Molly relished the next five or six minutes of silence in the room and she was sure that Dan had altered his breathing to be shallower, as if he were trying to go unnoticed in the chair next to her.

To break the nervous tranquillity, Molly wanted to ask about the line a minute or two after it had passed simply to make Dan squirm, but she realised this was slightly cruel, and also there was the fact that she could not think of anything to say which she would find sufficiently humorous to make it worth her while. She also would have needed to think about the tone of voice needed, the pace of delivery to ensure that she would not be asked to repeat herself and whether she would turn her head towards Dan or simply stay looking at the screen. All of these thoughts distracted her from the film so she decided to leave it for now, safe in the knowledge that she would go back to thinking about it later in order to be quicker with her wits the next time a similar situation arose.

This Jarman chap seemed okay by Molly and she vowed to read more about him in the future so that she could get a better idea about interesting people, but also because he may have written about the cottage and life in Dungeness and therefore she would have been afforded some connection to William.

If Derek Jarman had written about the area in a more poetic way than she could conceive then this may help her to place herself in William's feet and in his mind, a feat that was becoming something of an obsession in the months since she walked out of the bookshop with the photo album in her arms.

Her mind now wondered how many connections her little adventure would uncover, and she briefly thought about asking Miss Jarman if she was in any way related to her artist namesake. Molly wondered how she would begin such a conversation in a way that would reassure the often-prickly teacher that she was being serious, and also, she didn't know whether scientists had any time or energy for art as in Molly's mind the two things were irreconcilably divided on her devised Logic-Disposition spectrum.

These thoughts did bring her back round to considering the reason why she actually asked Dan to drive her down here – to walk on the same beach, likely even the same pebbles, as William. It was at this moment that she felt an uncompromising feeling come over her, like a blanket of absurdity which made her question her motives for the journey. What was she thinking in coming all this way?

Was she expecting some sort of epiphany, as if by standing and looking at the same view that William had likely once looked out upon that there would be some form of awakening in her which would connect her to a boy long gone?

She wondered what it was about the frozen-in-time images in the photo album that had resonated with her so much, and these thoughts were swiftly followed by others which centred on whether her questioning of her feelings was a sign that this was all just an infatuation rather than a connection based on something a little more substantial and meaningful. It wasn't as if she were retracing the steps of an ancestor to better gain an understanding of herself.

Maybe she had used William as a form of distraction away from her own misery and loneliness and as other girls of her age were exaggerating their first loves she also was overstating this connection. The next thought she had was to determine that the bleak landscape where she stood was beginning to affect her cognitive processes – she was merely interested in William as he had no story and she was an artist who needed to better understand others and herself. Things didn't need to be more complicated than that.

In the days that followed, Molly would berate herself that this was the mannerin which William unceremoniously seeped into her consciousness while she was there.

An unexpected shudder came over Molly and she knew that if she believed in spirits and destiny then she would have seen this as a significant moment, and may even have been willing to feel that this was William's soul reaching out to her.

She didn't believe in such things, however, but she did think of those moments in films where an eerie hush was used in a battle scene just before the first shout of 'CHARGE!' The wind would die down, the birds would stop tweeting in the trees and there would be one or two camera shots used by the director, in case the audience missed the significance of this moment, where close-ups would be used on a couple of the soldiers who looked towards the trees in a questioning manner. *As if,* Molly thought, *people who were just about to be slaughtered thought 'Ooh, why have the birds stopped their lovely singing?'*

There was a degree of comfort to be taken from this shudder as it acted as a reminder to Molly to do up her coat. There was always something so satisfying about zipping up against the cold, but Molly had perhaps not realised just how cold it was and therefore her hands were now red and purple claws which were not responding to the motor control commands of her brain.

There was no dexterity in her left hand at all and although this frustrated Molly it also allowed her to remember that the Latin for 'right' was dexter.

Her right hand was not much better, but there was enough precise movement to allow her to clump her hand around the coat's zip like a chicken claw being used to crochet. Intricacy was not possible now, which led to Molly's right hand losing its grip on the zip while at about the level of her sternum. The force needed to move the zip halfway up the coat meant that when her hand slipped the momentum resulted in Molly whacking herself in the chin. A quick look around reassured her that there was nobody around to see her do this, yet she knew that she would beat herself up about it later when she had time to consider her day.

The enveloping warmth of the coat allowed her to forget the rapidly deteriorating weather conditions in which she now found herself, and to more fully focus on the idea of William. Molly realised that he was no more than a concept for her, a phantom projection. She looked up towards the pathway which cut across the beach and imagined William walking towards where she stood, a distance of around eighty metres and a hundred years.

She imagined the sound of the pebbles being displaced under his feet, heard him whistling (people always used to whistle to themselves in the old days before the cocooning effect of headphones) and saw the wind blow his scarf. He was alone, ten years old, and looked full of life, energy and positivity.

The mirage faded and then Molly realised that she had been standing stock still for a minute or so in the direction of Dan in his car, the windows steamed up most likely due to the coffee he had brought with him in his trusty flask. She could see him, but his head was facing downwards, probably at his newspaper or book that he had with him. The contemporary broke the spell of the past, as it always would, and Molly wished to be somewhere else in time.

Molly placed her hand into the right-sided pocket in her coat and pulled out the photo of William that she brought with her. She was at first unsure about taking out one of the photographs from its place in the album as it felt like an intrusion. There was a part of her that knew she owned the album and so she could do whatever she pleased with it, but she also felt a strong and strange pull to acknowledge that she was perhaps just keeping it for a while, a custodian of someone's treasured memories and that that someone would be back for them at some point and eternally grateful for the untampered and safe return of a family history long thought forgotten.

Even so, she felt compelled to take at least one photograph from the album with her and the obvious one had William alone, on a beach, with the inscription 'Dungeness beach, June 1918' underneath it.

He was squinting towards the camera, his left hand in the pocket of his shorts while the right arm was bent, hand placed in the region of his belly button with his fist clasped shut in front of his striped tank top. Molly felt at first that he was most likely holding a pebble in his right hand, but doubts started to creep into her mind the more she looked at the image. There was something increasingly unnerving about staring at photographs of other people and Molly had felt, for a couple of weeks now, that her analysis of each image had dramatically changed her initial impressions of this family.

There was now something unmistakeably dark and mysterious about many of the photographs that would no doubt be overlooked by the casual observer and this meant that she was now more intrigued than ever.

There were some days when Molly believed William to be a virtuous and decent sort of a chap, whereas there were also those where her excellent character profiling skills changed his personality to that of a sadistic, violent bully who was scarred by the loss of his, albeit unloving, father in ways that were irrevocably to his detriment. *There would not have been the support networks in place in those days like today*, Molly thought, *and he would have been expected just to get on with things, the poor sod.*

This made her sad for William, but also for the victims of the imagined intimidation that he involved himself in to make himself feel like a man. *The abused abuse.*

The clasped fist became the centre of Moly's latest fixation with William as she wanted to understand him better and she had only a few images in which to develop her appreciation of him. Perhaps it was simply a cold day, and this was his way of keeping his hand warm. Maybe it was his attempt at asserting his masculinity by suggesting he was ever ready for what was no doubt then called 'fisticuffs'. Alternatively, he could have been holding a small creature in it, one that he would nurture back to health or one that was going straight into his killing jar.

Molly realised that the reason she had become so transfixed by it was the fact that, like a number of the other photos, there was an unnatural element to the pose which needed deciphering rather than just a mere glance which would result in no information, knowledge or worthwhile interpretive data whatsoever. Life was rushed these days and it was about time that somebody investigated, pondered and dwelt on William rather than assign these photos to the scrapheap of indifference and inconsequence.

Molly wondered whether she would be able to pinpoint his location in the photo by landmarks and hold the photo up in front of the same spot where it was taken so as to place him very much in the here and now.

The thought sent a little shiver down her back, as if her subconscious being was trying to intervene in the decision-making processes of its physical carrier. Molly enjoyed the idea of standing in the same spot as the anonymous photographer over a hundred years ago and aligning the slope of the beach and the background sea with the photograph, and she wondered how long she would stand there looking at it in that way. Two, three, maybe four minutes?

She started to worry that the longer she held it in place the more likely it would be that she would feel an overwhelming sense of disappointment and dejection when she finally moved the photograph down only to reveal the landscape, and not William himself standing in front of her. Another thought flashed through her head, which was that this was a macabre exercise and not altogether entirely different from trying to summon the dead through a Ouija board or a séance or something.

Here, the vessel for communion was a faded photograph which would invoke the imagined spirit of a boy through the creative capabilities of a cold and lonely girl. Was she the fool looking for comfort from a sense that the dead live on, or was she the deceiver, the clairvoyant who preyed on the needs of the still grieving?

A sadness crept over Molly, both for herself and for a missed friendship that she could never truly feel. In the weeks since she took the album home, she would often contemplate on what this new object meant to her and why she cherished it so much. She had, in fact, become obsessed with it of late – she often found herself waking earlier than usual with an adrenaline buzz that was entirely alien to her. Her tummy would flip over, and she wondered if this was how other people viscerally manifested their understanding of the culturally ascribed notion of romantic love.

It was, she suspected, the same sort of feeling that she had as a young girl on Christmas Eve, but that was a long time ago and she had worked hard to eviscerate herself of pleasant childhood recollections so as to linger in her more naturally becoming morose state. Life was so much easier when you just disengaged certain memories forever.

Molly studied the background of the photo rather than focusing solely on the human subject within it. There were a few plants poking out of the surface of the beach and so she thought that William was probably closer to the path than she was at that moment in time. There was a white fisherman's cottage in the background, maybe 100 metres or so behind William, but when Molly looked up and down the beach from where she stood she could not see a cottage of this colour. The building in the photograph looked a little taller than some of the others on the beach and even looked like it had a second floor rather than the bungalow style that marked the cottages that Molly could see in front of her. That particular landmark would serve no purpose in helping Molly ascertain where William was standing as it was clear that it had not survived.

To Molly's right she saw the power station, a lighthouse and the station for the miniature railway. The nuclear station served as a constant form of distraction to Molly's attempt to grasp the feel of the early twentieth century. Its relative newness was a blot on the empty landscape and Molly was sure that there was a thrum in the air, a sense of vibration that came from the facility that William would never have felt. Perhaps it was the area itself that shuddered, in self-acknowledgement of not really belonging to the rest of England and the movement felt in the atmosphere was simply the location's slow attempts at dislodging itself from its host country.

The small but perfectly formed station made Molly think of nuclear experiments in films and how they usually ended up with an oversized monster which would wreak havoc on the streets of New York or some other vastly over-populated city. Here, though, a nuclear leak had resulted in the down-scaling of the local transport hub which had no subsequent catastrophic denouement which would threaten the planet. Molly thought of the Lyddiputians and hoped that she would remember this pun.

There was a rising curiosity in Molly to find Church Road, where William and his family used to live. She knew that, much like her William-connected thoughts here on the beach, she would be disappointed when she got there only to be denied any great sense of revelation. And besides, she had sworn to herself that this trip was not to find out facts, but to discover likelihoods. How William may have felt or where he may have walked were more important now than the banal certitudes of facts.

Molly had been on the beach for ten or fifteen minutes now, maybe a touch longer. There was a contradiction, Molly thought, in her underlying anxiety that she never felt the need to wear a watch. The precision of time would only add to her own sense of inadequacy. She looked back to Dan in the car and was surprised at how far away he was.

She felt as though she had drifted with the emotional current, increasingly unaware of her surroundings. She would stay just a few minutes more before heading back to the relative warmth and comfort of the car.

CHAPTER 7

William

Molly had set her heart on writing a story about William. She saw it as an opportunity to immerse herself in his world and his family. This would hopefully develop in her an understanding of his personality which had escaped her up until this point.

She had often heard that people who were connected would know what the other person was thinking and would demonstrate this by finishing one another's sentences. Molly felt glad that nobody did this to her as it would be exhausting to be constantly thinking of alternative endings to what she was saying so as to disprove any bond that someone else misguidedly felt they had with her.

If anyone was ever stupid enough to want to fall in love with her she hoped that they would not be sufficiently obsequious and fawning as to hang on her every word but also not confident enough to try to guess where her sentences were headed. Molly felt that her personality and habits meant that it would be cruel of her to allow someone to love her, though. She knew she was unlovable and she didn't need someone else to tell her.

She found the journey to Dungeness more enlightening and enjoyable than the visit, although she had always had the suspicion that she would be disheartened with her stay there, regardless of how long she had spent on that windswept beach.

In fact, she willed herself to be disappointed in the idea of the trip even as it was beginning to gestate in her mind all those weeks ago.

The only surprise of the trip came when she got back in the car and all Dan said was 'You ready?' She nodded, and he started the car. No subsequent questions came. She didn't even look back as they drove off. There was both a comfort and a disquiet in Dan's simple acceptance that it was perhaps not his place to ask why she wanted to go there.

The initial ideas for the opening chapter of a book came to Molly surprisingly quickly. Unlike with most, if not all, things in life she felt no major pangs of anxiety before starting the task in hand. This was all the signal she needed to suggest that it would at least be a relatively pleasurable experience for her to engage in for a while. She sat herself in front of her laptop and simply started to write down what had been formulating in her mind these last few weeks.

She vowed not to tell Dan, but she used the internet to check some facts. Just one or two for the sake of accuracy. He would never know because she felt no desire to tell him about the book and she would likely ask him not to read it if it were ever published, anyway. There was a passing inflection of guilt, but this wasn't sustained as she felt her allegiance to William was increasingly becoming more important than the painfully static, mundane yet safe routine of her life with Dan.

Writing, she thought, was fairly easy as the first two words take care of the issues of the empty page. She typed 'CHAPTER ONE' and lost herself in William's world.

* * * * * *

CHAPTER ONE

When the telegram informing the family of father's death arrived, we saw it as something of a mixed blessing. No longer would we wonder, no longer would we not know which, surely, is the hardest thing to deal with when one considers a missing loved one. Here it was in typed words on a shoddy piece of yellow paper –

Joseph Cardew dead. Body being brought home. Family will be informed when arrives. Stop.

How he died or what pain he must have inevitably felt were not matters discussed by the family. Mother was handed the note from Grandpa who was standing when he read it, leaning on the mantelpiece of our big fire which would never somehow again burn so brightly. Grandpa was a curmudgeonly man, toweringly tall and imposing without meaning to be either. He was of the generation where he had seen it all before and knew what was around the corner. One of his favourite sayings was 'As sure as rum is rum, the past will again come'. This always seemed like an odd phrase to me until I learnt when I was older just how much of a drinker ol' Grandpa was. Similar to how Johnners at school would always use analogies of having sex with young ladies to illustrate the weak point he was trying to make, Grandpa often used meaningless rhyming couplets that mentioned alcohol. The only difference being that Grandpa indulged in his habit regularly whereas we suspected that Johnners was all mouth and no action.

Before passing the telegram to mother, Grandpa checked the time on his pocket watch in his waistcoat, drew the paper closer to his bespectacled eyes to better see some aspect of the information and arched his greying, wild eyebrows. As he moved his right hand to allow my mother to read that her husband was no more, he breathed out of his nostrils in an exaggerated, long and ultimately disdainful manner. His son was dead, yet I suspect that Grandpa was more focused on the time delay between the telegram being written and when it was received.

My father was Grandpa's third son who had died in the last four years or so which possibly explained his disposition. Regardless, my father was dead, and it felt as though we were the last to know. In actual fact, of the five of us sitting in the room I was the last to be handed the piece of paper, so I actually was the last to know as nobody told anyone else what they had just read, the paper was just passed around in unerring silence. I knew what was coming when I was finally handed the paper though, not just because of the colour of the telegram, but because of everyone's reactions. It still shocks me to my very core today to think of how I was just given the paper, particularly in light of how my reading skills were not up to much at that age. Nobody hugged me after I read it. Nobody even asked if I was alright.

I remembered father fondly and often felt that I could smell him around the house after he had gone although as weeks turned into months the smell of his memory changed. Smell memories, like mind memories, are susceptible to alteration as forgetfulness takes hold and nostalgia shunts recollection out of the way. There was, for me, no nostalgia later in life for war. It cost me the one thing that I was supposed to look towards in order to build myself as a person. The folly of rich men, empire builders one and all, had resulted in many families being left distraught as mine was.

Father simply was not young, old or rich enough to avoid being called-up to serve his country. He was an honourable man and, to my recollection, went all too willingly. I heard him talking to mother a few nights before he left to join up with his cannon fodder compatriots and there was a clear sense in his words and his tone that this adventure held no fear for him and he seemed convinced it was all a lot of fuss about nothing and he would be home before anyone missed him. I remember lying in my bed, shivering under the blanket and praying that he was right. But now we all know just how wrong he was.

The little boy who lost his father seems distant to me now. I often see myself, the person that I am now, as being far removed from little William and, as such, I do not seem to be able to clearly recollect much by way of the funeral, the bereavement process, nor the tears that I must have cried alone at night. Such things have possibly been seared from my memory, but I suppose that this may well be a blessing and simply the way of things.

Once the war was over, many of the men returned but, for some time, there seemed to be a steady stream of isolated cases where the men came home long after the last guns had ceased to scorch the earth. Some had suffered the most horrific injuries, legs and arms had been lost, memory and persona held hostage by the mustard gas that had been used in the latter stages of this most inhumane of conflicts.

For my part, I mostly saw the response of the wives who were more visible in the streets or in the shops than their returned husbands. Despite their men being alive, their remained a sense of grief about them and there was an understanding in the local community that the body may be back, altered as it may be, but the spirit of the man had been left behind on some blood soaked soil or other and there remained an empty husk of introversion and spite. Such instances made me wonder whether it was better for us all that father had died.

Morbidly, I would ponder from time to time on how it was that he met his end, but such thoughts were not helpful for me with regards to the expectations of the family wherein I were to remain strong in the face of this great trial that had been sent us. And yet how difficult it was to keep my resolve when it was only human for my mind to wander to that foreign field and to play out the scene of my father's last moments.

I liked to think that he had taken a wound to his stomach and slowly bled to death in the arms of a newfound yet trusted trench companion. That he was able to pass on a message to this other soldier to tell his wife and child that they were loved very much. That he was able to realise when the time came and that he would simply find peace in his own passing and his eyes would close of his own volition. In such a scenario, the other soldier would need to be blown to pieces in order to justify the fact that father's dying words had yet to be relayed to his widow and only son. In my nightmares, though, father was often seen to be meandering along a vacated trench, the sound of gunfire in the background, the flames clearly visible in the reflection of his eyes. He merely walked in a haphazard manner, mud and blood covering his face, whispering my name over and over and over again. The seductive whistle of an incoming bullet can be heard, one that lodges itself right between my father's eyes as the blood begins to flow to his still moving lips. May God have mercy on the souls of the fools who perpetuate war.

There were things that father did around the house which left a gap in our lives that nobody dared attempt to plug. His chair remained empty as mother refused anyone to sit in it as if he was at any point likely to come back from the dead, as though he were merely returning from the pub. He had left a pair of brown braces hanging up from his bedroom door before he went abroad to die for

King and Country, and that is where they stayed and would not be moved for some years after. Those braces were often used on me when I had stepped over a line which he never clearly defined. He said I would thank him later whenever he thrashed me, but due to the circumstances of war this later never had the chance to occur.

There were many things that happened in the years after my father's death that made me wonder what he would have made of things and whether he would have seen it as progress or just change for change's sake. The echo of my father's voice was often in my head, a friendly and reassuring presence that I would use as a sounding board for my own ideas and thoughts as I grew into the man he would never know. I suppose however old we get we have our parents' voices in our heads to help us find the way and to warn us of the perils that lie ahead. Whether we choose to listen or not is another matter entirely. Father's voice was often one grained in doubt at my abilities, a harsh set of judgements often being delivered to ready me for the harsh realities of life.

Mother's instincts were, unsurprisingly, to mother more than she had ever mothered before. I felt suffocated by her constant attentions and questions as to my potential whereabouts and my plans for the day. As far as I can remember, mother wore black almost constantly for maybe seven or eight years after father's death was announced and to her dying day always wore one black garment on her person.

She was a strikingly attractive woman, with an asymmetry to her face which compelled people to comment on her overly pronounced features. Mother's deep green eyes, cat's eyes as father called them, changed colour slightly with her mood and darker green meant that she had been crying or was in a melancholic frame of mind. Mother's eyes were rarely anything other that deep green although we all knew they had the possibility of change within them.

There was always a reliance on father from this woman. When he was alive, from what I can recollect, she was always at his beck and call and always seemed in need of his attention. With his passing, she now fell into the singular dimension of a life of mourning. Rarely would I see her laugh or raise a wide smile after father had gone off to war, and these simply did not happen at all post-telegram. There were times when I wanted to shake the sorrow from her, to raise a hand to her face in order to slap the pity out of her or to shout so hard that it expelled the gloom yet perhaps this, I thought at the time, was what married life and love were really all about. Perhaps my mother was the perfect symbol of how we are not single beings but more closely reflected God's will that we were to be units together as man and wife until the day we die, entwined before His eyes to live, if needs be, an empty shell of an existence if this was required to please His demands upon us.

The marshes, where I lived my childhood days, seemed

to stretch out in every direction forever when I was young. It seems strange now to think that the landscape there is bereft of hills or tall buildings and so the horizon is an ever-present spectre in the lives of those who 'live' in this Godforsaken patch of land. The horizon would remain at a constant impenetrable distance despite an individual feeling as though they were moving towards it and this is one reason that I felt entrapped in this environment without fully being aware of it. I now look back on my childhood and feel as if I were the village idiot – unthinking, unreasoning and simply being – enveloped by a warm home life yet with a suffocating mother who hindered my movement away from the marshes in the same manner that the horizon laughed at those with dreams of escape. I suppose now, as I am older, I realise that all children feel the need to leave their home town, their loved ones and the quiet comfort of familiarity in order to feel in control, in charge of one's own destiny. Alas, so very few get the chance to do so.

As a child, I suppose I was somewhat clueless of what had passed and what was to follow. My father's loss did not really sink in for many years to come as I was told not to cry – I was now the man of the house. There are, I suppose, few sights on this earth more pathetic and rare than that of an Englishman crying in company. There was not one person that I knew who was not affected by the Great War. Death and news of death were commonplace to us, and yet not once did I see any man resort to the distraction of tears. Of course, I heard mother's occasional sobs through the thin walls of our house at night, but this was forgivable as she had lost the love of her life and she was, after all, only a woman.

As a young boy, albeit the newly crowned king of this dilapidated castle, my life seemed to centre on running, shouting and occasionally sitting and looking. I was a very active child, as I suppose all boys are, but I also very much liked to simply sit on the grass outside St Nicholas's Church and look to the heavens for some answers of how to truly become closer to God. As a child, however, these attempts at maturity and seeking the answer to the most important of questions were often scuppered due to my thoughts drifting to the undeniable truth that the church looked somewhat like a snail, with the long brown roof of the nave representing the shell and the pronged spire which were reminiscent of the eyes of the gastropod. How interesting that gastropod is an anagram of god pastor. Interesting, perhaps, but likely not in the thinking of the church's architect.

The analogy of the snail shell is, however, one which resonates with me with regards to my faith as I feel that the shelter of the church acts as a form of protection against the vulnerability and uncertainty of existence. This allusion leads me to believe that slugs must be atheist and therefore they deserve their slithering form of suffering.

My Christian faith has helped me overcome many things in my life and has brought me great comfort which other sources would not have provided. I do, however, worry from time to time that my sense of the divine is not as pure as others, or that I am in some way lacking some connection to God Almighty. It may be, of course, that when speaking of such matters, others exaggerate their feelings, their solace in Him and their unquestioning natures. I will never be comfortable with the idea that we will never be able to truly know another, and we can never therefore be assured in their sincerity.

I ask God what plans he has for me, or whether his design is for me to make my own. I am confused as to the role I have in my own life and the degree of culpability that I should possess. 'He will lead your hand' I am often told while also being repeatedly and forcibly instructed to get off my backside and look for work. I cannot continue to blame God for my lethargic manner, I suppose.

Was my father's death a part of God's plan or is there an element of life on this planet which He cannot interfere with? Is this all a part of his test to see who is righteous and who is not? How can evil exist so abundantly in this world if all things come from God?

I find these thoughts troubling because I know that I am never going to find a solution to these quandaries on my own, yet I feel that there is nobody that I can turn to in order to ask such questions without being seen to increasingly be a non-believer. If I ask my mother or grandfather I will merely be hushed down and told not to ask such silly questions. I cannot ask the vicar as he, too, will say the same while also informing my mother of his concerns for me which would only double the sense of isolation for me. I have nobody to turn to but myself, and I know nothing of such things.

Thinking is all very well but only if one has an answer to settle on soon enough. I try not to think too much anymore, as thinking only seems to get in the way and nobody got a job just by thinking about things. I am the man of the house now, and I need to be a man of action who has enough grit about him to get out of the safe confines of the house and get work. Yet I still feel like a child.

One summer, myself and mother were on the beach at Dungeness, not in itself unusual for us. That bleak landscape of undulating greys and the penetrating wind seemed to mirror mother's constant affliction of sorrow, loss and continuing to live when all the life had left her. I suppose this was perhaps one or two years after the telegram and so I would have been 11, maybe 12. The beach was covered with driftwood, seagulls pecking at all and sundry and broken yet somehow functioning fishing boats. As I idly walked across the pebbles my eye was caught by a shell which, surprisingly, stood out from the other million or so in front of me. I realise that this now seems somewhat ridiculous, but at the time I felt my childish mind drawn to this one particular, nondescript stone for reasons I knew not. As I bent down to pick it up, there was a peculiar tingling sensation in my extended left arm, as if numbness had all of a sudden set in. In that moment, inexplicably, I internalised a shout of 'FATHER' which was, and remains to this day, the loudest thought I have ever had and will ever likely have.

My mind, limited as it was through lack of education and reason, raced with ideas that here, in this stone, was the spirit of my dead father. I kept that stone with me for nine years. It was either in my waistcoat pocket or under my pillow. After a year or two my connection to the stone was just one of habit as I had grown out of the idea that the essence of my father existed within this rock, and yet I could not contend with the idea of discarding it. I had been to the beach many times before, and have been numerous times since, and that was the one and only occasion when I have felt an unnerving and unerring draw to such an object. For two years this stone became my father in symbolic form – unmoving, solid and entirely detached from my own life. A strong presence but a dispassionate one. Twice, as far as I can recall, I seriously contended with the idea of taking a pencil to the light grey surface and drawing a face upon its surface and the only thing that stopped me on both occasions was my inability to draw accurately in a manner which matched how my mind saw things. There seemed little point in trying when I already knew that the outcome would disappoint me and would feel like a disparaging retort to my father's absence.

At night, I prayed to the stone under my pillow to

replace all of the hurt and hate in the world with either kindness or wild disinterest. Either way seemed like a better manner in which men should live so as not to harm others. I worried for a while that the stone was becoming a totem for God. I was replacing my regular prayers and thoughts with requests to a lump of rock which lay inanimately under my pillow. When I was much younger, mother had scolded me for trying to put a tooth under my pillow for a penny or two from the Tooth Fairy. She chided me that believing in fairies or sprites was unholy, so I am sure that had I told her of the pebble with my father's spiritual essence encased in its entirely unremarkable outer being she would have carted me off to the asylum to bark at the moon. I had heard word at this age that lunatics cast no shadow and so I would regularly check that I produced a silhouette in the appropriate lighting conditions. I did and so I felt assured that I remained in control of my critical faculties. The power that the pebble held over me soon waned, as all things eventually do, I suppose.

I was fortunate enough as a young lad to have a bicycle with which I could move from town to town within the confines of the marshes. Summer days could see me go as far north as Dymchurch and towards Dungeness in the other direction. In 1927, a miniature railway was opened between Hythe, Romney and Dymchurch which allowed me to more freely traverse these locations without placing undue stress on my right knee which, by 1929, was good to neither man nor beast. My bicycle afforded me the opportunity to visit some lady friends for an hour or two as well as wandering, both physically and in my mind. I suppose I have always been something of a daydreamer and I often found that I could be cycling for an hour, maybe two, in an almost hypnotic state before coming to and wondering what had happened as I had no recollection of passing various landmarks or places along the way.

I would take my bicycle at least once a week to Dungeness, regardless of the weather. We had lived in this part of the marshes for several years during my childhood before relocating when we had to move in with Grandpa. The place, odd though it undoubtedly was, always gave me a warm feeling in my tummy as I approached it. The harshness of the landscape lured me back time and time again. Even with my own eyes, which had no need for spectacles, I saw this place in black and white which in my mind's eye replaced the various tones of grey that were commonplace here. I would sit for hours on end near the sea, sometimes throwing pebbles in from my position twenty or so yards from the water, more often than not simply staring out to sea with my thoughts beyond the furthest reaches of my vision.

The persistent wind would chill me to the bone, regardless of the season. Yet this was *my* place and by being here I felt at my most contented. Time here was not important. People rarely came by – the occasional walker with their dog chasing a stick or fishermen with better things to do were often my only companions. Along the beach there existed cottages, wooden structures separated from the next by some distance highlighting a sense of loneliness and emotional disconnection in this headland. Each cottage was distinct in colour but not in shape. There was a uniformity to them which the residents attempted to negate with splashes of colour in an otherwise barren panorama.

On the beach, towards the road, there were occasional and seemingly sporadic chunks of grass that peeped out from the pebbles that formed the tedious tundra that was so familiar to me. They were inconsequential in themselves, yet significant in their intrusion and the shock of colour, even in my black and white interpretation of this space, made for a welcome reminder of life and nature's attempt to reclaim the empty, barren vista in front of me. An unwelcome presence, the shards of grass served to remind those appropriately attentive that vestiges of existence and potential can overcome, briefly, the inevitability of decay which defines life. When we as humans feel we have peaked we have long ago lived our best day. I, however, cannot imagine the dissatisfaction that comes with believing that the best day of my life has already been lived.

Many of my friends now point to their wedding as their best day, but invariably only when they are within earshot of their wives. I remain unsure as to why you would put yourself in a position, for the sake of romance, when thereafter you were compelled to state that no day would likely match that particular solar cycle? Better to die with life unfulfilled than live for many years knowing that everything is a poor substitute for what had gone before. Or die in an act of unparalleled bravery saving a school full of orphans, a story which would be long remembered. I have thought, for as long as I can remember, that I would likely die in the middle of my best-ever thought. I have always felt like a disappointment to so many, so why not slip off this mortal coil in the most personally frustrating way? I would have a story to tell in Heaven.

When I was a man of no more than 18, I had an encounter on the beach which I will forever remember. For all of the times I had visited Dungeness to revel in its gloom and wallow in my own form of pleasant despondency, this was the only time I can recall holding a conversation of any kind on that stretch of mutated and fragmented rock.

I had bicycled to the beach in a manner I had done time and time and time again on a nondescript day like many others. The weather was overcast but the sky was filled with the threat of rain rather than its actuality – in fact I cannot recall a time when it ever rained on me in Dungeness. I sat myself down not 50 yards from the incoming waves as was usual when a haggard fisherman sat down beside me. This was quite obviously a considered move on his part as there was open space aplenty on the beach. Yet here he was, as bold as anything, deciding to sit in my proximity. Worse than that, he engaged in conversation with me. I had, up until this point, not considered my sacred contemplative space to be fitting of chit-chat, yet I found myself passing time with a stranger who made comment and uttered phrases that I would take to my grave.

The fisherman, around six foot in frame with an eight foot radius of repugnant smell, sat down three feet away from me. This was far too close and I immediately felt uncomfortable, yet the reticence learnt by all Englishmen that permeated my every ounce of being could not inform this individual of how I felt. The speed at which my right hand swept through and over the pebbles in my proximity was the only factor that would have made somebody suspect that I was uncomfortable in this instance. The man was of the type where he could have been anything between late 50s and early 70s, I have always had trouble in singularly identifying the age of those older than 35. Wrinkles, and their absence, can be deceptive.

This man of the sea leant to his left, holding out a pink and white striped paper bag as he offered me a hard boiled sweet, without uttering a word. The gesture was one of kindness as he attempted to reach out to another human in the only way that he perhaps knew. When I refused to respond to his offering, he leant in towards my face in order to engage in conversation. Due to the fact that I was overcome with a stinging feeling in my nostrils, I fail to recollect his initial greeting. Once I regained a sense of emotional equilibrium I could speak with the fisherman as an equal.

The first phrase that I can recall which fell from his lips was 'And so we see the horizon, yet when we move towards it, she moves away. As with sand, the more we grip the more we lose through our enclosing fingers. We set traps for others yet only we are aware, and our knowledge is that which encircles us and is the fault with which we have to move on'.

Needless to say, my response was lacking. 'I'm sorry – what?' I replied. 'You see,' said the vestige vagrant, 'there are but three types of people – those who can, those who can't and then those who are for now undefined'. The stinging odours from his person made it hard for me to determine whether I was now engaged in a conversation with a drunk or not. Rather than reply, I felt it best to stare out to sea in an attempt to erase him from my presence as I knew that drunks could turn nasty without warning and I had no desire to extinguish the hatred of another. After some minutes passing, I inexplicably felt the urge to converse.

'What,' I asked, 'are you talking about?'

'When did you last see a reflection of yourself that did not look like your own idea of yourself?' asked the fisherman.

'Erm…yes. So…' came my less-than-witty reply. I began to feel somewhat panicked by this man's presence although he himself was doing nothing that could be deemed to be untoward.

'My friend, you do not understand my reasoning. When you touch an object what is it you feel, the sensation of the thing or the impression of your finger'.

'What would be the difference, and does it matter?' I could sense a quivering in my voice as I forced the words out.

'All things matter. When you have done anything there is always an action afterwards so without the first moment of inconsequence there can be no instant of exquisite realisation'.

At this moment, I considered picking up my coat which lay behind me, thanking my companion and escaping that moment in time, never to be recalled again. However, there was a compelling element to this man which to this day I cannot explain and so I remained, somewhat transfixed, in his presence. After considering him drunk, I listened more attentively to the tone and flux of his voice and found no reason to believe him to be anything other than entirely in command of his sensibilities. What spewed from his mouth, however, made me question my judgement.

'When did you last love?' he asked.
'Romantic love or otherwise?'
'Either or.'
'I loved my father' I said, 'I believe that he is the only

person that I have ever and unfalteringly loved.'

'And did he love you, young sir?'

'I believe he did.'

'And did he show his love for you?'

'Rarely.'

'Well then, I don't see that his love could ever be considered as true.'

'Then I disappoint you as much as I am disappointed myself.'

'When love is all there is, there can be no result but hatred and intolerance.'

'How?'

'The essence of all, of everything, is nothing.'

'Pardon me?'

'In the middle of the room you are as close to one wall as the next, yet which is the one that draws you closest to it? Yet your father is gone, that is clear as you say you loved him. Not love. Loved. Maybe the fact he is gone makes the loving all the more easier as, unlike some other relative like a mother who may still draw breath, he can no longer dissuade you of your affections by his actions.'

'Your questions, however fanciful, make no sense'. I tried to make myself seem more intelligent than is perhaps the case in the hope that this would diminish his enthusiasm. With each passing question the speed of his words became more and more hurried and the pitch of his voice became higher, suggesting an increased enjoyment.

'I live over there,' said the fisherman waving in a non-specific manner behind him 'and this is all I see day in, day out. As such things exist one is left to ponder on them and see the lines that connect all and separate those that no longer belong. I see you'.

'Meaning?'

'Meaning is only open to those who enquire'.

'I am afraid that I must go,' I said, tiring of his riddles. After my initial good-humoured intrigue, I realised that my interest was very quickly on the wane.

'Then go you must, but where to, when all you do is take yourself back to where once you had been and will go again, makes the going more about returning than moving ever on.'

'Do you work here?' I ventured, waving my arm towards the water in a desperate attempt to change the course of the conversation.

'I am here, I work nowhere. Work means venture, and hardship, and pity and only two of these could be said to be related to how I see this here. You can never lose what you never found – these opposites are immutably intertwined and all that is now will at some point be lost yet what is now has not necessarily been found.'

At this point, the fisherman pulled some tobacco from a leathery pouch in his shaggy coat's breast pocket and snaffled it into his pipe. His actions were overly deliberate, as if my observing him doing this were more important than the act or the outcome. Indeed, he did not, to my recollection, light the pipe or even pull it towards his mouth yet he seemed to take great pleasure in the action of filling this previously empty vessel with cheap shag.

'So, you do or you do not work? Are you not a worker on one of those boats there?' I asked once more.

'Yes, I am. I fish, yet I do not work anywhere as the sea is a rolling thing which does not stand still. From the shoreline there is a sense of belonging and points of reference but on the water, after a while, you see the sense that the sea you were previously on has moved even if you have not. I cannot think of a better view of life than the sea as everything looks the same, yet nothing stays as it was. It is ever changing yet seemingly consistent. A wave is simply water droplets that were once not noticed, and which will be again. There is no top, no bottom, no middle to the sea, it is all one and yet not. We talk of surface, yet no such thing exists in reality as it is not fixed. The sea is life as this is where all things live and where all things die. Being alive and living are not one and the same. Water brings and sustains all life and eventually takes some. Learn this, young sir, and you will be as happy as anything that is aware of its own demise can be'.

Not once had this man looked at me throughout this exchange. He mirrored my gaze towards the rolling sea which seemed to be increasingly unsettled. Astonishingly, this man then stood up and walked away without a word of goodbye. As he talked in his slow, monotone manner I considered ways to end this façade of an encounter and yet it seemed that he held in his possession the right to unnerve me and the authority to abruptly end our meeting, as if he were the injured party.

I sat, still looking out to sea, for some time after he had gone and contemplated, seeing the horizon as the metaphor for one's own life, that sense of visible destination which one can never reach. When you take a step forward, the horizon takes a step back.

The encounter with the fisherman gave the place, for some months, a sense of foreboding that I found difficult to shake off. As I cycled, on seeing Dungeness beach in the distance I became apprehensive each time I returned. Indeed, for some months after the meeting I questioned whether I ever wanted to go back there as I had developed a fear of this man which was not present on the day of our exchange, if that is what it could be called. It was more like a monologue with the occasional interruption from myself.

I had entirely produced a picture in my mind's eye of this man that was not how he had been. I knew this as from time to time I would have moments of clarity that contradicted the alterations I had unwittingly made. Why such changes had been allowed to manifest as a false memory I cannot rightly say. He became older, more grotesque and with a foul stench which was unjust and unkind. Such amendments did, however, reason to give this man a heightened sense of ugliness which is always helpful when conjuring up an idea of an evil person. Cruelty comes with neither a pleasing countenance nor an agreeable aroma.

I was unsure as to why I had altered this man's being. What was my mind trying to achieve by doing so? Was this man, perhaps, the devil incarnate, and I was being warned against him by spiritual intervention? I pondered on this for a while, knowing very well that many people who I associated with on Sundays (but not during the rest of the week) would have believed such nonsense but I was not to be persuaded that this was a reason. It felt to me as though many people wanted the devil to intervene in their lives as this would force God into action by rescuing them in whatever way He could. They would not only then be reassured of God's presence but also of His view of them. In my own mind, this is not how God works and this is just one of the reasons that I feel I cannot talk through matters of the Christian faith with people who know me.

What was peculiar to my mind was that this image of the fisherman only ever came to my mind when I was within about 600 yards of where we met. He did not appear in my dreams, nor did he present himself when I contemplated getting on my bicycle and making the trip to the beach. He only ever haunted me when I was in the vicinity. When I go to church, I feel God's presence more acutely, too.

I have, of late, come to consider this man to be a phantasm of manhood. My reason for saying so is that I have not been able to recall a moment when another man has spoken with me at such length. I have been spoken *to* and spoken *for*, of this there can be no doubt, but with hindsight I perhaps think that this was the only occasion when a man had listened to and responded to my utterances. Admittedly, his replies were unusual, but they were preferable to my previous experiences of feeling ignored or unworthy of attention and thought. This sounds a little cruel with regards my beloved father, and Grandpa, but their undoubted love for me manifested itself in ways which they felt comfortable with rather than taking into consideration the needs of a child. I felt their protective hold, but never an actual embrace. They would have perceived such things as women's work and, I suppose, they would have had a point. Father's attention was often harsh, critical and brutal but I always believed they came from a need to protect me, to save me from myself and to push me in a righteous direction.

I wondered whether this lack of affection from the male members of my family had in any way detrimentally affected me and I could not reach a satisfactory conclusion on this matter. I feel that I have grown into a gentleman of the sort that father would have been proud, yet there is an idleness in my personality which, had father still been alive, would have been the undoing of me. He would not have suffered a slack, indolent boy yet I feel that his strong presence in my life would have sufficed to ensure that such traits would not have been a concern for me had I not been semi-orphaned by war. My being raised for many years by mother alone has no doubt resulted in a softening around the edges of my mannerisms and motivation which would not have been the case had father avoided the draft.

Poor mother. Forever the self-preserved widow, wallowing in her own sense of loss and quiet despair. As I grow older, I question whether I have become a burden to her and I ask myself whether she would have been altogether happier had I, in fact, never been born. I know that such thoughts are sinful and so I very much keep them to myself. It must be inescapably lonely being a parent when the burden of responsibility is so dramatically and brutally doubled. I must resolve to let mother know how much she means to me one of these days.

My bicycle helped me to secure my first job as I was hired to be the delivery boy for the local grocers. I was perhaps a little old to rightfully be called the delivery boy, but the label soon stuck with all of the subsequent jokes that went with it. I didn't in all honesty mind as it allowed me to bring a few pennies home and Mr and Mrs Wilbers often allowed me to take home food that would only otherwise have been thrown away as unsaleable. Stale bread is not stale once it hits an empty stomach.

I cheerily toured the streets of Dungeness on my trusty metal steed, playing pretence at being a cowboy from one of the tales from America that so intrigued us as young boys. The open landscape near the beach was as close in my mind's eye to a lawless American shanty town as ever I could imagine. As I am now older, topographically accurate imagery of the American wilderness is more vivid in my mind's eye but at that time I used the open expanse of the region to play out my fantasies of being the Western hero. I often needed to remind myself that although it was obvious to all that I was perhaps a little old to be a delivery boy, there was a requirement in me to remind myself that perhaps I was not too old to play make believe games to drive my mind away from the all too often boring nature of my life.

Excitement came in fits and starts; there was no longevity for me in amusement and joy. This was, perhaps, a fault within my own personality but I was aware that many others around me were not what one would call contented.

The huts on the beach served my purposes of representing the various dwellings in the town of my imagination – the bar, the sheriff's office, a hotel or two. All were seen in my mind's eye as having horses tethered to posts outside, with variations of noise spilling out from each location. To ensure that my story remained honest yet taking into account the real-life prohibitions of trespassing that confronted me, I ensured that the outlaw who I was hunting was called out to meet me on the strip of dirt that existed between the different sides of the street. This fugitive would come out ready for a duel, yet I had other plans in store for him. Maybe my aversion to guns, even imagined ones, could be quite simply explained by those who care to look into the minds of others, yet I felt at the time that talking these people out of their hostility using my wit, guile and humour was a more certain bet in my main aim which was to woo the pouting and powerless woman in my imagined tale. At various times, this fantasy woman was no more than my latest real-world fancy placed into what I considered to be the appropriate costume of the era. In subsequent years, I have seen many films and photographs from this period of American history and my projected clothing of these objects of my desire were nowhere near as immodest as they were in my head.

It was not uncommon for me to be chased away from my play by whichever local resident was unhappy with my presence. Rarely did I make a noise of any note other than my footsteps on the harsh pebbles, and so I suppose it was just in being there that they took offence to me. It surprised me just how quickly the vivid imagery of the occurrences of a far-off continent were replaced with the vision of a sailor in grubby long johns and braces shaking a fist at me. 'I know where you live,' they would invariably shout which was often not the case as rarely did I see these salty old men in any location other than the beach. They seemed entirely rooted to this location, as if their very core would crumble if they were ever to vacate it. They spent their days in wooden boats, their sleep in wooden beds, their meals in wooden chairs, and they were likely ever to only leave this place in a wooden box.

I was perhaps never happier than in focused play. I do not mean in the games of a child, as I was some years passed being rightfully termed a child at this point in my life, but rather my world of make believe was often preferable to the one that I saw around me. In my world, nobody was ever irreparably hurt and my swooning affections to the female form were always returned to me with more attention than I ever could have gathered from real women. I was undefeated in this fictional world. I was strong, resilient and brave.

I was all of the things that I was expected to be but would always fail to be as I knew enough about myself to know that I had neither the energy nor the personality to convincingly persuade another that this was nothing other than a shameful act of inauthenticity.

CHAPTER 8

The death of all the romance

The most significant moment in Molly's life was the day she realised that she wasn't the only one who wanted to cry all the time. In fact, she began to realise that this was a common trait in humans and was possibly the very factor that separated them from animals. And it annoyed her beyond measure as she didn't want to feel the comfort that comes with shared experience. Hers was to be a solitary life, a unique journey.

When she wasn't sad, she wasn't really anything, or at least that was how she viewed it. Sad and exasperated in equal measure. With a dash of ennui.

The constant emotional numbness began in Molly around the age of twelve for no reason that she could put her finger on. She just suddenly became immune to true, pure and unadulterated enjoyment, as if a switch had been triggered from which there was no going back.

There were a number of occasions before the gloom set in when she could remember laughing so hard with friends that she wet herself and, on two separate instances, almost stopped breathing. Molly couldn't remember what the source of the initial giggling was but on all of these occasions it was the laughter itself rather than its instigating source that perpetuated the feeling and made things worse.

There is a cut-off point of self-awareness where laughter

initially derived from an external element is usurped by the internalised appraisal which is sustained in ever increasing circles by the sound of one's own convulsive howling, often resulting in aching sides or hideous porcine snorting, which only serve to further intensify the ensuing boisterousness. Molly felt those times were long gone and were unlikely to return any time soon.

Why, Molly thought, were the teenage years in this culture in which she was accidentally born so beset with a foreboding and inescapable sense of miserabilism?

She had read a few books on anthropology in recent years and none that she could recall attempted to make the claim that the teens in far flung cultures were wallowing in a sort of existentialist crisis that only prescribed medicines or counselling could cure. Had she grown into the conventional habits of teenagers as the culture surrounding her had told her over and over and over again that this is what it was to be a kidult? Was this some sort of self-fulfilling prophecy that she had somnambulated into? Were the forces of despondency external, or did she have a say in how she felt these days?

Molly had always considered that there were four stages of human life: child, teenager, adult, and old. The first was relatively happy for most, the second was fraught with the onset of change and the realisation that life was about to really start happening, by the third stage people calmed down and got their act together and the final stage was filled with getting up super early in the morning to make the most of what little time was left, while also wasting an extraordinary amount of time by hedging your bets and going to church.

She started to realise that there was little distinction between stages two and three, other than the requirement to pay tax.

The blissful and cherished childhood memories that a lot of others had were denied to her by nobody but Molly herself. She wasn't much enjoying this current life stage either, as she didn't feel that preparing for the latter periods was a worthwhile use of her time when there was little that made any logical sense to the activities that she was required to undertake in order to move to the third and longest phase, which just seemed to consist of sleep-work-eat-repeat.

The alternatives on offer seemed impossible to realise, facile even. She wanted to step apart from this culture, to be different and to disengage for all the right reasons. There was a bravery needed in standing in opposition to things, a sense of extroversion which she did not possess.

Her own sense of sadness stemmed from the knowledge that she would die, likely without much prior warning. It was less about her own mortality and more about the fact that her end could come at any point. An aneurysm does not make an appointment, a heart attack can be a surprise guest, and cancer can hide until it is too late.

Rather than use this knowledge to live life to its fullest, Molly realised that she had spent the last few years contemplating death more than she considered life. Death, for Molly, wasn't the end of life – life was just the precursor to death, a long ceremonial plod towards decay and being forgotten. Those who were remembered long after death had their stories rewritten and were analysed, dissected, and scrutinised like a cadaver on a slab. Live honestly, leave little by way of marks on the Earth, and then die alone in a metaphorical sense. Be utterly disregarded when dead.

Molly reasoned that it was better to make no emotional connections of any kind with other humans, as all that provokes is a sense of sadness when one party is no longer able to draw breath.

A life entirely separate from others – both geographically and mentally – was the ideal future scenario that Molly dreamed of. Then, when the inevitable end came (of starvation, probably), there would be nobody left behind to mourn her pitiful body which would quietly rot away on its own, perhaps offering some nourishment to the local wildlife.

In her mind's eye, Molly thought of Snow White and how her loneliness made her have hallucinatory visions of woodland creatures cheerily helping her clean the house only for those same animals, years later, to more than likely feast hungrily on her eyeballs, her cheeks, her thighs and calf muscles, their saliva dripping over the necrosed tissue of her still recognisable carcass as the sound of their devouring filled the forest. *Do birds dribble?* she wondered.

What is it, then, that made people want to connect and be heard? Is it the idea of humanity's general insignificance that propels an idea that the larger the number of people who know us the more immortal we will become? This would address why people in her class used to try to outdo one another with the number of friends or followers they had on social media. This would also address why people believed in an afterlife, as this one currently being endured was not sufficient.

All religions had end time scenarios, Molly thought. These were moments in holy texts which described the final days, the impending battle between good and evil that would, once and for all, sort out the just from the unjust. Of course, the idea of the end times being front and centre in a number of religions (*THE END IS NIGH!*) meant that the fools were easier to control. Watch out, they would say, for your god is watching and he needs to see pleasure in you if he is to let you into his part of the afterlife. God cannot tolerate any sort of behaviour which is deemed unworthy because seemingly although your god may be all things, your god is lacking empathy and will cast you into eternal damnation simply because you chose to follow a god which had little by way of patience.

God, in this instance, is best pictured as one of those parents on the train who keeps their child belted into their buggy, placated by cheap, non-descript flavoured crisps so that they can be left undisturbed to scroll through pages and pages of 'Which Disney character are you?' or 'Is this dress black and blue or peach and cream?' type RUBBISH on their phones. Once the child raises its voice or wishes to communicate with its carer in some way it is swiftly dealt with by a tut and another crisp shoved into its mouth. God, in this instance, is love but only on its own terms and don't you forget it.

Disaster movies, the Book of Revelations, fear of nuclear war, the Day of Judgement, the Rapture, zombie films, dystopian apocalypses and whatever else were connected in the idea of humanity's desire to be there at the end of days. They were all stories concerned with making people feel more significant than they were, as what could be more powerful than knowing that nobody lived beyond you?

Whether it was an ecological disaster that would wipe out all life on Earth, or some spiritual entity who was hacked off with someone for something, or the devastation caused by the weapons of maniacs, the need of humans to feel valued not in the respect that they might outlive others, but that it was impossible for others to survive them.

To die alone would be sad, to die by your side would be okay, but to die with everyone else on the planet at the exact same moment would be the most satisfying thing ever.

Molly considered more recent history to also point to the idea that people needed some sort of dread of the last days to really make them feel fulfilled. There was the Cold War from the 50s to the 70s, the threat of AIDS and acid rain in the 80s, Mad Cow Disease in the 90s, the millennium bug, bird flu, Ebola, and more recently the Department for Work and Pensions that would lay waste to all human life on Earth as we knew it.

None had come to pass, obviously, although perhaps it was a little too soon to really judge the accumulated effects of the DWP just yet. These scare stories were just that, tales of paranoia to unknowingly gladden the heart of all idiots.

Narratives of the future were almost always dystopic; there was no sense of idealism, joy or hope in what lay ahead. This was, Molly reasoned, true of all times, cultures and traditions despite the omnipotent 'happy ever after' of children's bedtime stories. Probably easier to get a kid to sleep with a nicely sterile, anodyne ending as opposed to the more realistic 'and they tolerated one another in public for the sake of their children and to save the embarrassment of their own life choices being ridiculed even though their fire of intimacy had been self-doused and extinguished years ago'.

Perhaps it was in this central aspect of inevitable fear, which was so ingrained in society, that aspects of depression emanated.

Although most people would not live their day-to-day lives

in conscious acknowledgement that their culture was centred on pessimism, it was so fully ensconced that there was no escaping its pervasive, and perverse, appeal. Everyone is heading towards death, and if that wasn't at the forefront of someone's mind, then the issue was made worse by knowing that what lay ahead before death was a life which was only going to get steadily worse and worse and worse – the prolonged delay before the inexorable decay.

It was hardly a surprise to Molly that more and more people were being diagnosed as suffering from poor mental health. The culture was almost set up to make it so. And who was suffering the most? It seemed everyone was.

Teenagers seemed particularly susceptible to feelings of inadequacy and the futility of it all. Molly's sense of pain, internal confrontation and her aura of pointlessness was, she concluded, likely to be more pronounced than others, but this did not mean she lacked empathy for others who suffered in the same way (but not the same depth).

Most teens these days were being funnelled towards dead end, zero hours contract jobs or a university education that came with the burden of thousands of pounds' worth of debt before the working world had them in its grasp. No wonder there was a sense of worthlessness for a whole generation of people.

Molly often had to listen to Dan telling her how easy kids had it these days as everything was accessible – music, films, books, company – all were there for the taking via the internet. The trouble was, Molly felt that this made more people unhappy in the long run as those things that were instant were also forgettable, nothing was cherished as much as perhaps they once were.

She used Dan's record collection as evidence of how people used to build their possessions, and the identity that often went with it. 'That's the original pressing' he would often say to her, with obvious pride. Many of these objects encapsulated not just memories but a sense of self, perhaps even of a community. Maybe this is what teenagers of today lacked as they talked facelessly while gaming or projected only the very best of themselves on social media to help portray a life of fulfilment, companionship and, ultimately, pretence.

Molly saw them in parks or in the windows of pubs as she went by – those kids who were with others but just stared at their phones, most likely feeling unhappy with themselves after looking at endless images of airbrushed no-mark celebrities or 'randoms' having a good time. Social media, Molly thought, led to life comparisons that never worked out favourably for the one looking.

Perhaps Dan was right that the issue of immediacy was problematic. The things in life that he had put value in – records, comics, books, videos – were almost now devalued by how ridiculously easy they were now to access. Downloading a few albums from the internet was not a record collection that people were invested in; it cheapened the art and the artist as it made the work disposable. And there's the rub – if culture is more expendable then what do people have to live for?

Their cultural artefacts are presumed of no value and, even if they were, people could ill afford to part with the money needed to engage at anything deeper than a superficial level. Even information is now instantly attainable, though often used incorrectly to preserve someone's cognitive bias.

Too much of Dan's thinking was seeping into Molly's consciousness, a fact that there was no denying. In many ways, this gave Molly a momentary feeling of familial warmth as she appreciated that this mindset was not just passed down as some form of hereditary hive-mind, but that there was a link between the emotional desires of her and her father. Life was simply too fast for Molly, and this was perhaps the absolute centre, the ground zero of her anxieties.

She felt as if she were the static body in a photo of fast moving, blurred others. She was a thinker in a world of people being far too busy doing.

Dan's tales of a slower world were often delivered for comedic effect yet there was a truth in what was said. The business hours of shops were an aspect that Dan would draw upon, although Molly didn't quite know whether to believe him when he said that shops used to close at lunchtimes on Wednesdays. Why would they?

Other examples included facts about how television transmissions shut down during the day and at night, 'party lines' on the home telephone meant that if a neighbour was using their phone you could not receive or make a call, and there was kudos to be had if your cassette deck ejected slower than anyone else's.

Dan also wanted to talk about how potential girlfriends could only be reached via telephone and the young men of the era would first have to go through the vetting process of the mother, yet he knew that this would only raise questions in Molly's mind that he was not yet ready to address. It was a shame as he had some good material here to draw upon. His favourite part was when he said that the maternal intervention meant that in his day it wasn't so much Tinder but Hinder.

That probably would have raised a laugh in a comedy club if he had the motivation to actually write the stand-up routine that he secretly felt he could deliver with aplomb. Maybe one day. Likely not.

All of Dan's examples – apocryphal or not – gave rise to the idea in Molly's mind that life had become a hurried procession with intermittent events before the weariness was finally eased by death. There just seemed so little time now for people to interact at any meaningful level and simply to be, to exist without the constant pressure to document the highlights of your life on social media as a pretence of contentment. *Why*, Molly thought, *was it not usual to take photographs at funerals*?

Molly's developing hypothesis read that an emotional disconnect between people and culture (rather than cultural products) leads to a sense of displacement and dissatisfaction which is exacerbated by huge debt, low paid jobs, and almost no hope of buying a house before grey hair is a dominant feature just above an old-before-its-time overly creased brow. In other words, there is no deep engagement with the present and no hope for the future. It's almost as if those in power have designed it to be so.

Molly had noticed a push in recent months from more companies to promote themselves as being conscious of mental health issues and many ran campaigns to raise awareness. These were the same companies, however, whose drive for capital allowed shareholders to benefit from the work of those underpaid workers at the bottom of the pile. *Probably better to pay your workers more and staff their working environment appropriately so as to get your house in order first before paying lip service to the latest thought trend, chaps.*

More teenagers, in fact maybe even more people in general, were now taking anti-depressants than ever before and Molly saw this as a double-sided coin where the pharmaceutical companies win regardless.

Was it, she thought, simply now easier to be diagnosed with mental health issues because society was increasingly filled with empathy, or was this an induced twenty-first century rite of passage as promoted by those most likely to make profit from it? Prescriptions for anti-depressants were the current belief in transubstantiation where the chemicals represent the body of scientific knowledge instilled in capsule form for the deliverance of the despondent at the altar for the heavy-hearted.

* * * * * *

For some time, Molly felt as if she had fallen in love with William, a quietly creeping chemical imbalance of attachment that entirely surprised her. Perhaps it wasn't love as others felt it (how could anyone ever know how others experienced their own sensations?) but she certainly felt in love with the idea of William.

That, she reflected, was all people ever really fell in love with somebody else for, the idea, the concept, the thought, the notion of them. Molly had seen it herself time and time and time again in the firebrand romances of some of the kids at school who went about their ritualistic flirtations and the ensnaring of their often-unsuspecting targets as if they were existential house flies with a nagging knowledge of how long they had to live, while knowing full well that they would inevitably end up in the shit. The chase was the important factor for so many of these people; the end result was fun for a while but they soon tired of their latest victim and so moved on to other targets.

Molly felt no real sense of self-ridicule when she thought about the burgeoning love that she felt for William as she knew that the reality of her situation with this ghost boy was not that different from other, more conventional romantic enterprises as she had spent an inordinate amount of time thinking about this boy, constructing an idea of who he was and what thoughts might have gone through his head.

On one or two occasions, Molly lost herself so much in this idea that when things of note happened to her she reminded herself to tell William as he would no doubt enjoy the story. There was a dizziness to the feelings that she felt which momentarily allowed her an excuse to forego the rationality and clinical logic which she felt underpinned her as a person.

Molly felt that these were all perfectly reasonable activities for her and marked her as no different from any other pining lover who was wondering where the focus of their attentions was at any given moment, or the affection-lacking beau who constantly concerned themselves with what was being thought by the quiet person lying next to them at night.

It was a little easier, Molly thought, to be infatuated with someone who was not only dead, but who she guessed had also not been alive during her existence on this planet. Her relationship with this boy brought up all the usual questions that people who are attempting intimacy must have, while being safe in the knowledge that William did not possess the ability to leave her disappointed. For this, she would be eternally grateful to him. Hers was a purer form of love than many others felt, she decided. More innocent, it would remain constant and unspoilt forever.

There were times when Molly became frustrated with William, which she found to be an interesting development in her one-way propinquity.

She often wanted answers to questions about him that he obviously could not deliver, but again she reasoned that this was not wholly dissimilar to most human interactions where one can never be certain of the intentions and honesty of another so she did not see this as a signal of some worrying madness developing in her. In fact, she took the view that this was likely a sign that she was able to form bonds with people and that perhaps she wasn't as unlike others as she had thought for many years now.

There was both a sense of relief in this realisation but also a significant degree of disappointment as she had tried so hard to not be like the others around her. Perhaps these feelings were helping to humanise her a little, to calm her down in the constant and exhausting rejection of societal norms and values which had become a habitual form of self-imposed distance for her, as if her contradiction of conventions gave her a valued sense of agency, of control in her own life and her performance of self which she was all too aware of.

The fact that she had let the idea of this little boy creep into her very being was tantamount to a miracle.

The frustration towards William often turned to bursts of hatred over the most facile of things. Molly hated the fact that none of the photographs were clear enough for her to really penetrate his gaze. The more she looked at the images, the more she thought they were deteriorating in quality, although in more emotionally neutral times she felt that this perception was most likely down to how she envisaged the photos in her mind as she thought about them much more than she actually looked at them. But she did look at them a lot.

There was, Molly felt, something quite central in human relationships in eye contact. She knew this because she was awful at it and was more often than not chastised for this lapse in her social skill set by teachers, other various adults, and sometimes even Dan. People her own age seemed not to be bothered by her inability to return someone's look, however.

Social etiquette and expectation were maybe changing due to teenagers' propensity to look at screens rather than at their immediate environment. Molly had seen enough films to know how important that first look across the bar was (look – look away – count to eight – look again – hold the look a little longer – look away – hope for the best) and also how those long, lingering looks signalled love to an audience who needed more than nuance. The photos in her hand, however, did not allow her access to William's eyes and this caused Molly more pain than she would have admitted to had anyone ever asked her how her relationship with a dead boy was coming along.

Had Molly only committed more to this relationship perhaps she would have got more reward from it. With hindsight, she often doubted whether she was right not to research more about William than she felt comfortable with at the time. She was content in her decision, however, because she knew that it would have inevitably led her to his grave, a fact that she could not bear thinking about.

She felt as though starting on this road of investigation, no matter how curious she was to know more, would have merely broken her heart. There would have been a finality to her relationship with William underscored by the eventuality that she would set some flowers down on his overgrown and long forgotten place of burial. All the time she did not see such a place it did not exist, and the idea of William could live on a little longer as a result.

It was at the moment of this realisation that Molly decided to leave the book about William unfinished, so that she need never think about how to end it, thereby keeping him in some sort of cryogenically frozen imagined memory. She reasoned that if she didn't write any more then the mythical version of this boy that she had constructed could be around forever.

There was no denying that Molly's affection for William was a ridiculous state of affairs to get into. She was possessed of a range of feelings towards him over time, none of which made any sense at all in the cold light of day. She had unwittingly morphed into all of the girls at school that she used to sneer at, those with overwhelming infatuations for Harry Styles or BST or whoever was the flavour of that particular month (Molly couldn't keep up with some of the other girls when she was at school, another reason for her sense of disenfranchisement).

She imagined some shapeless, faceless and nameless girl sitting in her bedroom for hours on end looking through a self-assembled scrapbook of photographs cut from newspapers and magazines of the distant object of her affections, gazing at the posters neatly collaged on the wall, while crying herself to sleep every night with the rushing realisation that this was the absolute definition of unrequited love. Molly was perhaps not quite at the stage of weeping every night over this strange fixation, but there were times when she was restless into the early hours of the morning as her head was filled with thoughts of William.

What did he smell like? What was his favourite food? What would he have thought of vlogging? How deep was his voice? Could he read? What colour were his eyes? How many pairs of socks did he own? Did he prefer dogs to cats? Which way would he have put the toilet roll on the holder? What annoyed him? What made him cry? What made him laugh? What made him angry? How compassionate was he? How big were his hands? What shoe size was he? What were his political views? Would his mind have melted if he had seen VR technology? Did he have any scars? Did he brush his teeth (at least) twice a day?

All of these questions would obviously go unanswered which was exactly how Molly liked things in this relationship, despite the occasional sense of inescapable frustration that resulted. It was in the unknowing that interest was conceived.

Where Molly stood apart from the teenyboppers was that they could easily access every fact about their beau from magazines or internet sites, whereas she had to ponder William's essential character profile traits herself with the knowledge bearing down on her that she would never be able to confirm her answers.

In some ways this was a positive, as at least she was not at the behest of the mediated machinery that manufactured lies to the masses, like ideological lactation for the suckling dupes who would lap up every last drop of nourishing information about so-and-so and such-and-such and who-the-hell-is-that.

Molly found it weird how absolutely and intensely fixated some of her previous classmates were to certain pop stars only to jump to the newest starlet at the blink of an eye. Looking back, Molly also found it interesting that the two biggest stars when she was in Year 7, Miley Cyrus and Justin Bieber, were as androgynous as you could get, and she was sure that this said a lot about pop culture and sexuality at the time although this thought would need to wait for another time when she could give it more focus.

Female obsessive behaviour towards boy bands seemed to be a lot more culturally accepted than other autistic human traits such as the overly enthusiastic devouring of and reciting of train timetables that often manifested itself in boys. Molly had read that autism was a masculine trait, that the male brain was more susceptible to it which was why there were loads more boys at school who had been diagnosed with this condition than girls (a factory default, perhaps). She obviously wasn't privy to the special educational needs of every kid at the school, but it was apparent to her that more boys had labels of autism or OCD or ADD or ADHD or ODD or whatever initialism was in mode at the time put upon them.

Molly had no real reason to disagree with the opinion of those who were in positions to diagnose, but she thought the disproportionate number of boys to girls was pure hogwash. It had to be if her ideas held water.

She considered it for a while, rapidly weighing up all sides of the argument, and felt that the answer lay in the expectations of behaviour that the parents had for their offspring. A boy gets obsessed with numbers and statistics of seemingly useless information? 'Get him seen to.'

A girl spends hour after hour after hour making up a fantasy where she, all of twelve years old and with tissues stuffed into her bra to make up the shortfall, are dating a famous man in his early twenties? 'That's what girls do.'

Here was another example of everyday sexism, that boys should have their minds on useful things whereas girls were being unknowingly trained to dote and depend on men.

'*Look at your mother*,' the man in Molly's imagination that she used to help these thoughts along would say, '*Look at her. She used to fantasise about [insert name of relevant male band member here] and it did her no harm. She would cut and paste photos into her scrapbook, write letters to him for years without getting any form of response back apart from a fan club form. She had mildly abusive relationships when she was younger as she didn't understand how they worked in the real world after being hopelessly embroiled in a one way relationship with [insert name of relevant male band member here] from [insert name of relevant band here] for years.*

She started to automatically associate feelings of neglect with love and aspiration and so that feeling she has in her stomach every night when she sees me undress in front of her and scratch my balls in my dirty pants before jumping in to bed and ignoring her unless I want something from her while she catches a whiff of my smelly vest for the first time since the same time the night before is one she is used to, one she appreciates.

It's a form of comfort to her. She was taught to be left disappointed, and so here we are. Patriarchy is a wonderful thing because even as I am saying this now you can tell that she can hear. She's listening. Listening but not agreeing as she doesn't want to feel like some sort of cultural dupe at the whim of the machinery of white male corporate oppression.

I'm not [insert name of relevant male band member here] but the system beat her down to the point where she feels that she can't get any more than she already has, and she has been so deadened by society's gaslighting culture of female subjugation and passivity that she has no more dreams left.

In fact, she is now in denial that she ever had any, and all she says is that life is what it is. The fire in her has been extinguished, and I make no claims to being responsible for that, but I'll be damned if I intend to help reignite her in any way.

And all because of a barely pubescent boy looking directly down at her from a poster in her wall that was held up by just three bits of unevenly distributed blue rubbery adhesive sticky shite. What would [insert name of relevant male band member here] think about that, eh?'

Molly was sure that just as many girls as boys would be diagnosed to have these supposedly problematic conditions but all the while their obsessive behaviours were just seen as natural, a passing phase of developmental growth, appropriate diagnosis would not be carried out. Of course, this meant that the subsequent support systems could not be put into place and so maybe there was a net loss for the undiagnosed in terms of life chances and support.

There must be, Molly thought, some reason why young teenagers had all these passionate feelings of displaced love for complete strangers.

Perhaps it was a standard rite of passage for people who were required to play at love before the 'real thing' came their way. Airbrushed images were not, however, appropriate training ground for sharing intimacy with a real, flawed human being. Pop stars, however, had served a purpose for many years of pushing an agenda of girls being trained to wait patiently for their love who would be required to be put on a pedestal by the grateful recipient of their attentions.

Wasn't this why girls were trained to focus their attentions on male pop stars and boys also covered their walls with images of men, but of their sporting heroes – the boys would see the images as aspirational targets that would push them to achieve their aims, whereas the pop stars would pacify the girls into a life of waiting until being beckoned. The man would save the woman. Classic Hollywood narrative.

Molly knew that these were overly trite generalisations in many ways, but there was still a valid point in there under the mass of assumptions.

There was a purity to her feelings for William which she supposed was how many people felt in the early rushes of romance, a sensation that she knew she would never herself feel in the real world of interaction with living human beings. William was *hers*, in the purest sense of the notion.

Although she had burning questions that she realised would never be able to be satisfactorily answered, she was in control of developing an idea of William – his personality, interests and habits. Such things would not be devised to disappoint.

This construction of the identity of another from very few facts, Molly reasoned, was not as creepy as some would think and she was certain that this was how most people began their engagement with others, by assembling a composited picture of the significant elements which combine to make a person someone of interest. There must be a sense of falsity to early dates, thought Molly, as people try to be the best version of themselves they can so as to avoid another doomed relationship.

Once those early pretences had worn off, all that couples were left with was a degree of tolerance. If you could bear the sight, sound and smell of the other then you would probably be alright. *What a way to live!*

Perhaps these feelings of love, these hitherto unheard-of qualities within the frame of her body, were early warning signs that she was going through the most unexpected of transmogrifications from Molly, and all that being Molly was, to a normal human being.

She was the caterpillar getting ready to metamorphise into an alternative being. Butterflies were often seen by people to be the more beautiful state, but Molly found caterpillars to be fascinating and so, if she were ever to be given the chance to decide, she would have stuck to being the caterpillar that she was with all of the strange, awkward movements, hairiness, colourful yet hidden qualities and their seeming lack of direction that came with being one of them.

This analogy would have been even better had she had the sleeping habits of many of her teenage peers as her bed could have served as the visual metaphor for a cocoon. She didn't spend huge amounts of time sleeping, but this visual similitude was still a good one.

Molly felt that a change was coming. Maybe her subconscious was beginning to be more comfortable with the person she was. Like a pair of new shoes that rubbed for a while, she needed to wear herself in to feel comfortable within herself. The early years of life were the wait to finally stop growing to fit into the shoes of life, and the teen years were mostly concerned with shaping the shoe by whatever means necessary so that it no longer hurt.

Maybe William would be seen by Molly in later years to be the catalyst between the romantic ideals of the early years of human life and the move to another version of herself. He had become the cocoon that she had become ensconced in, a process that was required before she could alter, change, progress.

Do other people pretend as much as I do? she thought. Her form of pretence often came by way of reassuring people that she was fine and dandy, that she had no worries, that she was content. Molly felt recently that perhaps she was beginning to believe her own lies about herself and as a result that she was actually becoming the person that she pretended to Dan that she was. Maybe, just maybe, Molly would start to feel happiness in her life again. *Jeez, what then?*

Would induced happiness be fulfilling? If Molly had the power to move objects with just her mind, as one day she surely would, then there was no doubt that she would be able to convince her amygdala that things were fine. She was good at persuading others, so she was sure she could fool herself.

Molly always wondered why, when she was feeling down, that she could never convince herself that things would be okay again, yet when she was happy there was always a tiny little voice inside of her chipping away at that moment, persistently telling her that there was little point in enjoying herself as it wouldn't last.

You'll look more foolish when the feeling passes, she heard that part of her brain proclaim. That was the hardest part of herself to shut down, particularly at night when she only had herself to listen to.

She had tried listening to music as she drifted off, but she liked her choices too much and would stay awake listening. She had tried audiobooks but none that she liked were read by the author so that was no good to her.

Dan had often told her when she was young to think of the sound of waves lapping at the shore to soothe her to drowsiness, or to count sheep or clouds, but none of these ideas worked, in fact they made things worse.

She could easily hear waves in her auditory imagination, yet she got frustrated with them and tried to count the gaps between the sea coming in and out again so that she may be able to work out whether the illusory tide was going to be low or high by the time she woke.

With the sheep, she worried about why she was there in that field with all those animals and whether they would be stationary for long enough for her to account for them all or whether sheep attack, and the cloud counting just made her worry that it would rain, and she was not dressed appropriately.

Such things made Molly who she was, and, in a way, she liked it and had no real desire to change them at all.

Molly would often lie awake thinking about the woman she was going to become. She thought about her hair thinning out, her face getting fatter, and her body being stretched due to the vagaries of time.

Would she end up as she always thought she would? That was a question that Molly was beginning to challenge in herself as a feeling of uncertainty had started to creep into her which did nothing but surprise her.

Perhaps staring at those images of the long dead boy had resulted in changes that Molly had previously not foreseen. Perhaps she was not as wise, as complete, as finished as she had thought. Maybe she would see herself changing in ways that were not expected or pre-planned. Perhaps adulthood was not as one-dimensional, as monolithic, as *certain* and lacking in the romance of raw emotion as she had always thought it was and would be. Perhaps she was, and would always remain, a work in progress.

How would she change in terms of her clothing choices, music or film preferences, tastes and opinions? Would the Molly of today even recognise the Molly of twenty years' time? Would she ever make it that long and, if not, how would she go? Hit by a car? Eaten by a shark? By her own hand? By the hand of another? Digested for over a thousand years in the belly of some sort of sand octopus that buried itself deep in the desert? By choking to death on a potato? At the End of Times with everyone else?

All were satisfying in their own way. They would no doubt afford the opportunity to tell wonderful stories about them when the altered, beauteous adult raconteur that had been growing inside Molly was revealed. Her rapturous audience in an afterlife that didn't exist would be raised to their feet to salute a tale regaled with wit, integrity and which touched everyone who heard it go their very core, whatever that may mean.

Molly thought back to the bookshop and the hours spent in that little room upstairs, amongst the dead knowledge, darkness and the smell of long forgotten dreams.

She was reminded how she felt a slight sense of unease with the number of globes that were there, gathering dust and becoming increasingly irrelevant with each passing day. There were also a number of books with old maps in and she was sure that she had likely flicked through some of these without paying particular attention or, more likely, the act of browsing through them had not been sufficiently important to have left an indelible mark in the jotting pad of her long-term memory.

These books were the mustiest, mangiest and most moribund in the whole place and likely for good reason. There was very little value in a book whose facts had long ago been replaced with new truths as countries, borders and flags were all reductive forms of human engagement which made no sense to Molly whatsoever and, as far as she was concerned, were just links to ownership and a false sense of identity that were given to those at the bottom from those at the top who were as disconnected to the ideas of collectivity as could be imagined.

Molly didn't know any young people that she could talk to about this, and she knew that it wasn't particularly good form to strike up a conversation in a random playground with a child ten years younger, but she was intrigued to know what a child would make of the idea of countries and of imagined lines in the earth which demarcated space as allocated property.

How hard would it be to explain the concept of borders to a kid who was in the 'why?' stage of questioning? Molly saw this as the best stage where the communication abilities, patience and tenacity of parents was really pushed to the limit. Such a shame that so many people move out of that life stage too soon. The world would be a much better, healthier and altogether more sensible place if people just asked 'why?'

The accident of Molly's birth meant that she was raised in a county by the sea, and the distant image of France could be seen on the horizon across the water when she ventured to Dover or Folkestone, and the French cliffs would maybe have been visible from Dungeness but for the eerie weather.

This twenty-odd mile stretch of water was a tangible mirage of separation as it was a visible sign of severance between the English and French landmasses and, therefore by default, the people who just so happened to live on either side of the busiest shipping channel in the world. It was perhaps to be expected that the ignorant rulers would use this divide by way of more fully exploiting those they had under their control, stoking a sense of intolerance for those others who lived closer to them than the people in their own capital city.

Molly wondered what life must be like living near, or even on, a land border. How would a person's identity be conflicted as a result of their proximity to another country? Would their externally ascribed sense of identity be affected? Would they be more liberal in their ideas to the others just over the border, people who they may well have seen, spoken to, smiled at on an almost daily basis?

Were there any homes that had their front garden in one country and their back garden in another? Why was the world made up of imaginary fences and walls as tools of keeping people apart? Who gained the advantage for doing this?

Molly had read enough about war, history and the such to understand that there was a contemporary attempt to colonise people's minds and the easiest way to do so was for the wealthy to appease the burgeoning hatred in those lower down the socio-economic scale of this supposed meritocracy by leading them to scapegoats for their ills.

There was plenty on the news and in the 'papers these days to see a rise in nationalism which scared Molly. How could people be so blind to the commonalities they shared rather than the things which were different? And what was the major problem with being different?

As the few at the very top became ever richer, it seemed as though there was a direct link to the degree of hatred for those who were mistakenly perceived to be at fault for the worsening conditions for those at the bottom.

How could it be anything other than racial bias that English people believed they had more in common with Americans over 4000 miles away than the French who were just twenty miles away?

There were clear degrees of separation in place within the culture in which she grew up, and these divisions were created through fear. A white skinned individual who spoke the English language was often not seen as a foreigner, but as some distant cousin, a charming rogue of the Anglo-bloodline which had been spread around the world for reasons probably best forgotten. As the skin tone altered, so did the reception from others. If skin tone *and* language were different, then heaven help us all! *Jeez, some people are so incredibly stupid.*

Molly felt that her own image of herself had been affected and subsequently formed mostly from the idea of her that others held. She was a number of things that were just labels given to her for ease of classification, and she was expected to perpetuate the restrictions of performance that each codified form of being assumed. Anything outside of these would be seen as a form of inability, incompetence and dysfunction.

Even her name offered a sense of roundness, softness and passivity which she hated. She knew that there was no particular malice intended on the part of whichever of her parents decided on this nomenclature, but it was a slight on her potential personality that she was given the, perhaps intended, self-fulfilling prophecy of a very 'feminine' name.

She felt that the only two words in the English language that were impossible to say in an angry tone were her own name and 'bubble'. Maybe 'poodle', as well. But that was the kind of company she was keeping through the semantic association of the tropes and quirks of the language she was surrounded by. She would not have her whole life, personality and aspirations mapped out for her by a name that was pre-ordained to her by a partnership that had long ago ceased to be. She, however, was the entity that spewed forth from that coupling, and she was determined to no longer be ashamed of this fact.

* * * * * *

Dan took the deepest, most meaningful breath in his entire life and for the next thirty-two minutes and seventeen seconds, with only a few pauses to gather his thoughts, he explained to Molly, in more detail than she would ever need, what exactly had happened for Caroline to go away.

Molly cried her heart out for almost exactly half the length of time that it took Dan to disclose the information to her. She didn't know which of the three main characters in his story she was crying for. She moved her hands away from her face as she felt the initial pain subside so that she could see the last tears falling onto her outstretched palms.

She had never given this side of her hand as much attention as now.

The world continued to turn.